Trepanation of the Skull

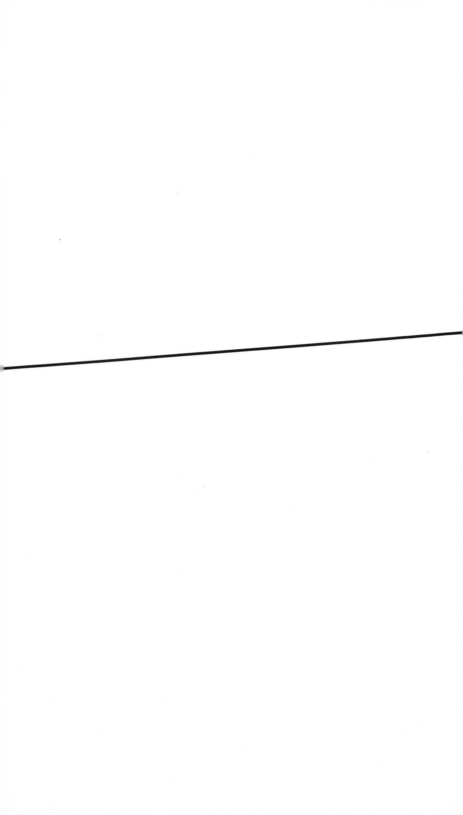

Trepanation of the Skull

SERGEY GANDLEVSKY

TRANSLATED BY SUSANNE FUSSO

NIU Press *DeKalb, IL*

© 2014 for this book by Northern Illinois University Press
Published by the Northern Illinois University Press, DeKalb, Illinois 60115
Manufactured in the United States using acid-free paper
All Rights Reserved
Design by Yuni Dorr
Sergey Gandlevsky holds the © for his novel.

Library of Congress Cataloging-in-Publication Data

Gandlevskii, Sergei
[Trepanatsiia cherepa. English]
Trepanation of the skull / Sergey Gandlevsky ; translated by Susanne Fusso.
pages cm
ISBN 978-0-87580-715-7 (paperback)—ISBN 978-1-60909-171-2 (e-book)
1. Gandlevskii, Sergei—Fiction. I. Fusso, Susanne, translator. II. Title.
PG3481.A4584T7413 2014
891.73'44—dc23
2014025215

CONTENTS

ACKNOWLEDGMENTS

Many people have helped me during the time that I have worked on this translation, beginning with Sergey Gandlevsky, who kindly gave me permission to translate *Trepanation of the Skull*. He has also been a generous interlocutor, patiently answering all my questions. His answers have often been so eloquent and profound that they warrant publication themselves (some of them are reflected and at times quoted in the notes). As a scholar who works mainly on nineteenth-century literature, I have found it inspiring and exhilarating to be able to carry on a dialogue with a living writer, especially one of such genius.

The translation could not have been brought to fruition without the help of my dear friend the artist Olga Monina, who worked on the text with me in detail, explaining slang, proverbs, and cultural references. She also designed the maps for this edition. She has been a wonderful teacher and guide to contemporary Russian life throughout the twenty-six years of our friendship, and I thank her from the bottom of my heart.

Suzanna Tamminen, Director and Editor-in-Chief at Wesleyan University Press, offered assistance and needed advice at a crucial

moment. Catherine Ciepiela, Howard M. and Martha P. Mitchell
Professor of Russian at Amherst College, also offered invaluable
help at a key stage of my work on this translation. I would also
like to thank J. Alex Schwartz, then Director of Northern Illinois
University Press, for his encouragement of this project at an early
stage. Linda Manning, Director; Amy Farranto, Editor; Susan Bean,
Managing Editor; and Shaun Allshouse, Production Manager at
NIU, have been helpful and responsive at every step of the process.
Yuni Dorr created an evocative cover design using a photograph by
Elena Gandlevskaya.

Wesleyan University has provided generous support in the form
of research grants and sabbatical time. I wish to thank in particular Andrew Curran, Dean of the Arts and Humanities, and Joyce
Jacobsen, Dean of Social Sciences, who provided a grant for the
design of the maps. My colleagues in the Russian, East European,
and Eurasian Studies Program, Irina Aleshkovsky, John Bonin,
Yuri Kordonsky, Priscilla Meyer, Justine Quijada, Peter Rutland,
Sasha Rudensky, Victoria Smolkin-Rothrock, and Duffield White,
have provided an environment of fruitful ongoing discussion of all
things Russian that has been of incalculable assistance. Whatever I
know about modern Russian culture has been enriched consider-
ably by my friendship with Yuz Aleshkovsky.

Sergei Bunaev, Kim Diver, Nancy Pollak, Stephanie Sandler,
Alexandra Smith, Michael Wachtel, and Matvei Yankelevich provided most helpful comments and suggestions. I would also like to
thank Konstantin Kandror for first putting me in touch with Sergey
Gandlevsky about sixteen years ago.

In this as in all my projects my husband Joseph M. Siry, Professor
of Art History at Wesleyan, has helped and supported me every step
of the way with his wisdom, his brilliance as a reader, and his love.

INTRODUCTION

Sergey Gandlevsky (b. 1952, Moscow) is widely recognized as one of the most important living Russian poets and prose writers. He has won numerous prizes, including the Anti-Booker prize for his book of poetry *Holiday* (1996) and the Little Booker (best prose debut) for his "autobiographical tale" *Trepanation of the Skull* (1994). His novel *[Illegible]* (2002) was nominated for the Russian Booker Prize. On April 13, 2010, Gandlevsky received the sixth Russian national "Poet" prize, the most important prize for poetry in Russia, "for the highest achievements in contemporary poetry." One Russian critic has called him "a magnificent lyric poet and artistic storyteller, one of the few champions of authenticity of feeling and purity of tone in contemporary literature."[1] Gandlevsky's poems have been published in English, both in journals and in the collection *A Kindred Orphanhood: Selected Poems of Sergey Gandlevsky*, translated by Philip Metres.[2] The present edition is the first English translation of *Trepanation of the Skull*, Gandlevsky's most important prose work.

As the poet Alexei Parshchikov and the literary scholar Andrew Wachtel explain in their lucid introduction to the poetry anthology *Third Wave*, Gandlevsky belongs to the generation of poets that emerged in the late

1960s and 1970s, who reacted against the public popularity of the poets of the "Thaw," Andrei Voznesensky, Bella Akhmadulina, and especially Evgeny Yevtushenko (who makes several unflattering appearances in *Trepanation*). While the Thaw poets benefited from the brief period of relative freedom under Khrushchev, when they read their poetry to enthusiastic crowds in stadiums, "the poets of this new generation shied away from public and universal pronouncements, meetings in large halls, and public readings." Parshchikov and Wachtel describe this choice as partly driven by lack of opportunity, but also as an aesthetic decision, "a conscious artistic reaction to the excesses of the previous generation." They describe the new generation as producing "chamber music in contrast with their predecessors' symphonies."[3] The new poets gravitated toward small groups, informal poetry clubs, and studios in which they could read their poetry to each other and issue their work in *samizdat* ("self-publishing," usually typescripts with multiple carbon copies passed from hand to hand). As Parshchikov and Wachtel explain, the refusal to publish in official venues freed these poets from censorship as well as other potentially corrupting influences like the need to cultivate mentors or to do assigned translations of poets writing in the other national languages of the Soviet Union.[4]

Gandlevsky's work was nurtured in several of these small-group venues. As a student at Moscow State University, Gandlevsky participated in the literary studio "Luch" ("Ray of Light"), which had been founded in 1968 by the scholar Igor Volgin (and continues to this day). In 1972, Gandlevsky and his friends Aleksandr Soprovsky, Bakhyt Kenzheev, Aleksey Tsvetkov, and Aleksandr Kazintsev founded the "Moscow Time" group. Unlike Russian poetry groups of the early twentieth century such as the Futurists or the Oberiuty, the "Moscow Time" poets did not issue manifestoes outlining the new aesthetic principles that united them. As Gandlevsky describes it, "We were friends, drinking buddies, we all were writing something and we would read it to each other, so sooner or later the idea arose of putting out little typewritten collections and declaring our literary community." Rather than aesthetic principles, they were brought together by what Gandlevsky calls reasons of general worldview: "We were all idealists. We thought that death is not really the end. We did not think that there is no design and that the Universe is a confluence of some kind of molecular circumstances. We did not treat poetry as a simple variety of human activity—one person makes boots, another writes in rhyme."[5] As the original members emigrated or gave up writing poetry, Gandlevsky joined other groupings such as the "Almanac" group and the Club "Poetry." The whole atmosphere of the fluid, somewhat chaotic literary life of coteries, studio readings, and self-publication is captured beautifully in *Trepanation*, as is the exhilarating but sometimes traumatic move these writers made during perestroika into previously unthinkable activities like publishing in official venues and joining the Union of Writers. As a matter of general principle, Gandlevsky shuns literary self-aggrandizement and self-dramatization. As the narrator of *Trepanation* says, "Literature was a personal matter for us. In the kitchen, in the watchman's booth, in the boiler room, there was no room for any abstract reader, people, nation. There was no one whose eyes had to be opened or who had to be made to understand. Everyone knew everything without that. There simply was nowhere for civic duty, precisely as an external obligation, to come from. And if someone wrote anti-Soviet stuff, then it was because of a sincere inclination" (47).

The aesthetic principles of Gandlevsky's poetry are well described by his translator Philip Metres. Metres explains that like many other contemporary Russian poets, Gandlevsky writes in the standard syllabotonic meters handed down from the nineteenth-century poets of the Golden Age: "Gandlevsky's persistent use of classical form suggests his longing for connection to a Russian poetic tradition that had been buried by Soviet imperatives, one which Mandelstam dreamed would be part of a great world culture." This crystalline form is provocatively combined with often "low cultural content," which "creates what [poet Mikhail] Aizenberg has called the 'explosive mixture' of Gandlevsky's verse."[6] As Evgeniia Izvarina puts it, "Notoriously *anti*poetic realia and *extra*literary phonemes resound in Gandlevsky's verse in a powerful chant, an essentially Homeric surf of precisely lyrical energy, which is by definition the most intimate kind."[7] A telling moment occurs in a 2012 interview, when the interviewer Lev Danilkin quotes Coleridge's definition of poetry as "the best words in their best order." Gandlevsky replies, "That formulation of Coleridge's that you quoted is excessive. There are no best words—there is only the ordering of words. The word 'crap' is in no way worse than the word 'rose.' The whole trick is in putting it in the right place."[8]

The poem quoted in full in *Trepanation of the Skull*, "Everything is ticking loudly. To lie fully dressed," is a good example of Gandlevsky's poetic
method (56). The original poem in Russian is cast in slow, solemn lines
of iambic hexameter, with alternating feminine and masculine rhymes—
a noble form for what is in essence the description of a hangover. Some
of the rhymes exemplify Gandlevsky's tendency toward piquant contrast
of high and low, such as *"postel'nogo bel'ia"* ("bedclothes") rhymed with
"dusha moia" ("my soul"). In his essay "The Metaphysics of Poetic Cook-
ery," Gandlevsky speaks of the way a poem emerges from an overheard
turn of phrase that becomes "a splinter in one's flesh, a tuning fork-phrase
to which—over the course of a week, a month, or a year—fragments of
speech that are of kindred tonality will be attached."[9] In "Everything is
ticking loudly," that initial generative phrase is "So that is death itself.
You've really blown it, bonehead," which combines the terrifying confrontation with mortality that is the poem's main subject (deepened later
in the poem by a reference to the metaphysical teachings of Dostoevsky's
Father Zosima in *The Brothers Karamazov*), with the lowest and most
banal level of diction ("you've really blown it, bonehead"). The word
"smert'" ("death") is amplified in the next line by words that rhyme
with it: *"zherd', krugovert' i tverd'"* ("pole, whirling, and firmament").
I have rendered this phrase as "meth, Nazareth, and breath," in order
to reproduce both the rhyme with "death" and the way that the words
range from the mundane to the cosmic—the hallmark of Gandlevsky's
poetic universe.

Gandlevsky's turn toward autobiographical writing in the 1990s was
part of a larger literary phenomenon. Marina Balina has analyzed the
ways in which the genre of official memoir in a socialist-realist mode that
arose in the 1920s and 1930s, which focused on a linear presentation
of supposedly objective facts and served a propagandistic purpose, provided a persistent template even for the dissident memoir of the 1960s:
"The dissident memoirists charged themselves with the same task of writing or rewriting history as did their socialist realist counterparts. . . . They
often referred to the same factual materials used in official literature, pro-
viding their own ways to prove the 'correct' readings of the facts."[10] Balina
shows that by the end of the century, a different sort of memoir writing
had come to the fore, developed by writers like Konstantin Paustovsky
and Iurii Trifonov, in which "facts" and linearity yield to personal life ex-

perience and a disconnected narrative marked by chronological breaks and discontinuities. She sees *Trepanation of the Skull* as following in this tradition: "It creates an image of the chaos of life, the preferred topic of postmodern literature."[11] Gandlevsky's "tale" is built around a watershed event in his life, when he was diagnosed with a benign brain tumor in late 1993 and had an operation for it in January 1994. The memoir does not proceed in a linear way. It jumps back and forth in time in an intentionally disorienting fashion, but always circles back to his illness, his diagnosis, his confrontation with death, and his operation and recovery. In the process he provides a vivid picture of the life of bohemian writers in the 1970s and 1980s, but also delves into his family history as far back as before the Revolution. The narrator's grasp of "facts" is often tenuous, thanks not only to his neurological symptoms but also to his alcoholism, which is described in loving and excruciating detail. Perhaps most importantly, the epigraph from *Crime and Punishment* signals the narrator's devotion to "talking nonsense"—the delight in free, unfettered, sometimes nonsensical storytelling with scant regard for verifiable fact or for logical connection. As Dostoevsky's character Razumikhin says, "If you talk enough nonsense, you'll get to the truth!"

The word Dostoevsky uses for "talking nonsense" is "*vrat*'," which is sometimes translated as "to fib." It signals a kind of lying or fabrication that is less serious and malign than "*lgat*'" ("to lie"). In *Trepanation of the Skull* Gandlevsky often uses the word *vrat*' to describe his narrative method, his refusal to be enslaved by the bald, unadorned "mother-truth" ("*pravda-matka*"): "It's not really a mother to us, it's a stepmother at best" (40). Dostoevsky's Razumikhin asserts that a deeper truth, a deeper self-revelation, is to be found through "talking nonsense": "Talk nonsense to me, but talk nonsense in your own way, and I will kiss you then. To talk nonsense in your own way—that's almost better, after all, than offering the truth in someone else's way; in the first case you are a person, and in the second you're just a bird!"[12] For Gandlevsky, this deeper kind of self-revelation and self-understanding is a property not of *pravda* but of *istina*, another Russian word for "truth" that he describes as the goal and essence of true art: "Through the magic crystal of art one suddenly is able to discern what is hidden to the naked eye, just as through smoked glass one can see the waning sun during an eclipse. We cease to be characters, figures on a chessboard . . . and for a brief time we see the whole match. We become co-Authors . . . . I will venture to call this precious type of awareness *istina*, understood not as a formula or as a guide to behavior but as a *state*."[13] In employing a free-form narration that jumps from one topic to another without regard for consequentiality or versimilitude, Gandlevsky is following in the footsteps of the narrator of Dostoevsky's *Notes from Underground* (1864), as well as more recent examples like the alcoholic narrator of Venedikt Erofeev's *Moscow to Petushki* (1969, not published in the Soviet Union until 1989).

In 1999 Gandlevsky participated in a roundtable devoted to the memoir genre, organized by the journal *Problems of Literature*. As the editors wrote in their introduction, "Memoirs have become one of the most popular literary genres."[14] In his contribution, Gandlevsky asserts,

> I do not consider my tale [*Trepanation*] a memoir in the exact sense of the word. . . . For the conscientious memoirist, considerations of authenticity, even if a subjective authenticity, simply must take precedence over aesthetic intentions. My concerns were the direct opposite. Every time I was faced with the choice: to tell the "legendary" version of some incident or the documentary one, I was guided not by truthfulness, but by the appropriateness of the given version to the conception of the narration—and without hesitation I preferred a "legendary" recension of events if in my opinion it was aesthetically advantageous for the work as a whole. I wanted to convey the pathos of a past era, not to recreate it in scrupulous detail.[15]

Nevertheless, Gandlevsky acknowledges that his work is part of a flowering of the memoir genre, which he sees as coming into its own both because people born and raised in the now defunct Soviet state have become "historical personages" who need to document the realia of their lives, and because after the falsity of Soviet life, in which seedy diners at train stations were called "Daydream" and the harvest was never just a harvest but a "battle for the harvest," "literature has a need to call things by their own names anew and soberly, to return cogency to reality, so as not to get lost in the bad infinity of the imaginary."[16]

In a more recent interview, Gandlevsky reiterated his view of the artistic—not strictly factual—nature of his autobiographical writing:

In art only plasticity, talent, mastery survive. Facts, life conflicts, etc., are a good thing, but the sensitive reader will hardly feel like returning to a book whose content is exhausted by facts and life conflicts. In such a work there is no unpredictable accretion of meaning, as in a truly artistic book. We reread Herzen's *Past and Thoughts* not because life buffeted Herzen around, but because he is a beautiful writer, and his best pages are devoted precisely to the most general and unexotic experiences: the death of his father, his wife's betrayal, etc.[17]

The translator of *Trepanation of the Skull* certainly experiences the "unpredictable accretion of meaning" that Gandlevsky speaks about here. This is not a work that is exhausted by its factual content; it grows upon each reading, like the best works of literature. It is a poetic work in the best sense of the word: in its complex form, in its rich allusions to Russian and world literature and culture, but above all in its language.

Gandlevsky is a true artist of language, who incorporates into his style the cadences of Pushkin and Tiutchev, the folk wisdom of proverbs, and slang in all its varieties—schoolboys' spoofs, writers' professional cant, alcoholics' in-jokes, Communist functionaries' jargon, criminals' argot, and the great Russian tradition of *mat* (obscenity). Part of Gandlevsky's ethical code during the Soviet era was a refusal to participate in official literary life; instead, he supported himself by working in menial jobs, including night watchman, museum guard, stagehand, and manual laborer on a series of expeditions throughout the Soviet Union (one of which is described in hair-raising detail in *Trepanation*). All along the way he listened carefully to the people around him and imbibed the multifarious richness of the Russian language. Metres's description of the difficulties of translating Gandlevsky's poetry is apposite to his memoiristic prose as well: "He forces a translator to scramble between retaining cultural particulars, at the risk of losing the American reader, and opting for some American equivalences, at the risk of effacing the original contexts."[18] Translating *Trepanation of the Skull* has been a humbling task but also an education. To attempt to translate "exactly" by using American dialectisms, which have their own regional, ethnic, or class associations, or to translate literally word for word, would produce misleading and sometimes ludicrous effects. Although I have used slang where appropriate,

I have concentrated on reproducing the intonation of Gandlevsky's narrator, which has its own peculiarities that are more susceptible to being captured accurately in English. I have also sought to render a general sense of the way he combines the highest and the lowest levels of language. I have provided aids for the Anglophone reader in the form of annotations: endnotes to the text, as well as a list of geographical names mentioned and a list of persons mentioned who would be known to the educated Russian reader.

A note to help orient the reader in the complex chronology of *Trepanation of the Skull:* the time of narration is 1994, after Gandlevsky's January operation. So, for example, a reference to "two years ago" should be read as 1992, and so on. In a few places where the shifts in chronology are particularly confusing, I have used italics to signal the transition. The action on the first page begins in summer 1993, as Gandlevsky's symptoms intensified.

Trepanation of the Skull was first published in the journal *Znamia*, No. 1, 1995. This translation is based on the text published in *Opyty v proze* (Moscow: Zakharov, 2007).

In the text I have used a modified version of the Library of Congress transliteration system. In annotations I have used the Library of Congress system.

In the course of my work on the translation, Gandlevsky answered my questions about the text in great detail. Some of his answers are cited in the endnotes as "personal communication."

Notes

1. Evgeniia Izvarina, "'Chelovek srednikh let . . .'" (Review of Gandlevsky, *Poriadok slov: stikhi, povest', p'esa, esse* [Ekaterinburg: U-Faktoriia, 2000]), *Ural*, 2001, No. 1 (http://magazines.russ.ru/ural/2001/1/izvar.html, accessed July1, 2013). The Russian Booker was established in 1991 as the first nongovernmental prize in Russia after 1917; it is awarded every year for the best novel in Russian. The Little Booker was a "branch" of the Booker Prize from 1991 to 1999, when it became independent; it has not been awarded since 2002. The Anti-Booker was established in 1995 by the newspaper *Nezavisimaia Gazeta*, and went out of existence in 2001. It was awarded in five categories, including criticism, playwriting, and poetry. The "Poet" Prize was established in 2005. All these prizes have (or had) major Russian writers and critics on their juries.

2. Zephyr Press, 2003.

3. Alexei Parshchikov and Andrew Wachtel, Introduction to *Third Wave: The*

New Russian Poetry, ed. Kent Johnson and Stephen M. Ashby (Ann Arbor: University of Michigan Press, 1992), 3.

4. Parshchikov and Wachtel, Introduction to *Third Wave,* 3–4. See also Elena Trofimova, "Moskovskie poeticheskie kluby 1980-kh godov," *Oktiabr',* 1991, no. 12.

5. "Konspekt," interview with Anastasiia Gosteva, *Voprosy literatury,* 2000, no. 5 (http://magazines.russ.ru/voplit/2000/5/gand.html, accessed July 1, 2013).

6. Metres, Introduction to *A Kindred Orphanhood,* p. xii. See also Dunja Popovic's illuminating article, "A Generation That Has Squandered Its Men: The Late Soviet Crisis of Masculinity in the Poetry of Sergei Gandlevskii," *The Russian Review* 70 (October 2011): 663–76. Popovic's discussion of how "late Soviet oppositional masculinity drew on nineteenth-century gentry culture" with its "high standards of honor, authenticity of behavior and speech, exercise of personal freedom, and a cult of exalted male friendship" is particularly apposite to *Trepanation of the Skull,* in which Gandlevsky repeatedly invokes Pushkin and Lermontov and even fights a duel in the center of Moscow. See also Alexander Zholkovsky, "K probleme infinitivnoi poezii (Ob intertekstual'nom fone 'Ustroit'sia na avtobazu . . .' S. Gandlevskogo)," available at http://dornsife.usc.edu/alik/rus/ess/etk.html (accessed January 5, 2014).

7. Izvarina, "Chelovek srednikh let."

8. "'Mir vygliadit sovsem propashchim, v tom chisle i tsivilizovannyi.' Poet Gandlevskii o mitiingakh, Bykove i sostoianii russkogo iazyka," interview with Lev Danilkin, *Afisha,* October 22, 2012 (http://magazines.russ.ru/ural/2001/1/izvar.html, accessed July 1, 2013).

9. Sergei Gandlevskii, "Metafizika poeticheskoi kukhni," in his *Naiti okhotnika: Stikhotvoreniia, retsenzii, esse* (St. Petersburg: Pushkinskii fond, 2002), 213.

10. Marina Balina, "The Tale of Bygone Years: Reconstructing the Past in the Contemporary Russian Memoir," in *The Russian Memoir: History and Literature,* ed. Beth Holmgren (Evanston: Northwestern University Press, 2003), 186–209, cited passage on 190.

11. Balina, "Tale of Bygone Years," 201.

12. F. M. Dostoevsky, *Polnoe sobranie sochinenii v tridtsati tomakh,* vol. 6 (Leningrad: Nauka, 1973), 155.

13. Gandlevsky, "Metafizika," 218.

14. "Memuary na slome epokh," *Voprosy literatury,* 1999, no. 1 (Jan.-Feb.), 3–56.

15. Gandlevsky, "Vernut' iavi ubeditel'nost'," in "Memuary na slome epokh," 13.

16. Gandlevsky, "Vernut' iavi ubeditel'nost'," 15.

17. Gandlevsky, "Mir vygliadit sovsem propashchim." Gandlevsky has recently given a more "factual" account of some of the episodes in his life that are described in *Trepanation of the Skull,* in *Bezdumnoe byloe* (Moscow: Astrel', 2012).

18. Metres, Introduction to *A Kindred Orphanhood,* xvi.

Trepanation of the Skull

A TALE

To my wife

W HEN I OPENED MY EYES, it would already be hurting. Or maybe it was simply that the headache would wake me up. My white boxer Charlie, of faulty pedigree, a product of unplanned breeding, would jump onto the bed in a single bound. Out of habit I would shield my solar plexus and groin: the little shit weighs almost ninety pounds and is as strong as a street-gang tough. My wife would turn onto her right side, and I would fight free of the dog's camaraderie and squeamishly pull on my pants and shirt that had gotten damp overnight. With sneakers on my bare feet I would go down to the glassed-in porch. I would walk on tiptoe past the children's room, not out of fatherly solicitude, but in order to grab another fifteen minutes of quiet.

There was noise in my ears. When it was new to me I used to look around and ask: Where's it coming from? Until I caught on that the source of the noise was me. Charlie would spin fawningly around me, and we would reach the back gate. The forest started right there. I would pause by the trunk of a birch tree that we'd felled the day before. Nice job. Too bad, of course, especially since the birch tree is the symbol of Russian spirituality and Russia's special path, but nice job. Although Swedish birches would be a little better looking. When Rubinshtein and I were slouching around Stockholm in September of 1992, I was taken aback by the preponderance of roses on the lawns. I started showing off my intellect. "Lyova," I exclaimed, "this is a northern country, just like ours! That shows how important it is to be near the Gulf Stream!" Rubinshtein

agreed with me in principle, but remarked in passing that in the courtyard of the Swedish Embassy in Moscow there were also so many roses
you couldn't spit without hitting one.

Charlie would mark the nearest fir tree, balancing on three legs, then
start fussily circling in the undergrowth, finally find his spot, and looking like a hunchback grimacing in martyrdom, would take a soldier-size
dump. He would jump sideways two or three times with relief, grab a fir
cone in his mouth, and invite me to play. Forget it, it's my turn now.

I would lock myself into the outhouse at the edge of the property,
smoke, press my palm against my unbearable forehead, and read the
headlines on the scraps of yellowed newspaper out of habit. "In the
immense expanses of the Motherland." That's clear. "We must restrain
. . ." Torn off, but also clear. "Disgrace . . . ," and again a ragged rupture.
"The Young Pioneers' Bonfires Are To Burn!"[2] Let them burn in hell.
That means, oh, how our homeland is wide, with its Papuans, lakes,
and canoes too. Guten Tag, cheerful bonfires at night! And of course
the disgrace we're all used to. The day has begun, what to do today?
Take off my pants and run away. There was another kids' joke like that,
with funny phrases inserted into a song. Oh, right! "From the Ukraine,
Moldova, Russia (in pants) the children of the Soviet land (without
pants) threw wildflowers (in pants) into the crest of the Danube wave
(without pants) . . ."[3]

I can tell from the squealing and mutual accusations that the children
have woken up. At breakfast I'll sing the boring daily tune: "Aleksandra,
there's no such word as 'groovy'; Grisha, you hand someone a knife with
the handle facing them, etc., etc." I've turned out to be a gloomy papa, a
boring one. A person is like a fly on a ball—I did my imitation of Ecclesiastes—and at every stage of his life he thinks he's located on the main
point of the sphere, but he doesn't see the whole ball, not ever.

I can hear Lena's "Good morning" and the neighbor's answering military greeting. We were walking with him along the street of the dacha
settlement the other day, and he kept talking about how upset he was
that in the spring his fence would be heaved out of the soil: the men did
lousy work, they didn't dig the posts in deep enough, and the frost line is
about eighteen meters down.

"Are you a builder?" I ask, disingenuously, because the profession of
the local inhabitants is a zone of silence and suppression.

"Everything's relative in this world, Seryozha, everything's relative."
Relativism.

My Lord and my God! By what "rule of the screw" does my head split like this every day! A-a-a-a-h. Maybe I should wrap my head in toilet paper and walk around like that. So the bastards would know how shitty I feel.

No, the neighbors are not hangmen—they're engineers recruited by the KGB organs, just house servants. But all the same, those "Cherepanov Brothers" are going to get vicious after they've finished their post-breakfast burping, when the whole department of vampires starts in on their yard work, digging their teeth into my blackly ringing skull, using whichever tool they choose—drills, power planes, lawn mowers, and "Friendship" brand chain saws: Okay, slimeball, spill your guts.[4]

There aren't any hangmen, but there is a spy. The station chief in São Tomé and Príncipe.[5] Rumor has it that Andropov once screamed at them in a general meeting: "The Americans," Andropov screamed, "work hard for their money. And you sit there in the embassy like a mouse under a broom, you aren't worth the hard currency you spend!"

After eight years of reminders, the spy brought our settlement chairman the miserly sum of eight rubles for electricity.

"Are you kidding me," the chairman said in amazement, "didn't you study physics in school?"

"That's what the meter read," the spy said, putting an end to the discussion.[6]

It was from him that another colonel, with the tipsy assistance of the watchman, swiped seventy cubic feet of grooved beams.

Relations with the neighbors to the east and south are quite decent, and you don't have to ask them twice to pull on the rope when the birch tree has already been sawed partway through and has started to tilt. And if they have room in the car, they're glad to give you a lift to Moscow.

What have I come to: to sit carefree with an officer in the state security apparatus. To gradually get into a little talk about life . . . just what I was deathly afraid of back in December 1981, when three indiscriminable and undiscriminating triplets in leather coats burst into Olya's place in Fili at the crack of dawn.[7]

They just wanted to have a little talk! Don't even think about it! In the kitchen I hurriedly smeared my wrist with green Magic Marker as a reminder: you have a mother, you had a childhood with a bicycle and Robert Louis Stevenson, you love Pushkin, and the main thing is, you'll be very ashamed of yourself.

They were hurrying me, the car was waiting downstairs. As I walked by I whispered to Olya to distract them with talk, hid some beer under my sweater, and locked myself in the bathroom. Damn, I forgot the opener! I turned on both faucets full strength in order to muffle my fuss with the bottle, and ripped off the bottle cap using I don't know what, maybe the toothbrush. Sitting on the edge of the bathtub, I swigged from the bottle to the sound of the two faucets. It's all my fault, why did I lose my nerve, diddle around? As if I didn't know that in the end they would just take me by the throat? I already knew that back when I called home from Choboty and in a strange voice my mother hinted as clearly as could be that there'd been a search at our place. And then I spent two more days walking around the empty settlement, rehearsing. Until Olya asked me straight out, "Don't tell me you're afraid?" This was too much. We made our way to Moscow, decided to have a little fun. We went to the Mir Theater to see the Damiano Damiani film *I Am Afraid*.[8] People were being thrown alive into wet cement; the judicial authorities shut their eyes to these pranks. As we were leaving the theater, seeing that I hadn't cheered up, Olya suggested, "Shall we buy a little bottle of wine?" We bought three bottles of dry wine and took a bottle of beer as change.

"I'm ready," I shouted to the visitors, pushing the bottle behind the door with my foot.

We zipped along the centerline of Kutuzovsky Prospect. The antenna was bent by the speed. We sailed past Borozdina's house. Youth. Dunaevsky Street. Childhood and boyhood.[9] The triplets gallantly helped Olya get out at the Dzerzhinsky subway stop: she had to go to work on Tsvetnoy Boulevard. They circled a few times around the main building and anchored alongside a two-story nineteenth-century structure. "Here we are. Please get out."

Fuck it, there are a lot of you, a city within a city. Black "Volga" cars. They're dragging canvas bags, probably from searches. The employees run from entryway to entryway, from building to building, traveling light, without their coats. They slap each other five, grinning: How are you? And how's the wife? They shiver a little in the cold. I'm up shit creek!

They lead me to an unremarkable room on the second floor. I sit down, look around—nothing special: just an ordinary room. My Porfiry comes rolling in, introduces himself: Major Kopaev. A disciple of Albrekht, I mention a record of proceedings.

"Well, you're quite the professional, Sergey Markovich," the major laughs. "How could we do without a record? Everything according to the rulebook."[10]

Little by little we get to Kozlovsky. I'd seen him once. Or twice. A fat man with a red beard, a receding hairline; you can't deny it, he looks like a prose writer.

"So what did you talk about?"

"About literature. About *The Violist Danilov*."[11]

"I'd like to read that, but I just don't get around to it. Does he write well?"

"I haven't read it."

"So how did you talk about it?"

"Sometimes you know you don't like it before you've read it."

"Did you read *Red Square* by Kozlovsky?"

"No."

"We've Met in Paradise?"

"No." And that was the God's truth. All the issues of *Kontinent* went through Kenzheev, and it wasn't my turn yet. He liked Soprovsky better, and considered me not too bright, the lousy little Tatar.[12]

"So how can you and your comrades get together to defend him, and write letters, when you haven't read him yourselves?"

And I start up my rehearsed nonsense about the difference between artistic invention and slander of the Soviet order.

"And where will they permit you such artistic invention? In South Africa? In Chile?"

"You're putting our country into an interesting category," I say, and congratulate myself inwardly.

The major chuckles and spreads his hands as if to say: my mistake. I ask permission to smoke and immediately regret it: my hands are unsteady after yesterday's wine, but he'll figure it's from fear. I excuse myself to go to the toilet, which is also a mistake, because he accompanies me along the busy corridor and breathes down my neck, and there's no door on the stall. And for some reason I just can't piss. Since schooldays I've known that I can't do it in front of people. To the sound of my classmates' cackling I'd go and stand idly over the urinal for a minute or two, then hold it until I got home.

We return and take up our initial positions. We're silent, for a long time we're silent.

"And what is this?" he exclaims victoriously, and like a trump card he lays out a piece of paper from a ruled primary-school notebook, covered with my own drunken handwriting.

I say with amazement and relief:

"So you must have all my documents too, my work ID, and my passport, and my draft card?"[13]

My God! And I'd blamed Chumak unjustly, I'd thought that Chumak had seen that I was out of it and had taken my map-case off me out of drunken concern, forgotten to return it, and disappeared. It's all just homelessness, gratitude, and chronic alcoholism. It's the fear of looking like that pig Pechorin when he met Maksim Maksimych, even though there wasn't much in particular to talk about.[14] It's the pride of an intellectual, even an intellectual who's let himself go the way I have, pride in having a friendship with a man of the common people, a man as simple as a stump.

Up to the last minute I didn't believe he would come. Chumak would call me every year, year and a half, now from Gazli, then from Chardzhou, then from Andijon. It was hard to hear him because of interference on the line and the seriously drunken state of the caller. The conversation would come to a standstill at "Hey there, brother," and "I'm coming to see you, brother." I had decided that that was his symptomatology, and why not? When he's drunk he has an urge to go to the office where you can make long-distance calls, while I, for example, get the urge to go visiting—and the farther the better, whether to see Kibirov in Konkovo or Koval in Otradnoe.

And then all of a sudden he shows up, and he's not alone! He's with his "slant-eyed girlfriend," as he says with simple-hearted racism. And with a brat. They're tired and dirty after three days sitting up in a train. My wife and child go quietly into the bathroom. Mama feeds everybody. But Misha Chumak didn't come here to bathe or to eat macaroni. He needs a continuation of our drinking bouts, but it's just impossible here: my mother is home, my father will get home from work any minute now, my brother will come back from the institute, and in my room the "slant-eyed woman" and the kid are sleeping. So under an innocent pretext and my mother's sorrowful gaze we slip out of the house, and after we've done our shopping, I call Arkady Pakhomov from the supermarket near the Yugozapadnaya subway station, and I take him by force, without any ifs, ands, or buts. He clearly isn't up for drinking, and I don't feel like carousing, but that's what's in the cards.

Thank you, Arkady, for understanding my situation. Your own parents were home, and Evgenia Sergeevna was playing music in the next room. We put three "Andropovkas" on the table.[15] You grimaced (a sign of cheerful disapproval), brought some black bread on the sly (your parents thought we were playing lotto), and—we got the party started! We were noisy, but I was the most enthusiastic of all. I don't think I let you open your mouth once. We were already high, we'd had a drink on our way there, and in general I'm big on talking nonsense, and I had to present Misha in the best light . . . . But the story I had to tell was worth it, you have to admit. So here it is.

You know, I always had a hard time getting set up for an expedition. If the personnel office asked for my draft card, I'd know I was screwed: Article 2B.[16] In 1978 I had bad luck, and that's all there was to it. The bureaucrats were seized with what Dostoevsky called "administrative ecstasy." It's the middle of May and I'm still floating around like a turd in an ice-hole. I had to drag myself off to the back of beyond, to Lyublino. Buses, transfers, the address on a slip of paper. Seems to be my street, I get out. The road is blocked off with a turnstile; it's crawling with police. I show them the address. Go around, they say, you can't walk this way. Finally I find it. The boss is a smiling guy of about thirty-five. He looks okay. We introduce ourselves. Yura Afanasov.

"What's going on around here?" I ask. "I had to wander around the back alleys, everything's closed off."

"Yeah, they're having a trial for some nut like you."

"?"

"Yuri Orlov."

I immediately confess that there are some problems with my draft card. That's no problem for us, Afanasov reassures me, as long as you have your arms and legs. And in a jiffy I've been registered for three months in Mangyshlak, but on one condition. That I escort two flatcars carrying machines and vehicles for the expedition. And I agree, or else where the hell would I go?

"Okay, bon voyage," my new boss says in farewell, "I hope they don't throw you off the flatcar."

"Has that happened before?" I ask with interest.

"Now don't you worry," good old Afanasov replies.

I got depressed about having to spend a week or two dragging to my destination. But then I thought, okay, I'll travel around Russia like Pushkin, at a slow pace.

And we set off like Pushkin. We spent almost a month on the road. There were four of us escorts. I was the only one who hadn't served time. In the first few days we drank away all our cash, and the fistfights started on the second day of the trip. Then I understood for the first time: you shouldn't try to make people like you, or to find a common language. They'll correctly understand that as weakness, and you'll be shown no mercy. This timely discovery saved me from being pounded. All I'd do was try to break up the fights, at which I had mediocre success. I was amazed at how infantile my fellow travelers were. In the evening they'd punch each other's faces in, or dump the grub onto the head of the cook Vitya Kukushkin, and in the morning they'd get together as if nothing had happened. Like three-year-old children acting up in the sandbox over their toy molds. I also couldn't believe their complete contempt for freedom. If I'd been even a week in the hell they kept reminiscing about, I'd be afraid to cross the street at a red light, but they couldn't care less. They were already selling some of the expedition's property, tempting the hungry town of Voronezh with canned meat. Were they sick of being free, or what?

But the main surprises began after we passed through Makat. They sold everything that wasn't tied down and drank up the proceeds. They finished off the pills from the expedition's drug supply—and now Vitya Kukushkin, like some Francis of Assisi, is having a heart-to-heart talk with his sneakers. I have nothing to do with it: I'm reading. One fine morning there was a strong smell of coffee. Overnight the train had been re-formed and a car filled with colonial goods had been attached right to our flatcars. The "council of war in Fili" didn't last long. My incorrigible comrades, like wolves, one after another leaped over onto the roof of the car in front while the train was running. The forty-car freight train was rumbling through a completely flat semidesert, and only a few camels enlivened the landscape, beautiful in its own way. One of the guys hung over the side and broke off the seals on the car. They rolled open the door and the looting began. A quarter of an hour later, five or six large crates of ground "Arabica" coffee were piled on the flatcar. The looters didn't even find time to cover the evidence with a tarpaulin. They straggled off to sleep wherever they could find a place.

The next morning at a junction we picked up two men. One of them, a lean guy with teeth in a checkerboard pattern, was called Misha Chumak, and I don't remember the name of the other one, a very young man with a shaved head. I only remember that he was richly illustrated: neck, chest, back, stomach—water sprites, eagles, torches—you couldn't count them all. He had the look of a nasty bastard. They weren't friends, they'd met by chance in the desert. Misha Chumak was chasing *saigak*, the Central Asian antelope, on his motorcycle, he lost control of the motorcycle on a dune, it twirled and whirled, he laid it down—and now Misha's here wearing only a shirt, and he has to get to Urgench to find a job. The second guy, with the illustrations, kept quiet, but as far as I could understand he'd gotten totally lost and only found the train tracks thanks to Chumak. Toward evening we suddenly stopped in the middle of the desert. For no reason at all. There was a junction not far off, we ran over there, and the attendant explained that the locomotive wasn't pulling. The train was heavy, the locomotive was a low-powered one, so it wouldn't pull. Already an hour ago it had decoupled, abandoned the headless freight train, and whisked back to Makat. No one knew when there'd be a high-powered locomotive. In theory there must be one.

"We'll be waiting until Good-Fucking-Friday," Chumak said, and he turned out to be right.

We stayed out there in the sun for one day, two days, three. And for the whole lifeless train, which stretched for about two kilometers, there were six of us, if you don't count the trackman in his hut filled with flies. I gave up and tried with difficulty to read an English book. The others furiously played the thieves' card games *bura* and *sika* with homemade cards, but I passed as always, since I'd been fleeced in Pevek.[17] It was boring as hell. Seeing me ruining my youth over a book, Chumak warned me, "You're making a mistake, Seryi, that shit's going to get into your head and fuck it up." And it's as if he was telling my fortune, the echoing answer to that prophecy came seventeen years later!

By Sunday morning we'd run out of water, food, and smokes. Misha took a forty-liter water can for want of anything smaller and went off into the steppe. I tagged along after him. He never shut his mouth, and he was really good at slinging the bull. Everything in his life was the same as it was for those guys back on the flatcar, but not really the same. They'd remember the joint constantly and with relish, endlessly retelling the horrors, but Chumak talked about imprisonment only reluctantly. Knowing you're not supposed to ask what somebody was in for, I couldn't help myself anyway, and it turned out that all his beefs were pure nursery school: either he beat somebody up when he was sloshed, or somebody beat him up. Or he fell asleep drunk in a trailer, and because of his cheap "Pamir" *papirosa* an "establishment of economic significance" burned down. Or he stole the Party regional committee's turkeys and barbecued them for some girls in an irrigation ditch. He's a hell-raiser. He talked without punctuation marks, like Aksyonov's Teleskopov.[18] "The world of animals"—he'd begin one of his innumerable amorous tales with artificial contrition, and like a foreigner I'd listen to the story of how he was working as a long-distance truck driver when they got a roadside hooker drunk, and how it all ended. And wandering about the steppe, gathering wild garlic, I rejoiced in this man and felt how sick I had gotten of that jungle on wheels, because for two and a half weeks now I'd been on guard even in my sleep: my fellow travelers made me nervous. So, little by little, chewing the fat, we stumbled onto the empty trailer of some drill operators. The trailer was lived-in and tidy, with a picture of a Japanese woman on the wall. Misha made himself a loan of some water, took a small quantity of dry biscuits and a couple of the packs of Prima cigarettes that were scattered around. We had a smoke in the shadow of the trailer and then set off for our freight train on the horizon. We cut across a *solonchak*, a stretch of salt-encrusted soil. The water can was so heavy it was painful to carry, and Chumak taught me how to carry it braced between us. We showed our companions what we'd scrounged up, and the whole jolly company cussed and tore off to retrace our path.

They returned with happy faces after about three hours, and from fragments of their conversation I realized that the bastards had really gone to town, hadn't denied themselves anything, maybe even pissed in the drill-operators' water can. They got an unsealed deck of cards and went off to lead with diamonds. We killed another day like this.

Toward night, I see that the cardplayers have finished their fun, but they aren't crawling into a truck as usual to sleep but are hiding in various places, and each one makes sure to equip himself with as heavy a piece of iron as possible. I don't get it at first. Chumak and I are having a smoke on top of the cab of a GAZ-66 truck mounted on a flatcar facing the sunset, and he suddenly says to me, with punctuation marks: "On Monday at five in the morning the drill operators will be dropped off at the borehole. They're all wild beasts and they're armed, and there are footprints on the *solonchak*. You do whatever you want, but three hours from now I'm getting out of here. They're not going to bother figuring out who's who." I answer him by telling him the story of the coffee. And he, a qualified correspondence-course legal expert, enumerates the counts and the sentences: robbery with breaking and entering, misappropriation of government property on a particularly large scale. He says, *they* aren't going to bother figuring out who's who either. For about two hours we hustle to unload the truck in the darkness, we put the coffee on the bottom and then reload it. And we smoke. "Well?" Misha asks. "I'm getting the hell out of here, wanna come along?" His proposition was drowned out by the sound of our train clanking, jerking, coming to life, and slowly, slowly, slowly starting off.

Two or three days later we arrived at our assigned destination, the Mangyshlak station. The four inseparable friends, huffing and puffing, rolled a little Gazik truck out of the train on two planks and rushed off to Shevchenko: to fuck some babes. And they told me and Chumak to keep guard. I keep worrying about that coffee. And I make up my mind and say to Chumak, "Why should we sit here with our kissers hanging out? We've found four great bosses for ourselves: 'Keep guard.' Let's dump this coffee. I'm losing my nerve."

"Shitting your pants?"

"Yeah."

And in the same way, along the same planks, we roll out a second Gazik. We extricate the crates of coffee from their hiding place, load them in the truck, and drive to the station. It's not far—about a kilometer. From the back door we bring the load into the storeroom of the station snack bar,

without haggling we get what's coming to us from the big mama, plus
four bottles of fortified "Gift of the Sun" wine. And everyone's happy.
We ride around the dusty settlement of Mangyshlak for a while and then
return to the classification yard.[19] Everything's safe. In the middle of the
relief tracks we set up an expedition table and canvas chairs, we put the
firewater, some bread and greens on it, and we drink without rushing, we
drink to the proposition that the children not fear thunder and we get
hard-ons into our old age![20] Twilight comes—we sit in the twilight, it
gets dark—we sit in the darkness, until our peaceful sitting, as in a night-
mare, turns into the beating of Misha Chumak illuminated by headlights.
It's the four cons who've come back out of the blue, sober and mad, with
aching scrotums. I jump around, blinded by the bright light, stick my extremities into the cursing melee, and call for help from anyone—people,
the devil, Chip and Dale, whom no one had even heard of back then.

"Help him, Arkady, he can't find it."

While I was blabbering, my Chumak had drunk himself helpless and
was now staggering in the corridor trying to find the door to the toilet.
And I too was getting swiftly bombed. Either I had worn myself out with
my solo, or Andropovka is truly a treacherous kind of vodka. I catch the
worried gaze of Arkasha Pakhomov directed at me. Don't get all hot and
bothered, mine host, we're getting up and leaving, and I swear we'll make
it home, and may the same happen to anyone who raises the price on
Texas pigs! Let's have one for the road.

Near the All-Russia Exhibition Center subway station, where there's
always a crush, we immediately lose each other. But I thought Chumak
would find his way back, he'd remember the address. Or rather I didn't
think anything but was woken up by the woman guard at the Belyaevo
station, the end of the line. I emerge, sobering up, onto the platform and
suddenly remember: my map-case. I definitely had it when we left Pakhomov's. And of course I had to put my birth certificate in there too, to
make a full set! Oh, my God!

And for four days—it wasn't enough that our place had been searched
in my absence and I was all wired up waiting to be arrested—now I was
dumbfounded by the prospect of housing offices, passport offices, military commissions, police departments, declarations, explanations, certificates, certificates, certificates! But the map-case—there it is, my little
fish, there it is, my little bird—lying on Kopaev's desk.

"So all right," Kopaev brings me out of my joyful confusion. "What does all this mean?" He sternly points his chin at the accursed receipt.

How can you explain something like that? I swear I don't know. The peculiar nature of some of my situations would make a well-disposed but sensible person vomit . . . . But this is a guy with dead eyes and a Komsomol paunch. How can I explain that it's possible to step out for three minutes with the trash can and return three days later, from Leningrad and without the trash can?

Well, okay, a week ago I was sitting with Kenzheev in Choboty, where we had rented a room and a kitchen at the winterized dacha of Nikolay Ivanovich, a former prosecutor of cases that always ended in the death sentence. Across the lane from the pharmacy. Besides Bakhyt and me, Soprovsky and Volodya Semyonov were there. Naturally we were talking about the arrest of Kozlovsky. Of course we were drinking. Energetic Soprovsky said we couldn't abandon our guild comrade in his misfortune. We had to write a letter. As a distraction we'd send one copy to the Union of Writers, and we'd "lose" the other one. Everyone expressed their opinions for and against, then we started composing the missive. We kept drinking. This Volodya Semyonov was a good friend who came to visit me in the Burdenko neurosurgery hospital, but he has a certain peculiarity: when he has a snort, he gets on his high horse like you wouldn't believe. It was the same this time—Volodya was smashed; here people are getting excited, they're rolling out a letter to the Turkish sultan, and he keeps droning: you shouldn't be afraid of anything, I'll scribble my signature on any piece of paper without looking at it—and he's saying all this right next to me.[21] This droning is driving me crazy, because I don't know how the others feel, but I'm scared shitless. And the main thing is that when he's sober Volodya has enough honesty and manliness to tell the story of how Bukovsky said to him in the 1960s, "Blame everything on me, they're going to put me in prison anyway." They were getting ready to expel Volodya, the son of an academician, from the Komsomol because he had allowed some sort of "incorrect" artists to exhibit their work in his father's apartment.[22] But now he'd knocked back his three-plus shots of vodka and was acting the hero.

"Is it true," I ask, "that you'll sign any piece of paper?"

"It's true," he says.

"Without looking at it?"

"Yes."

And drunken monster that I am, I use the edge of the table to write on a piece of ruled school paper: "I am familiar with the regulations of the fuzz. I ask to be considered a member of a terrorist fighting organization. I pledge to appear with a weapon at the indicated time and the appointed place." Volodya scribbles his signature on the piece of paper for me without looking at it, as he promised. Then I let him read it, and he good-naturedly brushes me off, saying, "Bullshitter." My anger disappears, and I say that at a difficult moment I will be there to extort cash from him with the help of this little piece of paper. How it got into my map-case, I haven't a clue.

I tell all this to Kopaev, but succinctly, without names or psychological analysis, and he writes it down as I tell it, repeating it aloud like a pre-school child, and with half an ear I hear: "with the object of extortion."

"What are you doing," I shout, "that's a criminal count!"

He smiles. But then he gets serious and says, "So let's do it this way. You bring your friend to us, since you don't want to name him without his permission. And we'll give you back your documents, okay? And please get a job, because look how long you've been without work—seven months. Keep in mind, we know everything, even about Klimontovich's carrot. They'll sign your pass downstairs."

"I don't have a passport."

"Oh, hell." And he accompanied me through the security gate.

Kolya Klimontovich had just told me a couple of days before that at the supermarket in Bibirevo where he lives, out of boredom he'd switched the price lists on the carrot crates.

I inhale the marvelous December air, light up a cigarette, and think that of course I won't say anything to Volodya Semyonov—it's shameful enough without that. Sooner or later they'll give me back my documents anyway. I also think: "Dissident. Liberator of the Fatherland. Prisoner of conscience. Piece of crap. Homeless alky." I also think, wiping the green smear off my wrist with a lump of snow, that I'm going to have to get a job, since I've been stupid enough to be exposed.

My biography is in a certain sense an exemplary and instructive one. All the signs of the outcast are present in it: inability to find one's way in life, drunkenness, friction with the authorities, constant work as a watchman, seasonal expeditions. Everything that the editorial bigshots make a fuss over now, those guys who began as the heralds of perestroika, who would frighten a renegade like me—this did happen—with sudden embraces, warm hospitality, and the cry: "Oh, my honest old buddy!" Now this biographical herd instinct grates on me, this life according to a template. Could I really not think up something of my own?

"But you're a seventh-generation intellectual!" my father would lecture me with anger and bitterness. "You've pissed away your best years, and you don't give a damn!"

But my poor papa wasn't completely correct, there were also some learning experiences. I'm hitchhiking with the standard poodle Maksim along the Afghanistan-Tajikistan border from Vanch to Osh. The contingent of troops would be sent into Afghanistan in December 1979, I'm traveling in October. The border is weakly defended. There are pickets every fifty kilometers, in places the posts holding the barbed wire have been knocked down. Maksim and I even took a dip in the Pyandzh River, running the risk of taking a bullet. In hitchhiking there is one rule: you can pay or not pay, but you cannot fall asleep. It's infectious. The driver will doze off along with you, and the car will go off a cliff. You have to entertain the driver, to earn your passage. The first night I spent in a roadside *kishlak*, the second in Khorog, in a hotel, no less.[23] A bust of Marx stood in front of it. I was flabbergasted. An obscure German economist, a nutty oddball, and now a bit over a hundred years later here stands his plaster gourd, almost in the Himalayas!

The woman manager of the hotel started to make a big deal about the dog, but I spun a tale for the aged denizen of the Pamirs about how this was a scientific pooch, transported to the high mountain region for outer-space research. I was young, I could talk the tail off a donkey. I was awakened by Maksim's whimpering. He was standing up to his belly in urine and turds. My shoes and backpack were saturated with fecal matter and were staying afloat with great difficulty: the sewage pipes had burst. We fled the shitty hotel without a backward glance and spent a long time washing off in the Gunt River, sniffing each other suspiciously. And at this point we finally had some luck. I stuck out my thumb, a gasoline truck stopped, and the driver, a well-built guy named Mukhammed Yakubov, picked us up on his way to Osh. It took us two days to get there. We bathed in a sulphur spring at the Dzhilandy spa. The first night we spent in Murghab and in the morning we set off along the high plains of the Eastern Pamirs, as flat as a table. Only Lenin Peak, Communism Peak, and other peaks rose like icy arrows shooting up in the distance. Sometimes there were yaks grazing by the side of the road, sometimes Kirghiz villages with their felt-covered yurts flashed by. I've gotten to see a lot of life, after all! Attaboy! I love it!

For the first part of the trip Mukhammed entertained himself by teasing the border guards with the poodle. It was forbidden to transport sheep from one region to another, either because of quarantine or some other sort of nonsense. And here's this curly-haired creature, a sheep if there ever was one. The guards who've stagnated in this hole with nothing to do, rubbing their hands, come running from their huts by the crossing to confiscate the sheep. And then the sheep starts barking.

But a bit later I see the driver's getting bored. By the Karakul lake, trying to entertain him, I point to the huge crows heavily soaring over the dead water, and I ask, "What is that bird called in Tajik?"

"You Russians call it a 'duck,'" the driver answers, livening up. "In general it's a crow, but the correct word is 'birrud.'"

Relativism yet again.

So one could pick up some good sense even while being degraded into the lumpenproletariat.

This was a whole science—how to answer questioning with abracadabra. Mukhammed Yakubov taught me the first lesson, and years later, Vladimir Yanovich Albrekht. He taught that one should tell the investigator something so truthful that the chances of putting you in a spot were reduced to zero.

"Whose Gospel is it?"

"It's the Gospel of Matthew."

But Albrekht's own know-how wasn't enough to save him from the camps. It was Prigov who talked me and Sasha Soprovsky into going to Albrekht's lecture "The Ethics of the Interrogation," in Leonid Bazhanov's apartment on Malaya Gruzinskaya Street. Do you remember, Dmitri Aleksandrovich? And do you remember, you and I were strolling around Zvenigorod when Vitya Sanchuk's little dog ran away, and he would rush to every sound of yapping and call, "Lapsik! Lapsik!"

We wandered near the monastery along the Moscow River, and you showed me the village on the other side of the river where you lived with your parents the summer after the war. And then for want of something

better to do we went to the dacha settlement Mozzhinka to shoot some
pool. I perked up when I realized that you had never in your life held a
cue in your hands, and decided to take revenge on account of Vitya, who
always trounced me.

You had a strange way of playing and getting into the game, Dmitri
Aleksandrovich! You were dead serious. Vitka and I turned the game
into a game. We slouched around the billiard table lazily, lightly muttered officers' obscenities through clenched teeth, chalked our cues in an
emphatically Onegin-like manner, took aim while parodically sticking
out our butts.[24] But for you a game is not something to be trifled with. It
was not pretty: you took the billiard game by force. You lay prone on the
table, you wheezed, you sweated. Sticking the tip of your tongue out in
your zeal and scraping the felt with your cue, you pushed the balls into
the pockets. Is that really how decent people behave? A billiard match
should click foppishly, as the lightning of the cue ball sparkles like the
electricity in a physics experiment! When you had won the first match,
I condescendingly congratulated you, but I inwardly resolved that there
would be no more giveaways. I racked the balls in "pig's head" formation
for a second battle. You did your same old thing, but soon the depress-
ing spectacle of your dilettantish efforts took on an ominous hue, and
I began to miss. By midnight you had beaten me in a shutout—13:0.
You had turned a ballet into a gang rape, and I began to look at you with
new interest.

Mozzhinka is a great place. They say the New Russians have taken
over now, but ten years ago Mozzhinka had still preserved its ambiguous charm.[25]

According to tradition, the name of the place derives from the smash-
ing (*mozzhenie*) of skulls, the favorite pastime of the local villains. An
asphalt road for internal use crossed the settlement and stopped short
at the forested slope down to the Moscow River. On the right hand we
passed the House of Culture with its four Doric columns and echoing
lobby, where the walls were hung with photographic portraits of the
academician-homeowners. The dachas were identical but opulent: two
stories high, with all the conveniences; Stalin respected science and hu-
mored it. The cornfield on the opposite bank of the river recalled the
capricious labors of Khrushchev.[26] It smelled of Russian history of the
Soviet period. The style of those times took the onlooker unawares, and

one might go numb and experience, without having actually experienced, the singing of *"Gaudeamus, igitur"* in an academician's bass and the reading of *Marxism and the Problems of Linguistics* at bedtime in the fabled past, when after summer storms rainwater laced with adrenaline ran through the roadside ditches.[27] As a *raznochinets* with the standard six-*sotka* dacha allotment, I wickedly noted the Latin American neglect of the Zvenigorod latifundia: fences broken down in places, nettles growing chest-high.[28]

It was an endless deep-blue September, and the golden uniforms of the oaks were falling underfoot like the rubble of the Third Reich.[29] The inhabitants of the preserve were allowing themselves the luxury of a sweet carelessness in housekeeping and an un-Soviet benevolence. If Vitya disappeared for two or three days and returned drunk as a Polack, Genrikh Eduardovich would say to a guest: "My son has taken the Twentieth Party Congress and all its consequences to heart."[30] I found his tone quite strange. In similar situations my father would blurt out, "Marry him off or castrate him!" Vitya's mama, Elena Isaakovna, had in her time taught literature in school to Vladmir Poletaev. And I consider myself to be the great-nephew of Poletaev in literary genealogy. Because he scolded and nursed two ninth-graders, Aleksandr Kazintsev and Sasha Soprovsky, and under their strong influence, after the death of the eighteen-year-old master, I let out my first squeak in rhyme.

The young Poletaev possessed exceptional poetic abilities, a rare erudition for his age, and a youthful impudence. Once when he was a first-year student at the Literary Institute, he brought an awkward schoolboy, Kazintsev, to the Central House of Writers. They were sitting having coffee and caught sight of Arseny Tarkovsky coming into the café.

"Arseny Aleksandrovich, could you come over here for a minute," Poletaev called out.

The old man came hobbling up to the table. Poletaev, like one peer to another, introduced Kazintsev, the sixteen-year-old hope of Russian poetry, to the old poet. Later it turned out that Poletaev did not have even a nodding acquaintance with the classic writer.

Before I met the two classmates named Aleksandr, I had not written poetry because I didn't know how to rhyme. Or rather, I did write it, but when I was nine years old: "We've fought and punched each other out. We've got no time to fuss about." "Poem of Love." Lyusya Vykhodtseva.

I wrote her a cowardly note: "Lyusya, I l—e you. If you guess who, then leave an answer in my desk." The written assurances of reciprocal affection were received by Zhenya Meshalov, and with bewildered rapture he imparted to me his unearned success. I listened to him, swooning with Salieri-like feelings.[31]

In 1970, contrary to the family tradition of technocracy, I was accepted into the Department of Philology at Moscow State University, purely by chance. The essay question for the entrance exam was "Romantic Nature in Lermontov's Narrative Poem *Mtsyri*." Three-fourths of the competitors went astray in their excitement and started describing shrubs-flowers-nature. Coached by my tutor Nina Aleksandrovna Berman, I got a death grip on the subject and for an hour—with feeling, with sense, with deliberation—I quickly filled the page. I was already getting up to turn in my scribbling when the woman seated to my right, later my classmate and now a single mother, Lera Andreeva, pointed out to me about a dozen omitted commas. So I got a four (second highest on a five-point scale) and was admitted to the oral examination. I did badly, but the examiner, A. I. Zhuravlev, had heard my name from his friend, my high-school teacher Vera Romanovna Vainberg, and gave me a five. "Your Gandlevsky's eyes are more intelligent than his answers," he said to Vera Romanovna. A year later Vera Romanovna stopped working and would have her favorites come to her house because she had developed brain cancer, and she is now lying somewhere at the Vostryakovskoe Cemetery, and I have never once visited her grave.

I applied to the Department of Philology because I had decided to make myself into a great writer. I had a pretty decent knowledge of Pushkin, Mayakovsky, Bagritsky, and Utkin—the same writers my father had a decent knowledge of—and I planned in my own works to achieve an arithmetic mean between Anatole France and Dostoevsky; such were my intentions.

I was the only man in the group, and I was hastily chosen to be the *proforg*, who would represent the interests of the group of students in the professional organization and with the university administration. I got hopelessly lost in the records of monthly dues payments and had despaired of ever extricating myself from this situation, when Soprovsky, an external student I hardly knew, disheveled, chubby, short, with huge slightly bulging light-blue eyes, came up to me and asked with unexpected sympathy, "What are you worrying about?"

At the age of eighteen I didn't know how to answer simply, so, coming out in spots, I said, "I tell You, man has no more pressing need than to find someone..."

And Sasha, the bookworm, caught it on the fly: "... to whom he can give up that gift of freedom with which he, unhappy being that he is, was endowed at birth."[32]

And we became inseparable for twenty years, with some interruptions caused by quarrels.

Aleksandr Kazintsev now spends his time being professionally concerned about the Russian *narod* [common people], and this is strange to me, because I had had occasion more than once, at Sasha's request, to accompany him from my birthday parties to the Sokolniki subway station: he was afraid of hooligans. My other friends and acquaintances and I myself never experienced any special feelings for the *narod*, but we walk the streets without escorts. And who isn't afraid of hooligans? A foster child of the Mozhaika courtyards, I sucked in the fear of street toughs with my mother's milk and have carried it with me to the age of gray hair, and not without reason. Just take for example an adventure I had three years ago.

Somehow I notice that most of my tales begin monotonously, "We went and bought," something like the fairy-tale introduction "*Zhili-byli* [Once upon a time]." Once upon a time, April 12, 1991, Vitya Koval and I went and by a miracle bought in a store on Serpukhovskaya Street, five minutes before closing, two bottles of brandy for fifteen rubles each. It was a gloomy day, and the headwind on Pyatnitskaya Street blew the street trash around, stirred my neglected beard, and lifted the Hutsul locks of my companion walking alongside.[33] Along the way I calculated that Lena's love for Koval would counterbalance Lena's non-love for drinking bouts, and I had really plucked up my courage by the time we turned onto our street, First Novokuznetsky Lane. Lena loves Koval, and for good reason. His shamanistic ravings are primeval and wild and have nothing in common with the square merriment of a charlatan who's read too much Huizinga.[34] Vitya has a woman's sensitivity to coarseness and barracks language, and so he can talk spicily like no one else. Aizenberg said that it's a little frightening to be friends with Koval, because it seems as if he's walking with one foot on the ground and the other in thin air. To masculine amusements common to the bathhouse and beachside card games Koval time and again answers with the caprices of delirium tremens and breaks up the party.[35]

He was in the army when the August campaign of 1968 started. His regimental companions were prepared for action and were rubbing their hands in pleasurable anticipation of making the Czechs shit their pants, when Koval took a snort too many out of nervousness and started wandering around the parade ground in his underwear, gesticulating and preaching pan-Slavic reconciliation.[36] The madman thought he was orating in the town square of a Central European city decorated with equestrian statues. The holy fool was saved from a military tribunal by the lynch-law punishment meted out by the more senior soldiers.

Or the time he went hunting at a nature preserve with his wife's Kalmyk relatives. On the way he was getting nauseated because of what awaited him. But here too his fiancée in a glass jacket (the bottle) came to her intended's rescue: he started acting up and was thrown out of the bus onto the blazing highway by the indignant hunters. He happened on the shack of a Chinese wise man just at the right moment, and an hour later, having been bid farewell by the old Buddhist, a barefoot Koval was tramping along the side of the road in the direction of Elista.

And when we were on tour in Sweden, we got a note from the audience: a young Swedish woman with Nordic straightforwardness came right out and said that she wanted to have a baby by Koval.

So it was with this man that I appeared before Lena's green eyes with two bottles on April 12 three years ago.

Lena joined us, the children were with my mother-in-law, we spent a wonderful evening and, long after midnight, we even sang multiple encores of a song from the times of fraternization and zeal at the First Moscow Festival of Youth and Students in 1957: ta-ra-ra-ra-ra-ra-ra-a-a-a / ta-a-a-ra-ra-ra-a-a-a (twice).[37]

The next morning I said with a significant air that there was salted fish in the refrigerator. We armed ourselves with three- and five-liter jars and went to the self-serve beer hall in Klimentovsky Lane.

Natasha Molchanskaya is right—a garden-variety drunk can stretch himself and say without ceremony: "It's gotten a little colder, isn't it time to have a drink?" An alcoholic can't do it like that. In order to slake his lust he needs a pretext, even a ludicrous one, a reference to the sanctity of custom. So all right, we had a fish. So is that a pretext to suck down eight liters of beer first thing in the morning, as if people can't eat salted fish just like that, without anything or with some potatoes, let's say? And if there hadn't been a fish, would we have all gone home? No. We would have searched out some beat-up apple and assured each other and Lena that fruit demands dry wine, some sour stuff that costs two rubles. If a moldy pickle had come our way, we would have raised a fuss about the lack of order: there's something pickled, and no vodka. Well, and what if the house had been bare as a bone? We probably would have guzzled cologne: it doesn't presuppose any accompanying victuals.

In the cattle pen on Klimentovsky Lane the hungover throng was bitching and moaning, and there was a whiff of punchfest in the air. A few guys had already managed to find themselves on the other side of good and evil and get their beer without standing in line. And there were two lines: first to get twenty-kopeck pieces for the machine, and then for the beer itself, in a crowded hangar on the left. We suffered for about forty minutes in the line for coins and then got into the beer line. The riffraff in the beer hall no longer seemed to all look alike, like Chinese, but were starting to fall into different categories. The larger category— hangdog drunks with dried-out mouths, like Koval and me. Jars, string bags, coins in our sweaty fists. And the second category, not numerous, but noticeable—five or six men with wolfish movements and the manner of petty thugs.

A cold lump of cowardice, like a tangle of snakes, stirred in my stomach. I wanted to leave—to hell with this swill—but the horse was already out of the barn. A gangleader had arisen, my two-meter-tall namesake, a real mountain of a man. He was blocking the entrance into the beer hangar and would let people in or not let them in at his own discretion, laughing and shooting the breeze with his own bunch. Vitya and I had gotten right up to our goal, and the beer dispensers could already be seen, when we came to a standstill. The gangleader turned his back to the line and got involved in a conversation with his fellow punks. I was becoming ashamed. I touched that enormous back and said that it was time to let people through. He turned around.

"You want some suds?" Seryoga said in amazement. "So go on in."

I could tell by his swaggering politeness that there would be trouble, and as I went in I took off my glasses and put them in my chest pocket. We filled up both jars and started off toward the exit feeling doomed. But

I couldn't have expected such a swift ass-kicking. Without giving us a chance to come to our senses, they shoved us into a service courtyard—a roofless storeroom lined with tin. I could hear Vitya cry, "What's the problem, guys!" It rang out and then fell silent. Heavy breathing, stamping, and cussing muffled our martyr-like squealing. I had two concerns: to stay standing and not end up under their feet, and to protect my new dental work, metal-ceramic crowns in the sides of my upper jaw. Under the hail of blows I leaned my back up against the tin wall to steady myself, shielded my head with my arms, and let the whole thing unfold. Seven or eight of them were working us over and wouldn't let us stand up straight.

"Look, a purse!" resounded over my head.

"It'sh emfty," I said through my smashed mouth, but they didn't believe me and pulled my wallet out of the gaping pocket of my jacket. Absorbed by the purse, the bastards lost interest in Vitya and me, and disappeared just as suddenly as they had descended on us. We straightened up. I couldn't see myself, but Vitya was unrecognizable: you couldn't see any features of a face, but what I'll conditionally call his physiognomy was turning purple before my eyes. We went out into the beer hall.

"The beer is leaking," Vitya imperturbably warned a tipsy well-wisher and pointed to the bag with the broken jar.

Under the unsympathetic gazes of the less refractory denizens of the drinking establishment, we crossed the place of execution as a graphic example of chastised willfulness, and I proposed, "Maybe we should go to the police?" Vitya nodded unenthusiastically.

But the employees of police station No. 47 performed miracles of efficiency. The policemen and the victims piled into two police vans and rushed to the scene of the incident. When the raid descended on the beer hall, it turned out that that gang of scum hadn't even taken the trouble to leave, but was still there sucking down beer. The bleating, weakly resisting hooligans were thrown into the cars. Along the way the police took me and Koval to the emergency clinic, where they hastily x-rayed our skulls and gave us tetanus shots.

In the police station there was a difference of opinion. The hawkish investigator said, "They're bastards, no need to pity them, they need to be thrown in prison." The dovish one, on the contrary, invited us into his office and sat with a vacant look as one after another the bastards promised us piles of gold as compensation for the punchfest. Five out of the seven men were born in 1973, that is, they could have been our sons. I was amazed as well by a certain kind of disgusting intimacy that developed in our relations with the hooligans. They went into all the details of the brawl, they confided that if they had let themselves go, they would have smeared us all over the asphalt, so it wasn't clear what all the hullabaloo was about. This kind of familiarity might exist between a gynecologist and his patient: once he's taken a peek in there, then why be sentimental, why use polite pronouns with each other.

After two hours of this tedium Vitya and I were ready to retreat, if only we could get out into the fresh air, but then a ranking police officer in ci-vilian clothes went a little bit over the line. He tossed out in passing (we were sitting in the hallway yet again) that he would lay a bet: even if we were to write out a statement according to form, and this case were to get going, all the same we'd be bought off. He'd give us no more than three weeks for that to happen. In his experience he was always right on the money about this. And he conspiratorially took a swig of Fanta, remark-ing on how dry his mouth was after celebrating Cosmonautics Day.[38] At this point the remnants of mettle started to revive in Koval and me, and to spite the officer in civvies we swore out the necessary complaints.

I wore dark glasses for about a week and a half, my scratches healed, only for about six months the skin on the top of my head kept twitch-ing. By the time they started dragging us to the regional office of the public prosecutor to see Investigator Kholodovich, a brilliant April thesis had crystallized in our heads. Here it was: since the fate of these bastards was in our hands, we wouldn't have them put in prison; after all, we had to pay tribute to abstract humanism. To let them pay us off would also not do, as if we were designating how much it costs to bash our heads in. We would get them in the pocketbook, not to our advan-tage, but to the advantage of the striking miners.[39] It happened that just at that time there was a collection in support of the miners' families. We expounded this idea to the investigator and the young oafs. We were never summoned again.

The analogy with Ivan Ilich couldn't help but come into my aching head two and a half years later, when my polyclinic martyrdom began.[40] In the story, a successful middle-level civil servant climbs up to straighten a curtain, stumbles, bruises his internal organs, and—what do you know: he dies. And here was a similar case. On an April morning my bosom buddy and I went out quietly and peacefully to freshen our weary brains with eight liters of diluted beer, and as a result—I had to die. Because of the frolicking youths of the Zamoskvorechie neighborhood.

By September 1 of last year we had returned from the dacha to Moscow, and I started going to the polyclinic on Aeroportovskaya Street and at the same time started a job.

At the end of August Natasha Molchanskaya had called me and said that in connection with the death of Lakshin, everyone had been shifted around and they now had an extra staff position. She went on to say that generally speaking this position would perfectly suit Grisha Dashevsky, but he was already working at the Russian State Humanities University. I got a little scared, but Natasha calmed me down: if I didn't like it, I could quit. I went to the offices of the journal *Foreign Literature* for negotiations with Grisha Chkhartishvili.[41] He greeted me warmly and even said that they were "eagerly expecting" me. I honestly admitted that, in the first place, my knowledge of English was catch-as-catch-can, and in the second place, I had only the most superficial acquaintance with foreign literature. Okay, in childhood I'd read Dumas and Stendhal, in youth I read Faulkner and Salinger, and this summer I had been plodding away at Ortega y Gasset in the commuter train, when I was able to get a seat, that is. He comforted me by saying that they were not expecting erudition but intellectual vitality and fresh ideas.

By that time, my level of intellectual vitality was the following. For example, through the thick mass of a migraine I would converse with Tatiana Vladimirovna Lanina about Brodsky's translations of Marvell, and she would say something comprehensible, and I would be pursuing an extraneous goal in the conversation: to hide from Tatiana Vladimirovna that her interlocutor was an imbecile. My extra task was to hold on with the remains of my memory to the identities of Marvell, Brodsky, and my interlocutor, and to strain all my powers to recollect at least a few verbs and nouns in Russian, in order not to be completely silent. Adjectives were already a luxury. And to look strictly between the two Tatiana Vladimirovnas, so that my unfocused gaze would not arrest the attention of the real, single Tatiana Vladimirovna. Because by that time for me everything visible had acquired a twin. I was quite capable then of crossing the cafeteria in the basement of the editorial offices with a bowl of soup in my trembling hands and knocking over one or two chairs off my starboard side. And the trembling in my hands was no longer a misfortune caused by a hangover, but a constant companion. First I had to give up my favorite Chinese fountain pen with a gold nib, a present from Lena. Then I couldn't master even a simple ballpoint pen, even if I pressed it to the page until my knuckles turned blue. Then even drawing a line with a pencil became too much for me. So that's how I worked as an editor.

In my free time I diligently visited the polyclinic to see the neuropathologist Avrora Ionovna Pikovskaya. I would tell her about childhood seizures and grown-up brawls, I would explain my symptoms. She would listen to me patiently and refer me to an oculist for an X-ray of my skull, to the ear-nose-and-throat doctor to check my hearing and sense of smell. She would prescribe pills—they did no good. She tried to get me an appointment for a consultation with a professor. Sometime at the end of the fall I bumped into Avrora Ionovna by chance in the hallway of the polyclinic and asked, "Have you forgotten about me?"

She said, "No. We can't come to an agreement with the consultants about the fee."

In the middle of December they called me for the consultation.

He was a real Doctor Dolittle, gray-haired and cozy. He even had the name of a gnome: Dzhano Nikolaevich. A star pupil of my illness, I immediately got an encephalogram out of my briefcase.

"Why do I need your encephalogram when you're here with me?" Dzhano Nikolaevich said with a smile and got out his little hammer.

All at once I felt as if a weight had been lifted off my heart, as if I were not a haggard forty-year-old guy with graying hair and a life made rotten by my own hands, but had come just as I used to come thirty years ago with my mama to the same sort of professors, with the very same sort of little hammers. Everything here was familiar to me: the questioning, and the tapping, and the touching the end of your nose with your index finger while your eyes are closed. I would have stayed there forever. But they asked me to go sit in the hallway. And then they asked me in again, and Dzhano Nikolaevich said:

"Here's how we'll proceed. You're going to spend all your money on CAT scans—at the Burdenko Neurosurgery Institute or the Oncology Center on the Kashirka—there are a lot of CAT scan machines around now. First we'll rule out all the worst possibilities, and then we'll devote our attention to your health, all right? They'll do it in two days and give you the results personally."

"Money in the evening, chairs in the morning," Avrora Ionovna elucidated his thought.[42]

I took the referral sheet and went away with new hope.

At home I read the referral. I understood everything except one word in Latin: *strabonus*. Like the deceived husband in Chekhov's story, I got up on the stepladder, got the dictionary from the shelf, and found: "Strabo, -onus (Gk.) (1) cross-eyed, suffering from a squint; (2) an envious person." It's probably the first definition, but I knew that myself. And the second definition isn't applicable. "No! I have never known envy . . . not even when Piccinni," etc. Even you, Alyosha, even in my youth I didn't envy you; I probably had the sense to realize that I myself wasn't born yesterday, I didn't just fall off the turnip truck.[43]

And that is the way, my strict comrade, in which I intend to write. In your fifth decade the tangle of your past is formless, like the "bird nest" on the spinning reel of an inexperienced fisherman, and you can pull on any knot in this senseless tangled mass; playing that game is a specialized taste.

On January 13 they performed a trepanation of my skull and removed a benign meningioma tumor that was five or six years old. They did not find the main Dostoevsky thought there, but twelve hours later, when the anesthetic finally wore off and I stopped having dreams and painfully trying to collect my bedraggled goods and chattels—little suitcases and 1950s leatherette bags with broken zippers—I had a breakthrough. Alyosha, in my forty-second year I sensed with full authenticity that death would actually come and that "I am real"; and all the trivial details of my not-too-clever life appeared to me as flagrant and precious.[44] Memory and the gift of speech returned to me, and I could not stop up the fountain. I was struck with the incoherence of Faulkner's Benjy, for I was thinking about everything simultaneously, and my thoughts ran in all directions like the mercury from a broken thermometer.[45]

As for me, I'm a lover of light reading, and I would like to compose something in that vein for myself. What are my ambitions for this scribbling? Oh, my pretensions are great!

. . . Early in the morning the scientific gardener of the near future will lower his scrawny, goose-pimpled legs from the cot. He'll scratch around in his

garden-variety head, he'll rack his pea brains. "Think I'll make a cellar. Two by two. According to that handbook I saw the other day. A really frigging good one. Time to stop guzzling rotgut." He'll pull on his athletic pants with the left footstrap torn off, feel for his galoshes like an automaton. He'll take a spade out of the shed and—the ball will get rolling: we don't mind a little labor, but we need a piece of ass. Getting the spade all the way in each time. Two by two. The booze will get sweated out of me, if my ticker holds out.

Soon the excavation work makes the time fly. At first you cut the heavy layers of turf and you grieve: oh, how thin the layer of humus, how poor! Then you hack your way into the clay and you cuss your way through the springy roots, three fingers thick; but now even they have been cut through, the work is going great, the day is at its peak. In the morning the sky was all a deep blue, but toward noon two or three small clouds are frolicking above the laborer like lapdogs. He's already in the pit up above his waist, and there's no end to the oily clay—now yellow, now veiny purple. Where are you, oh layer of sand, promised by the scholarly handbook? Now the spade clanks as if on bone and won't go any farther. The balding amateur gardener moves a bit to the side, sticks the spade in halfway, and—picks out the obstacle to his scientific digging. There's some real sand for you, fuck it! Wow, I'm really lucky! To have to rebury this thing—makes him regret his hungover labors; if he throws it away with his spade over the fence into the forest—they'll find it and drag him around the cop stations. He sits mournfully on his haunches over his ominous find. There you are, grinning at me! In the upper right corner is something metallic. Correct, all correct. It was put in for me at the Literary Fund by the maestro V. Yu. Gorshkov. The whole thing cost 17,000. The bastard was rich—my hero continues his examination—a metal-ceramic crown! But there in fact you're mistaken. That one was done under the table in Soviet times by the skilled craftsman Anatoly Evgenievich. It cost 700 of the old rubles. That also took a bite out of me, by the way. Everything's relative, as someone said in this settlement once upon a time. "But who split his gourd open?" the accidental exhumer will marvel, having noticed a patch in the bone about the size of a hand on the top of the human head he's dug up. "I picked the wrong day to give up drinking," the gardener will skillfully place his ripening intention on firm footing, look at his watch, groan, scramble out of the pit, and start jogging up the hill in the heat in his one-strap athletic pants all splattered with clay—to the Porechie glass-walled café.

"Hey, Claudy, let me in!" he'll beseech the local thought-leader in a dingy white coat standing at the cherished door with her hands on her hips. "My ticker's stopping!"

And Klavdia Fyodorovna, pretending to be stern, will take the bill and bring the suffering man a bottle with a label glued on crooked and, not devoid of a feeling for language, will mutter at him as he moves away: "His ticker's stopping, the shameless jerk. His dick stopped a long time ago."

He won't be able to wait until he gets home, he'll plop down by the side of the road in the blazing sun, and having taken one, two, three swigs there in the roadside fir grove, he'll sum up: "That's where we'll all end up!" The shadow of an onrushing cloud will cover the hard-luck gardener, and he'll shiver a bit: there's something awfully familiar about it, or I'll be a sonuvabitch! Getting warm. Warmer. Hot: school. A teacher with progressive tendencies, Maro Ashotovna, called by the kids Sharo Abortovna. Extracurricular reading. Some kind of gibberish with a medical title.

The thought of a Booker Prize came to me about twenty minutes after I filled my Chinese fountain pen with ink for the first time after getting out of the hospital and put a stack of fresh lined writing paper on the kitchen table.[46] But it is not for me, Alyosha, to open your eyes to the amusing peculiarities of our craft and the extent of its naïveté.

I'll finish my cock-and-bull stories, mark them all up, type them up in a clean copy, and again mark them all up; and then I'll hide them for a month in a desk drawer. At the end of the appointed period I'll get them out and again mark them all up with my own conventional signs and arrows in the margins: where to move what. And again I'll type them up. After all, I'm not a moneybags, I don't own any sort of special computers.

Rubinshtein swears that he himself heard one writer say to another in the café of the Central House of Writers, "My friend, I banged out such a fucking masterpiece!" So I'll bang out my fucking masterpiece, and if I'm successful, I'll go up to the mirror, as I always do in case of success. Where does it all come from? Salt-and-pepper, like a standard schnauzer. A reddish, crooked beard. Abundant eyebrows. Small eyes beneath eyelids at half mast. Glasses. Thick nose and lips. Asymmetrical ears. But the talent! A humongous talent!!! I'll encouragingly slap myself in the puss, and call my wife, and read the whole thing to her from beginning to end. "Very good," Lena will say, but I won't believe her, because she loves me even though I'm a jerk, and I'll begin in a roundabout way:

"Let's invite some people," I'll propose, "and arrange a reading. Not the whole thing, of course, but maybe just an excerpt or two?"

"Let's," Lena will say with an ominous premonition.

"But without acting like beggars," I'll bluster. "With a meat interlude. Or if worst comes to worst, some chickens." (And in fact I'm thinking of a case of vodka.)

"We only live once," Lena will say, stubbing out her cigarette in the ashtray, and her green eyes will grow dark as her pupils dilate: for my wife, my train of thought is not Newton's binomial theorem.

"Why are you getting so ticked off?" I'll ask. "After all, this isn't just some coffee-klatsch. A celebration is a celebration. All the more since people are doing us a favor, coming to hear my ravings. Are you saying we no longer have to thank people for their goodwill? Why is it that in such cases," here I'll raise my voice and light up my second cigarette in a row, "why is it that everyone: the Kovals, the Aizenbergs, the Kibirovs, the Faibisoviches—all put themselves out, and all we ever serve is little salads? No, it's all quite neat, tasty, and attractive, but after all?"

"You know how I feel about your love of vulgar display," Lena will say with loathing. "To try to keep up with the Faibisoviches and the Kibirovs is bad form: everyone has his own life and his own means."

"Militant poverty is also bad form," I'll say, and we'll fight, which is what I was aiming at.

It'll be the way I want it after all, but now my hands are untied for a double game: one bottle out in the open, in the sideboard, and two on the sly—behind the toilet tank, under the divan, etc. And I keep buying that way over the course of several days. Little stratagems. Then for about half a week I'll suck up to her and flatter her, because the date of the reading is nearing, and there's nothing worse than having guests when electricity is crackling in the household. And finally we'll make up, and the day before the party I'll start chopping vegetables for an Olivier salad, and Lena will bring home some imported chickens.

So now everyone's gathered. I'll cast an appraising glance over the tables pushed together under a single tablecloth, the little salads, the plates, the place settings. As a lover of and expert on symmetry, I feel visually offended by the motley collection of goblets and glasses, but what are you going to do, was it Pushkin who broke them?[47]

After a half hour of pre-party standing around and joking, the guests will take their seats. And I will make my way to the head of the table, lay out my pages, knock back a shot of vodka for courage and reader's inspiration, and take the floor. I'll say: "Thank you all, I'm glad to see you all. About seven years ago, when we were still living in a communal apartment, we had some guests, including a few of those present here, and I mumbled just for fun that I was going to delight you with prose. Poetic prose. Don't expect a plot—it's this and that, the dark passages of murky associations. A mass of allusions. Unexpectedly, that buffoonery came true. But I don't want any condescension to my weakness. For better or worse, I don't belong to the breed of frenzied writers who harbor malice because of the words of a critic. So if someone limits his response to something like 'It's shit,' I promise not to snap at you, I believe too much in your kind disposition toward me, which is completely mutual. So I'll get started. And please have a drink and a snack, as long as it doesn't affect the sobriety of your judgment."

It is with these words, Alyosha, that I plan to preface the reading, and I will not undertake to name the listeners individually. I'm afraid to jinx it and cause a quarrel accidentally, jealousy is rampant these days. And it's just about the season for people to be going off to their dachas. In general all sorts of travels are now happening. But if you—you or Kenzheev—are present, you are welcome!

Can you feel how exhausted I am? It resembles the second day of one of my binges . . . . It's morning, and I'm awakened by the sound of my own heartbeats filling the room. This second day is the most insidious, because the energy of anxiety takes control of me entirely. Chain me up right now, so that three or four days later I won't be lying with chattering teeth in sticky sweat under a pile of old rags, trying to grab my own reason as it keeps slipping out of my uncertain hands like a sliver of soap, and my torn half-dreams are monstrous. But there is no chain in the house, and the strength of my mother or wife is not commensurate with my sick stubbornness.

Spoiled by today's alcoholic freebootery, I can no longer remember in which years the stores opened at 11:00, and in which years they opened at 2:00. But since my story is a joyful one, let's say they open at 11:00 today—right on the dot the iron-reinforced door will open, because I won't make it to 2:00.

No showers, all that comes later. I make a search of my pockets: paper bills with paper, silver with silver, copper with copper. Now the empties. Take them all, and whatever will be, will be. 0.5 liters: beer bottles separately, vodka and cognac bottles separately. 0.8: scrape the foil off under warm running water in case of a salesperson with principles who won't accept a bottle that still has the foil. Oh, my hands! On the other side of Waterloo Bridge a local alky had said knowingly, "They're shaking," when I treated him to some Pegasus-brand Soviet cigarettes, and he offered me a can of beer he'd drunk some of. Tactless Lyova just couldn't keep his eyes off my hands during our trips together in the old days. Aizenberg, kind soul, forestalls my convulsions at the table when I try to pour spirits into various vessels, and Timur never asked superfluous questions when I asked him to fill out the customs declaration for me at Heathrow.

0.7: The last ordeal, but also the most difficult. Some blockhead—maybe me—has pushed the corks into the bottles, and now they're rolling on the bottom. Calm down, don't despair: it's only a hangover, not the end of the world. Get a shoelace and patiently pull them out, there's no other option. There's a good boy. Now count them up, multiply them by category in your head, add the results of the multiplication, memorize the total sum, and wrap them up. That's that. Dress as inconspicuously as you can. My God! Yesterday I was walking around the city in Dubovenko's hat, a bow tie, and a doctor's smock! What a disgrace, how cheap! Okay, enough of tormenting yourself, let's go.

With my heart stopping now and then, slipping on the ice, but impetuously, purposefully—with Goethe's "Dahin"—I go to the store.[48] The people in line at the approaches to the entrance are timidly grumbling, sharing meek suppositions about the selection of goods. At last. The criminal twilight of the liquor department. They're taking people out of order. Be patient. Cosmonautics Day of 1991 is still ahead, and you will still get yours. If it's now the beginning of the 1980s and I'm in Fili, then sooner or later I'll see the counter with a plastic contraption that resembles an unseaworthy sail of hope, and written on it will be: "You are being served by salesperson Ekaterina Rodina." If I've already moved to Choboty, in the store near the station there's a completely different sign: "Nothing do we value so dearly and obtain so cheaply as politeness and culturedness." And over the dictum is pinned a reproduction of Raphael's Madonna. Or the original. I'm not completely sure of anything right now. I had a theory that justified the mass Soviet drunkenness. Delirium, delirium and horror, were offered to the whole people—from the Kuriles to the Carpathians—as the regime of the day and of life. And the whole people, with rare exceptions, preferred to celebrate on the pretext of the three-hundredth anniversary of the faceted glass. I had another theory, a mystical explanation of the nature of the hangover. If you buy a truce with the world for three rubles 62 kopecks (the price of a bottle of vodka), or even for a ruble 30 kopecks (the price of a bottle of plonk), and not at the price of inner efforts, then it serves you right to have the shakes in the morning. "Hey, you with the beard. Gone to sleep?" I'm at the counter! Speak and act, act and speak! Good luck! Let everything go well, in the final analysis I can dream, can't I? Let me have enough not for two bottles of dry wine or one bottle of "port wine," but for a 0.7-liter bottle of dry wine and a 0.8-liter bottle of white port wine, and today, at any rate, I won't perish, and I forbid myself to think about tomorrow![49] Now just go on your way, only don't slip on the ice and don't break the bottles; the demon of hangover bad luck hasn't yet completely lost interest in you.

I'll begin with port wine, perhaps, not taking my eyes off the bed, in order to throw myself down on my back like a rabbit who's just finished copulating if my shuddering stomach gets the idea of throwing the rotgut back outside. Seven minutes, in the opinion of Sasha Borisov, must pass before the alcohol is assimilated by the internal organs and the hangover starts receding. I can stand that. I even enjoy these residual torments.

So that's "the most bastardly thingumajig"! It is so "cynical and spicy" to confess one's vice, but when on January 12 the form "Consent to an Operation" lay in front of me on the hospital nightstand, where in black and white the penultimate item read, "Notify the doctor about drug addiction or alcoholism," I was ashamed to tell the anesthesiologist Oleg Andreevich.[50] He asked me something else about my systole, placing interesting little discs on my chest, which had been shaved the day before as required. A masculine voice came to us through the open door of the operating room, saying that Konovalov would begin in twenty minutes. "And we will begin in twenty minutes," Oleg Andreevich said, and answered my curiosity: "No, systole isn't the same thing as tachycardia."

How can I not have a systole, when Sasha Soprovsky poured me my first glass of vodka in Misha Kozmenko's kitchen—let's see—twenty-three years ago.

I get up from the bed, the sofa, the ottoman, the cot, the divan—it all depends on where the action takes place. Even the limp grass in the vacant lot behind the supermarket near the Yugozapadnaya subway station can serve as my couch, if the season allows one to collapse onto the ground.

It's all over, I can light up, and just fifteen minutes ago the mere thought of tobacco was fraught with retching. I can interpolate some dry wine, which opens amazingly easily, because my hands are again obeying me. I will look out the window, wiping off the perspiration with relief; out there snow is coming down, or rain is distinctly heard, or the wind is pushing the poplar trees around; and there's so much goodwill in the world, and it was worth it to suffer a little for its sake. And I will begin an endless incoherent conversation with Sasha, Bakhyt, you, Misha, Timur, the other Misha, Viktor Oganesovich, Rita, Vail, Pushkin, my wife, Grisha, my father, Vitya, Brodsky, Khodasevich, Galich, the other Vitya, Irina, Masha, Kukes, childhood, boyhood, youth, Molchanskaya, Stevenson, Chesterton, Nabokov, Golovkin, Sorotokin, Magarik, and I will want to call, write, knock out an express telegram to everyone, everyone, everyone, and begin the message with the apostle's "Rejoice!"

It's a strange thing, Alyosha, experience and life have worn us out and unfettered us, and it turns out we know how to talk even when we're sober. Last autumn I was your guide to Soprovsky's grave. They didn't have any flowers at the Preobrazhensky Market, or any quarter-liter bottles for having a drink in his memory, and you bought a Snickers and a bottle of beer.

The leaves at the cemetery were settling like a silent explosion at a quarry, one could see the blackened marble gravestones of Old Believer merchants. On the way to Sasha a half-drunk old man tried to talk you into drinking to the memory of his brother, and you hastily waved your hand in my direction, saying, "He doesn't drink." When the old man found out that the long candy you were munching was called "Snickers," he exclaimed, "I keep hearing 'Snickers,' 'Snickers,' 'Snickers'—so that's what it is!" And bowing in the Japanese fashion, he stuck the remainder of the candy bar in his pocket as a treat for his granddaughter. We walked on, but we got a little lost until I recognized Sasha's oak cross. We put it up more than a year ago—Petya Obraztsov, Sergienko, Pakhomov, and I. We had had to reinforce the tin-covered foot of the cross at the head of the grave, and Petya Obraztsov, the only one of us, it turned out, who knew the technique of cementing, sent us three to get some broken bricks and cobblestones, and started mixing the mortar himself. We spent about two hours busting our butts, but it came out well, in my opinion.

I opened the beer using the neighboring fence, we each took a gulp, poured out the rest onto the grave, had a smoke, and set off for the subway, leaving the empty bottle in a prominent place on the side of pathway No. 10. On the way, I don't remember what prompted me, I said that the Greeks were not mistaken in their faith in fatality, and that it truly rules over those who do not know how to pray about their own free fate. It's just that fatality operates by degrees, and its power is not manifested all at once, but makes itself known as one ages. A lot of time is needed for the gears of inevitability to make their rotation and for a person to feel how long ago they snagged him and are dragging him along. I also said that Nabokov is close to Sophocles, for example, because in all his novels you can hear the steps of fatality. You answered not quite to the point, as happens with people who have long ago retreated into themselves, that life tests whether or not you're a louse through the fulfillment of your desires: through trips abroad, work, marriage, a car accident.

So while we're on the way, before I say a parting "vale" to you, let's recall some incident from our common past; the chiseled composition of this work will hardly suffer any harm from this. I keep remembering the story with the code name "The Blue Cup."[51] It's not devoid of a certain piquancy, is it?

You and Soprovsky were living in Vykhino then, renting a room from the widower Kamyshko, and you spent your time in scholarly wrangling over the *fortochka:* Should it be open or not?[52] In the guise of a graduate student, I was renting a one-room apartment on the first floor of a building at the intersection of Svoboda and Fomicheva Streets. I was twenty-one years old and had rented the apartment for rendezvous with an older woman. I was in love to the point of unseemliness. The day I moved in, the beauty dumped me over the telephone, without ever setting foot across the threshhold of the dwelling that had been intended for her. But my friends and acquaintances, black-humor specialists fond of sprinkling coarse salt into the wound of their neighbor, nevertheless christened the apartment "Rita's place."

You came to visit me from the Zhdanovskaya region in southeast Moscow to the Tushino region in the northwest, traveling on an electric suburban train without paying the fare. Either you didn't have enough money for an honest ticket, or life hadn't yet instilled respectability in you, and your convictions of those days permitted it. It's not clear why Sanya didn't come with you. I guess he had decided to make use of his solitude to carry out some libidinous plans, although you had strictly forbidden him this, in view of one of the main conditions of the rental.

Masha Chemerisskaya had given you, maybe that very day, a portable battery-powered radio of Latvian manufacture, bought on the installment plan for 109 rubles. In the nearest glass-walled café we settled on three one-liter bottles of Bulgarian "Gamza" wine in braided plastic sleeves for ease of transport. It was a bright winter day, and our mood was in harmony with it: I made the bottles jingle, you were radiant as you dragged your music box along. Grunting and complaining about our old age, we sat across from each other at the kitchen table. In a thorough and masterly way you pulled out the antenna on your new acquisition, segment after segment. You caught some Mozart on the air, and we got down to our favorite task, in a leisurely way and with clinking of glasses. If you killed me (and it's leading up to that), I could not recall the subject of our conversation. You too, probably, even though you hold in your memory eight languages and other unnecessary details.

"Ours is not to reason why, we just crash after getting high," was our motto then, which I did on the narrow red divan, a present from Valya Yakhontova.[53] It's boring to drink by yourself, and in order to wake me up you started tickling my nose with the end of the fully extended antenna. In my sweet slumber I slapped it away and bent it. Then you, with your innate or acquired tendency toward impressive gestures, quite forgivable in view of our profession—the tendency toward generous gifts and bloody sacrifices—crashed the radio onto the floor, and the new black receiver broke into pieces. Mozart fell silent. I kept sleeping as if nothing had happened, sweetly smacking my lips. You must have ended up next to the table, you poured a cup to the brim, drained it at one go, turned it around in your hand, and threw the blue thing in my direction, hitting the untimely slumberer in the left temple. Here it is, the mark of it. Material evidence of immaterial relations. Blood spurted in an arc, staining the wallpaper that belonged to someone else. You started wringing your hands—and I saw this with my own eyes, because I woke up instantly and rushed to the bathroom, where I was reflected in the oval mirror. I understood that I had been murdered, and ran to the telephone to dial the emergency number. And you were already crashing through the entryway door to flag down a car. But you had no success in flagging anything down, and the Soviet ambulance service could not be faulted for being in too much of a rush.

About forty minutes later, leaning on each other (you had grown weak from remorse, I, from the lassitude of death), the murderer and the murdered, in a towel turban, could be glimpsed on the dismal nocturnal Svoboda Street. The very first car turned out to be a drunk-reaper (a vehicle collecting candidates for the sobering-up station). It's true, I only found out about that the next day, when, after they hastily sewed me up, I was issued a fine of fifteen rubles for alcohol in the blood. You were going to have to pay it. And you, with a heavy heart after murdering your friend, like Onegin, got on the electric suburban train after midnight, returned to Vykhino, and told Soprovsky that, quote, if Seryozha were to die, you would hang yourself.

In the morning, with a sheepskin coat on over my naked body and with a bandaged head, just like now, I rang the doorbell to "Rita's place," because I didn't have the keys. But some kind of life could be sensed going on there, and poseur that I was, I expected to be the highlight of the program. They finally opened the door, but hardly anyone paid any attention to me; the carnival was continuing there in full swing, having lost, as Bakhtin teaches us, its universal character.[54] But even in this state of decline it was dear to me, since it welcomed me.

I had to somehow explain to my parents the origin of the scar on my temple. I said that the fresh abrasion was the result of falling off a horse.

Okay, you memory returned to me by the doctors, prove that the "Extract from the medical record No. 13/94," issued to me at the final moment by Senior Nurse Nila Semyonovna in the Academician N. N. Burdenko Scientific-Research Neurosurgery Institute of the Order of the Red Labor Banner, speaks the truth: "In his neurological status a regression of neurological symptoms is observed (his memory for words has improved)." The names of the slandered animals, please. I count to three: one, two, three. Varnak, an Orlov trotter. Agapka, a mare of Akhal-Teke breed. Amazing.

Hold on a second: memory is one thing, congratulations on its return, but it seems to me I've been running off at the mouth and gotten mixed up in my mutilations and my nonsense-talking.

Yes, there actually was a moonlit courtyard that resembled a stage set at the Bolshoi Theater. There was also a pair of horses nibbling loaves of black bread on the snow turned blue by the full moon. There was also the owner of the beauteous beasts—an artist later put in prison for anti-Soviet agitation and propaganda. But by the time I took advantage of the invitation of my friends who worked in the stable to take a horseback ride, Tsvetkov had already been living in America for three years, and the scar was a different one, in a different place, and of different origin. That's when I heaped the blame on the four-legged creatures. But I have no intention of expanding on this later scar.

"You promised to confess!" some lover of the truth out there will blurt out.

In the first place, there's no need to shout at me, you're not in a tram, behave yourself. In the second place, reread the epigraph. Dostoevsky, by the way, isn't chopped liver. And in the third place, don't interrupt, I don't recall interrupting you . . . . As I went along I invented two or three bicycles and tricycles. And discovered a continent in the Western Hemisphere into the bargain.

Inspired by the precedent of Dostoevsky's Ferdyshchenko, I thought, okay, let me spit out the mother-truth and tell it like it is.[55] But it's not really a mother to us, it's a stepmother at best. I'm just as suspicious about absolute freedom. I love the absolute only in the Swedish sense of the word (Absolut). Pepper Absolut, for example. I would give absolute freedom an inoculation against being rabid. So that it would know when to stop. The same goes for pure truth. You have to resist—drag your feet on the floor, dig your heels in, grab onto the furniture and the doorjambs, blow bubbles out your nose, head-butt the truth in the stomach, and bite its stinking hands. Our position is unenviable, and in any case it's not the not-rolling stone of truth that will get us out of trouble, but a certain unnatural component of the scalar of a boulder and the vector of our rabidity. But truth, what is truth?—an anatomical theater. I happened to observe the final victory parade of this pure, singular, complete, veritable unwed mother on December 17, 1993, in the lobby of the Burdenko Institute.

They were giving me a CAT scan. The whole process was beautiful and solemn, and resembled cosmonautics. The doctors sat behind a glass partition, and I lay on a mechanical trestle-bed, which hummed beneath me, rose, and pushed me headfirst into what seemed to me to be a kind of winking electronic womb. The electron is just as inexhaustible as the atom, dammit! When the apparatus had finished buzzing, I got up and put on my glasses and shoes. A bearer of bad news in a white coat came out from behind the partition.

"It's not good," she said. "A tumor in the frontal-parietal area of the brain and a large edema. Are you a Muscovite? Then with these results you can be admitted to the hospital, you need an operation. But now, go see our chief doctor."

"How do I find the chief doctor?" I asked hoarsely.

"Go out of the pass-through room and turn left, you'll see a sign. Wait for your images in the lobby."

I got up onto the stilts of mortal terror, set off for the lobby, and began rushing around the marble checkers of the floor like a maddened pawn. Two or three times I went out to smoke convulsively, returned, and again clattered on my new stilts from the heavy double doors to the rectangular mirror. "There it is, it turns out you're real," I silently quoted with gloomy ceremoniousness to my gray twin in Aizenberg's glasses and Soprovsky's cap. They brought out the images: six small negatives with my skull in various projections, no bigger than photographs for an international passport. The conclusion was attached. I remember the words "tumor-meningioma," and then the displacement of something or other there by six millimeters. I estimated by eye a gap of six millimeters between my thumb and forefinger. It turned out to be a trivial distance, not a meter anyway. But after all, it's—MY BRAIN!!! B-r-r-r. Then I remembered that today was Syoma Faibisovich's opening, and I'd be able to say farewell to some people who are dear to me and have a goodly amount to drink, given the circumstances. I went left out of the pass-through room and went into the door next to the sign "Chief Doctor."

Leonid Iurevich Glazman. Days and hours of reception. I waited on a standard-issue hospital chair for the previous visitor, who was wrongfully distracting the chief doctor from my chief newborn disaster, to come out.

Leonid Iurevich looked at the winter light outside the window through my monstrous film and said, "Such tumors are usually benign, but you need an operation. What's it like for you right now, does your time permit?"

"I'm completely free right now," I answered not quite appropriately and asked, pleading and trying to ingratiate myself, with false cheerfulness, "The whole picnic will take about a month, approximately?"

"Three weeks minimum," Glazman says. "Come with your images to the admission office at our polyclinic on Monday at 9:15."

"And should I bring the electroencephalogram and the certificate from the Literary Fund?" I ask conscientiously.

"Keep them as a souvenir. What's your relationship to Sasha?"

"I'm his brother."

"Well, good luck, don't lose your images."

And after shaking hands I pull Soprovsky's cap onto the second of two doomed heads, and go out onto Fadeev Street. I continue to mechanically twirl the Literary Fund certificate for a minute or two and then crumple it up and throw it into a trash can.

For some reason I took my daughter Sasha with me to the polyclinic, I no longer remember why. When I explained to her the reason for the unaccustomed and amazing cleanliness, courteousness, and lack of crowding, she asked, "You mean they're all writers?"

I nodded.

"How stupid," she said with a grimace.

About seventy people were accepted in absentia and en masse by the progressive Union of Writers after August 1991.[56] This acceptance in absentia was itself a slap in the face: it was just assumed that we all couldn't wait to get in. But you don't look a gift horse in the mouth. I had no relationship to the barricades of August.

The whole family was at the dacha when August 19th came. We had no radio, and the black-and-white dacha television was so reluctant to speak and to show pictures that we had given up on it. In the morning, when all six of us (my cousin and her three-year-old son were visiting us) returned after our ritual Childe Harold–like dip in the icy little settlement river Romanikha, our neighbor shouted over the fence that they'd removed Gorbachev and good for them. We rushed home and started trying to persuade the television, if not to recover its sight, at least to stop being mute. The appliance heard our prayers, and the flight school at Kubinka wasn't sending out too many student flights that day, which were the reason for our television's hiccups and blinking. The press conference and the flapping tremor could be discerned tolerably well.[57]

In the morning Lena and I set off for Moscow, entrusting our little parasites to the long-suffering patience of my cousin. We went both out of civic concern and by agreement with Nikolay Aleksandrovich, my well-wishing father-in-law, who had volunteered to help clumsy me mount shelves in our new apartment. On one of the granite pillars in the Novokuznetskaya subway station there was a sign announcing a demonstration at the White House. There was still an hour until the demonstration, and I accompanied my wife to the apartment. We gawked at the tank in the alley of the Committee for Tele- and Radio-Broadcasting. The tank crew were sitting without their helmets on the armor plating and drinking kefir out of cartons. I abandoned Lena to the domestic bedlam and went back. Next to the escalator somebody hurriedly gave me a leaflet signed by the courageous Yeltsin, calling for disobedience to the new authorities. I rode to the Krasnaya Presnya station and was absorbed into a huge crowd, but I could hear well. Elena Bonner was speaking; Yevtushenko said something, in root rhyme, as always; there were also other orators I've forgotten.[58] After about forty minutes my civic inspiration dried up, and the duty of a family man sent me on my way.

At home I was met with an awkward situation: my father-in-law had already come, and he and his daughter (who's about three feet tall in her stocking feet) were moving something that was too heavy for them to lift. With redoubled zeal I bustled about and was a jack-of-all-trades until dark: I drilled holes, shaved wooden stoppers, soaped screws. At about 11:00 we locked up the uninhabitable apartment and went out. The morning's tank crew were no longer drinking kefir, but were standing next to the tanks in their helmets and holding their automatic rifles in a horizontal position. At the Ring station we said good-bye to Nikolay Aleksandrovich; he was going home to Strogino, and we were going to Kutuzovsky Prospect to stay with Tatyana Arkadievna, Lena's mother. "I advise you to go to the dacha, who knows what might happen," my father-in-law said in parting.

At the Kiev Radial station I lifted my butt for a second from the leatherette seat when I saw men leaving the car with unambiguous intent, but
fatigue, cowardice, and my wife's weak resistance gained the upper hand,
and my butt lowered again. So I easily crossed the boundary, described
by Czeslaw Milosz, between decency and docility.[59]

That August night, falling asleep at my mother-in-law's place (there
were rumblings from the direction of the Parliament building, or it
seemed as if there were rumblings), I thought that I would be ashamed
in the morning if something had happened. And I was ashamed. The
television announcer said, "Unfortunately, blood was spilled," and the
mirror somehow was keeping me from doing my morning ablutions.
I remembered an illustration out of a children's edition of *And Quiet
Flows the Don:* Mishka Koshevoy is lying on his side with a blade of
grass in his teeth in the middle of an open field. In the distance are
hobbled horses. The caption read, "People are fighting for freedom,
and I'm pasturing mares."[60]

We passed the day of August 21 in righteous labor for the improvement of our dwelling. In the middle of the day I finally managed to reach
Petya Obraztsov by phone, and it turned out that he had spent three days
without budging from his post in the hottest spot. I asked how I could be
of help, and Petya said, "Relieve someone tonight." After a snack of bread
and kefir, my wife and I dragged ourselves, on legs feeble from fatigue,
into the children's room and started installing, braced between floor and
ceiling, three supports of a children's stadium with ropes, a horizontal
bar, swings, and gymnastic rings. We got utterly tangled up, but Timur
of the golden hands rescued us when he dropped by with his esteemed
insomnia and a bottle of port wine.

During the day Natasha Mazo called and said that the radio had just
announced that the insurgents had been captured on the way to the airport. My wife hurried to the dacha, and Timur and I finished drinking
and went out into the street.

The next day I continued messing around with the apartment, and
in the evening I had a meeting arranged with Petya Obraztsov at the
Dzerzhinsky station; he promised that I had never seen anything of the
kind: they were knocking over the monument.[61] But I didn't experience
any enthusiasm, either because I didn't have the right to it, or because
I was over the age for it. We gawked for about an hour and went off to

Petya's place, where people had gathered up to the very waterline. The next morning I knocked back a glassful and turned up at the dacha with a swollen kisser and a horse barn in my mouth.

How did we end up here in Kiev, oh my long tongue? Whose nephew am I and why mention the elderberry bushes at the dacha in Tuchkovo?[62] Here's how: I was recalling the mass acceptance into the Union of Writers.

So they accepted people and accepted people, easy as pie. A few months later, it turned out that you needed two or three recommendations from members, even if after the fact. Whaddya know! It's as if someone got invited to a restaurant and had a splendid meal in sincere innocence, and then it turned out that the person who'd invited him had no intention of paying and suggested that they go dutch . . . . Of course it was obvious that you just needed to ignore the whole rigmarole. Then we learned that Prigov had been accepted. That's his business. Then there was a rumor that the gourmand Lyova had been frequently caught dining in the restaurant of the Central House of Writers. I got up my courage and asked him point-blank: Was it true or not? He answered that it was all true, but that he hadn't submitted any recommendations, they just took his word. I secretly decided that he was lying out of discomfort. But when the turn came for my Fall, and it was discovered that I didn't have a full complement of recommendations, and I scowled and promised to bring them later, they reminded me of "my Rubinshtein" and his promises. One recommendation was given to me, sitting over tea at our place, by my Vilnius friend Vitya Chubarov, and the second one by Yury Ryashentsev. He was the classmate and oldest friend of my uncle Yury Gandlevsky. Ryashentsev had helped me more than once during my unpublished youth, and thanks to him (and not only to him) I have been living on my literary labors since 1985, and in general, I make ends meet.

Twenty years ago I showed Ryashentsev, the only professional I knew at the time, my best 7–10 poems and three or four translations. He found a few flaws in the versification and sent me to Chukhontsev at *Youth* magazine. Chukhontsev said that the work resembled Kushner. The evening of the same day I was at my uncle's house and again bumped into Ryashentsev. I had the shamelessness to admit to him that I had never read Kushner. Ryashentsev immediately picked up the phone, called Chukhontsev, and said, "Gandlevsky says he's never read Kushner." What weird people they are, after all!

But usually things didn't go so inoffensively, and there are a few scores to settle. In the beginning of the 1970s Kenzheev, Tsvetkov, Soprovsky, and I undertook a rather naive tour of the editorial offices. I remember that I was most struck by the fact that sitting before you would be not an old, inarticulate murderer from the secret police who had wasted his youth in torture chambers, but a quite anthropomorphic type. The literary employee would read the manuscript, upbraid you for your literariness, your Pasterna-krap and Mandel-shams, the absence of God and the wafting of death, and send you away empty-handed. At home or in a reading room you would leaf through the back issues of the journal you had been rejected by, and right and left you would run across such doggerel as this:

> "It warms my heart to rid my lines
> Of roses and of nightingales.
> My poems sing now of combines,
> Of tractors and of fertile swales."

Except it was even more clumsily rhymed than that, because I just now composed this quatrain for the needs of my narration. And you understood that you were sitting across from a janissary and having the wool pulled over your eyes—being deceived, to speak plainly.

Once I went with Tsvetkov to *Youth* to keep him company as he was going for a response. We were received by a huge man, Leonid Latynin, then a poet and now a prose writer of epic ambitions who has undertaken to encompass all of Mother Russia with a novel—from the times of Stribog and the primitive wooden plow to our days.[63] May God help him. The huge writer with his Soviet bungling had stuck Alyosha's manuscript somewhere and couldn't find it. It happens. Tsvetkov got nervous and gradually started to boil over, and I with youthful curiosity was expecting apologies. But Latynin lazily opened his desk drawers, squinted at some editorial file folders tied up with cloth tape; soon he got bored with this. He clasped his enormous paws, opened his mouth, and said, "I can console you: when the library of Alexandria burned down, almost all the tragedies of Euripides were consumed. But how the value of the remaining six increased!"

And that lesson was enough for us. For almost twenty years after that—right up to Gorbachev's perestroika—neither I nor any of the writers I knew, loved, or respected, stuck his nose into those libraries of Alexandria or came anywhere near them! Except maybe Kenzheev, but for him it looked somehow charming and not repulsive, because he is not just light but "lite."

I have the honor of belonging—and here I am not playing the fool but speaking completely seriously—truly, *I have the honor* of belonging to a circle of writers who have once and forever restrained in themselves the lust for publication. In the Soviet press, at any rate.

You could be a bore or a cutup, a coward or a daredevil, a penny-pincher or an "unmercenary anargyros," a drunk or a teetotaler, a debauchee or a prig, a womanizer or a monogamist, but you were not allowed to keep beating down the doors of editorial offices.

You could have a master's or a Ph.D., be a watchman, an elevator operator, an architect, a boiler-room worker, a parasite, an unskilled laborer, a gigolo; you could be a setter of locks and peepholes, take amphetamines, smoke pot, shoot up morphine, translate from any language into any other language, hand out books in the library, but to feel oneself to be a Soviet writing failure was forbidden. The very air of such failure was abolished, and that of course is a victory. Whining, lamentations, keening for the printing press were considered an obscene genre. The only thing that could be more obscene would be working for the KGB. That was our monastery, and that, just so you know, was our rule—that was the way we Romans did it. We didn't (for a second time in a row I will resort to the help of Aizenberg) try from year to year to break down the door of the editorial office, and we didn't tumble in there, cheerful and pitiful like Bobchinsky and Dobchinsky, when it was suddenly thrown open.[64]

I'm not idealizing this circle, I know it too well for that, and I'm not throwing this in anyone's teeth. It's just that I'm a native there and I'm telling about the strange mores and customs of my homeland. Literature was a personal matter for us. In the kitchen, in the watchman's booth, in the boiler room, there was no room for any abstract reader, people, nation. There was no one whose eyes had to be opened or who had to be made to understand. Everyone knew everything without that. There simply was nowhere for civic duty, precisely as an external obligation, to come from. And if someone wrote anti-Soviet stuff, then it was because of a sincere inclination. That's why I was so puzzled by Yevtushenko's story in *Ogonyok* about what subterfuges he resorted to, what he sacrificed, what ambiguous relations he entered into with high Party officials, just so that he would not be parted from his readers, and would be permitted to open their eyes. This is a mentality that is completely incomprehensible to me.

I have a long-standing and strange relationship with Yevtushenko, or rather I have no relationship with him, but all the same it is long-standing and strange.

I accidentally stole a brindle boxer, a little bitch, from Yevtushenko's wife.

From my youth I had a particular talent: to be able to borrow money from people I didn't know. I would return it, of course, so I didn't become a con man and my photos weren't hung at train stations and at intersections with the appeal to "neutralize the criminal." But I could have become famous; I had an undeniable talent for extortion.

When some group of friends had been drinking for a day, two days, three, had drunk up all their cash and started to get depressed, but couldn't bring themselves to go home, I would realize that my hour had struck, and everyone who knew about my talent would start looking at me hopefully. It would work this way: I would go out into the stairwell, take the elevator up to the upper floor (so as to walk downstairs, it's easier), and begin ringing the doorbells of all the apartments in turn and bum some money, whatever they could give me—five rubles, ten, twenty-five. Success would be my companion. For this you need sensitivity, a superficial charm, a feeling of moderation, and the main thing— truth in precise doses. The latter quality, by the way, is coming in handy now that I've set out to be a prose writer.

So I ring at a door and don't know anything yet, but I believe in my lucky star and await a surge of inspired effrontery. Who will open the door to me? A sullen family man in a tracksuit, with slippers on his bare feet? Then I need a manly confidential tone: you know, we're both guys and we know all about these scrapes. Or if it's a housewife in a housedress with arms lathered to the elbows who's just torn herself away from her laundering at the unexpected sound of the doorbell? Then the tone has to be completely different, and the legend takes a slightly different form: some sweet little student is awkwardly struggling with his embarrassment; asking for money is a new experience for him, but he doesn't have anything with which to celebrate the final exams, degree, or term paper he's just completed. The method makes sense, doesn't it? As Vitya Koval answered, when we were touring with the "Almanac" group in Yaroslavl, and a woman journalist asked him whether anyone else could read his poetry from the stage, "He can if I teach him how."[65]

That's how I'd answer, if some lady journalist showed an interest in my skill.

There are three rules of begging that you have to learn by heart and be able to rattle off even when half-asleep. The first and most important: never hide your true goal; you are borrowing money to buy alcohol. Not for flowers for your favorite teacher, not for a taxi so that you can bring your grandmother back from the nursing home for the weekend, not for the funeral of your best friend. Sentimental good intentions will only evoke suspicions of swindling, all the more since you can be smelled from a mile off. The second: indicate precisely the number of the apartment in which you're binging, this will lend conviction to your voice. The exact number, your own real name, in general impart to a half-truth the aftertaste of the full truth. And finally, repay the debt without fail, and preferably with a deadline—after all, you haven't completely lost your conscience.

I've explained as well as I can why a saccharine lie is doomed to fiasco. But why does failure await the tersely expressed truth? Well, who's going to give even a greasy ruble to a man if he says, okay, a band of renegades, artists who are starving for good reason, has gotten mired in days-long drunkenness, they all have problems with the police and the KGB, don't let them perish? I've chosen the golden mean. So you have to make things up in such a way that you're taken at your word, so that you're given money in general and a Booker Prize in particular. By the way, how are they given out? You have to ask Lena Yakovich so that you don't make an ass of yourself at the ceremony. Maybe the competitors stand in a special chamber with black blindfolds and they break a sword over the head of the winner? It's an English prize, and probably the queen or the rebellious Princess Diana attends. The curtain is drawn aside, and a blindingly beautiful hand covered with rings slips through the folds of crimson velvet. As if in a fog, I fall onto my knees, I bend to kiss the beautiful palm, but in an instant it has already been pulled away, and only the weight of a ring in my cupped hand allows me to believe that this all happened—in reality!

That hungover morning found a mixed company in Peredelkino at a playwright's dacha. Before this I had been in the writers' section only once, when I was totally green and Igor Volgin was taking a university literary workshop on an excursion to Pasternak's and Chukovsky's dachas.

Now everyone was messed up from yesterday's drinking, and we had to do something. Without our usual enthusiasm, without any happy craziness, Arkady Pakhomov and I set off for the hunt. I have to say that Arkady was also not without an aptitude for begging, but in this calling he is not at all my equal. He lacks a certain flexibility, his charm is a bit monotonous, he can be coarse with women, and most importantly, the dandyism of the high-quality extortionist is not inherent in his character. Although I can't hold a candle to him in subway-car socializing or street bravado. Once he and Volodya Sergienko were returning from a New Year's Eve party on the subway. Arkady infected the sleepy passengers with his example, and after they'd passed two or three stations, about fifty people broke out in choral singing. When Pakhomov suddenly got out at his stop, all the fury of the people coming out of their trance fell on Sergienko.

Not expecting success, just any old how, we started knocking at the doors of the writers' dachas. The family members would open the door to us, we wandering minstrels would drone out our chants, and—we were turned down flat everywhere. Either they could sense our hungover depression, or the men of the house, as writers, had trained their family members to live in a field of fabrication—we just couldn't take them with our bare hands. Squabbling and blaming each other, we walked into the next yard. This turned out to be Yevtushenko's dacha. His secretary, a young careerist, explained that the owner was away, refused to give us money, and languidly advised us to go to the next dacha, Mezhirov's. Only when we got to Mezhirov's yard did I notice that a young, frisky brindle boxer had come tagging after us. She would jump up to kiss us and was incredibly funny. Out from behind the corner of the dacha, pushing a wheelbarrow with something or other in it, appeared the owner. I always had a good feeling about Mezhirov, and at one time even liked him. I don't believe that "Communists, forward!" is simply a "locomotive," a piece of politically correct verse that drags along the poet's other, apolitical poems. Anything bitter you can say to Mezhirov, he himself knows and has said about himself, and his recent lines about the American black church made me smack my lips enviously:

"They all rise, as we say here in the USSR,
and they sing that we mustn't be afraid
Of anything, anything..."

We were totally exhausted and explained our visit succinctly. Mezhi-rov, stammering, answered that he had a twenty-five ruble note, but it was his last one, so we would have to return ten rubles the same day and we could return the other fifteen in a few days. We thanked him and rushed to the store, fending off the dog's kisses, like two housemaids fighting off the annoying advances of a high-school boy.

Now in a completely different mood, having returned the ten rubles, clattering and clinking the contents of a canvas bag, we arrived at the playwright's demesne. Our reputation was saved, and the cheerful boxer bitch immediately conquered the goodwill of our drinking companions with a *Sturm und Drang* of kissing.

A couple of years ago I ran across a reflection by C. S. Lewis that caused my heart to ache. Since the only thing that is immortal is the substance of love, the existence of animals beyond the grave depends entirely on us. If we truly love a dog, a cat, a hamster, or a turtle, then we thereby immortalize our pet. Without our participation the beasts are condemned.[66] Even if Lewis was wrong, God might pay heed to this opinion, approve of it, and introduce a few correctives into His creation; after all, He is a creator and not a dogmatist. When I'm in a good mood, I find it possible to believe that the mongrel Lord, the collie Mitchie, the standard poodle Maksim, the Saint Bernard Tom, and you, my gentle Charlie, will again begin to jump around me; after all, I loved you! And over our heads the linden and maple trees that I lovingly planted in honor of the birth of my daughter and son, Sasha and Grisha, will begin to rustle in the heavenly wind.

We had finished drinking everything that Pakhomov and I had brought, and no continuation was in sight. The guests started leaving the dacha. At the station I suddenly realized that the trusting dog would be run over by the train, or dognapped by some tipsy passerby. I took off my belt, lassoed the dog, and took her to the Yugozapadnaya neighborhood, under my parents' roof. I really gave my father and mother a treat: my eternal alcoholic reek, pants falling down, someone else's dog on a strap, when we already had our own. We dragged the snarling bitches off into different rooms, hell was replaced by calm, I collapsed with the boxer in my arms to have a snooze. After catching some z's, I got Yevtushenko's telephone number at the dacha and reported to the secretary what had happened. "Bring her here," he said sternly. But now I was the one in the strong position, and it was my turn to say no. I gave him the address and hung up. The dog spent the night with us. In the morning I went off to teach sixth graders some useful lessons, leaving the pack of hounds with Sasha, my younger brother.

My mouth was dry, and I was listening with delight to the frail Anya Sorokina tell me that her favorite literary hero was Andrii in Gogol's *Taras Bul'ba*, because he "dared to have a preference," when a foreign car pulled up to No. 121 Leninsky Prospect. A minute later a striking female stranger was haranguing my bewildered brother in broken Russian about Moses's eighth commandment.[67]

And I stopped thinking about Yevtushenko. I just got one more tale to dine out on.

In 1983, when all the initiated were impatiently awaiting the impending realization of the prophecy of Orwell-Amalrik, and it hadn't yet come to pass, but my uncle Gorya died in April 1984, and my mama on May 9, and her terrible future death clattered with its claws over the linoleum floors of our apartment for a whole year, and we had managed to get used to the loathsome invertebrate, I settled down, got married, had a child, and was working as a watchman at a building site on Aleksey Tolstoy Street, right where it runs into the Garden Ring.[68] The work was a piece of cake: on duty at night in a warm shed and two days off. You could always find someone to substitute, the other watchmen were my buddies: Alyosha Magarik, my old friend, and Seryozha, a new guy, taking a rest after prison (Magarik still had that ahead of him). Workmen of Bulgarian nationality were ennobling a prerevolutionary house, that is to say a Soviet communal menagerie, for future highly placed residents, making a silk purse out of a sow's ear. Beyond the fence around the building site stood a comparatively new nine-story building, the residence of Grishin, the first secretary of the Moscow City Committee of the Communist Party. The local old-timers would solemnly communicate whether the town governor was home or not, based on the degree of illumination in the third-floor windows. Thus do Londoners infallibly know whether the Queen is at home by the flag hoisted over Windsor Castle.

This lofty neighborhood explained the periodic visits to my building site of three or four identical young men in leather coats.

"Is everything okay?" they would ask, coming into the shed without knocking.

"Everything's quiet, are you from the KGB?" I would ask with affected naïveté, tearing my eyes away from some *tamizdat* (Russian literature published abroad and smuggled into Russia).

They would leave without favoring me, the uninitiated one, with an answer.

The advantageous situation presupposed that I would go on binges, and quite often on a wintry, inky-black, Moscow morning, awakened by a telephone call from my wife, I would extricate myself from a sleeping bag spread out on some chairs and rush to clear away the empty bottles before the arrival of the work superintendent Solomko, and then would go out into the darkness and wet my dried-out mouth with a gob of snow grabbed off of a pile of wood.

This Solomko claimed that if he were to go out onto a balcony to greet a procession of the women he had had carnal knowledge of, and raised his hand in exultation, his hand would go numb before the crowd of women would begin to thin out.

That winter my friend from Tbilisi, Mada Rozenblium, came to Moscow, and I invited her to Shteinberg's studio. The workshop was happening on a day I was on duty, but the watch shed was a stone's throw away from the Central House of Writers, and I allowed myself a two-hour AWOL. The workshop was taking place in the Oak Lodge, where once Galich had been "flogged," but now "reading in a circle" was going full blast under the command of Arkady Akimovich, a former prisoner.[69] The reading ended, the commenting was over, the studio members started heading for the cloakroom. In the lobby Mada took the opportunity to introduce me to her friend Vladimir Leonovich, and I invited him to my watch shed. We went to get our coats in a foursome, the fourth being Egorov, also called Volodya if I'm not mistaken. He was a writer or a translator, I can't remember anymore which; I liked him as a person. We put on our coats.

Leonovich held Mada's fur coat open for her. I was smartening myself up in front of the large mirror and saw Egorov in it, giving his ticket to the cloakroom attendant. In the mirror, next to Egorov, appeared Yevtushenko—tipsy, judging by all appearances.

"Congratulate me, they've given permission for the film!" he fired off to Leonovich.

"How's the writing going, young tribe?" This was now to Egorov, and I was observing in the mirror.[70]

"Well, any way but the way yours is," my classmate responded with adolescent daring.

Evgeny Aleksandrovich Yevtushenko flings out his arm, Egorov takes that arm and bends it behind him the way a policeman would do, Mada hangs on Egorov with a cry, trying to make him stop. That's it.

"Fascists in leather coats, you'll never become writers!" Yevtushenko shouts at our backs.

We go out onto the street and wait for Leonovich, and the snow comes down onto Mada's fake-fur coat, on my black corduroy one; I don't remember what kind of coat Egorov was wearing. Leonovich comes out and says, "After what has happened I cannot take advantage of your invitation."

He nods coldly and walks away. A week later Aleinikov calls me and says, "After the way you beat up Yevtushenko, Leonovich can't help you get any translation jobs."

I start to explain, but I give up halfway through, remembering that a poet needs a legend.

So in order to finish up this Yevtushenkoniana that has suddenly overgrown the place, I will report that about five years ago Lena came into our room from our communal corridor on First Novokuznetsky Lane and said, "Some jerk is asking for you on the telephone."

I go. "Hello," I say. And an impressive voice conveys nice things about my poetry, but mispronounces my unfortunate name, and I have enough pedantry to correct Yevtushenko. From time to time I say "thank you" and fall silent. Not out of pride or hostility, but out of constraint and an inability to carry on literary conversations with people I don't know. He asks me, as poet to poet, about my impressions of America. And I answer. He asks me to "dispatch" my book to him in Peredelkino. And I promise to do so. And on that we say good-bye. I wonder whether Evgeny Aleksandrovich suspects that the dognapper, the fascist in a leather coat, and his taciturn telephone interlocutor are one and the same person?

"Why 'jerk'?" I ask my wife when I come back in the room.

"He didn't say hello and he messed up your name," Lena says without turning from her desk.

The nature of prophecies and literary predictions is enigmatic. The worst fears, the horrible warnings of Dostoevsky have come to pass, and Constantinople has remained as Istanbul, just as it was then.[71] Or my case. It was precisely a writer that I became. I never became a fascist; I am too incapable of making generalizations, and my malice is too unstable, for that. But I did in fact get a leather coat, barely a week after he hurled his curse. Lena bought me the coat with her first large royalty payment at the Nauka publishing house. It just won't wear out, and I've been delighting in it for ten years now and will ask them to bury me in it or maybe will leave it to Grisha. It's Yugoslavian, very long, old-fashioned, with a fur lining and collar and a multitude of military-style rivets, buckles, and straps. It cost seven hundred rubles at a consignment store. We aren't rich enough to buy cheap things—I love these stale maxims. Soon I'll explain to my son that there are no plain women—there's just an insufficiency of vodka. And I've long been repeating to my inelegant daughter that it's better to have a wrinkle on your face than on your stocking, although she is a beauty in the Slavic style, like my mother.

But whatever is said, especially in rhyme, comes true without fail, only in an unpredictable way, never directly but sideways. For example, having in mind that I rarely write verse, about twelve years ago I wrote about the silence that lies in wait for my speech.[72] But just as I used to write two or three poems a year, I have continued to write the same amount. Not long ago, however, I almost lost everyday speech about ordinary objects, and turned into a dog: I would understand but couldn't say anything. I would look at the sideboard, would know the meaning and purpose of the object, but had lost the ability to name it. Or I'd say to Grisha, "Please give me . . ." and would seethe from helplessness. And Grisha, crazy himself, I know that breed, would mutter through his teeth, the seven-year-old wolf cub, "Give you what, Papa?" "Oh, that—" I'd howl, "that whaddyacallit!" And we're talking about a fork, not the *recognitio* of abstract ideas in the sphere of semantics. I would be talking on the telephone with an old acquaintance or even with my closest friend and would be afraid of not getting their name right. That's the kind of unpoetical and unpoetic silence I brought down on myself inadvertently through my prophecy.

I wrote that I like prison-camp songs, especially when performed by Alyosha Magarik—and he was put into a prison camp; I mentioned in a weak, slobbery poem, more out of love for details than anything else, the passenger ship *Admiral Nakhimov*—and it sank.[73] Was my almost first love, Irina Borozdina, right when she said I'm a magician, and everything I touch turns to shit? Well, okay, let's say I'm a bastard. But the others? After all, every poet who's worth anything is shell-shocked by these seemingly toy shooting ranges. The gun is loaded with rock salt, but the recoil is no joke. Everyone knows that you must approach speech with a certain wariness, just as it's recommended that you approach a horse from the front and the authorities from the rear.

This belief in the word brought me so much concentrated terror before my operation, when in the daytime, but especially at night, my thoughts would crowd in fear around the well-known boundary. Two of my last poems had been about death, the last one quite directly; this had never been my style before.

> "Everything is ticking loudly. To lie fully dressed
> On top of the bedclothes to the sound of match marches.
> Come on now, no more foolishness. But the feeling of terror is older
> And more long-lived than you, my soul.
> On the chair a cigarette butt flickers in the ashtray,
> And two keys glimmer in the winter twilight.
> So that is death itself. You've really blown it, bonehead.
> Meth, Nazareth, and breath: the torment of a rhymer.
> Then a nude woman rises from the bed
> And slowly puts a voluminous cassock
> Over her head, and walks aimlessly all around
> The empty dwelling place, which holds the memory of the bad
> Or the quite bad. Before a great parting
> Custom requires that one sit for a little while,
> And she will take a seat, not letting drop a single sound.
> Fathers, teachers—this is what hell is!
> She will pass in transparent darkness up to the very door,
> From the threshold she will cast a glance at the pitiful bed,
> And she'll note down the strange dream with her finger on the dusty
>   secretaire
> As she leaves, but you can't make out the words."[74]

"Don't trifle with that," Lena warned me.

So. I'm lying in the Burdenko hospital. It's night, two sweet pills have long ago melted on my tongue, but I am not in the least bit sleepy. It's pretty stuffy, my roommate is snoring like one of Röhm's thugs in the film *The Damned*, and I understand that it's a stalemate.[75] If I'm truly a poet, I reason, that poem simply will not allow me to survive. And if it lets me get out of here, that means I'm no poet at all, and my whole rotten, weak, no-good life is coming to nothing, because its only consolation and justification—poetry—is, it turns out, a fizzle, a soap bubble. There'd be some excuse if I hadn't been aware of the danger, if I had known not what I did when I traced out the word "death"! I knew it all perfectly well and was aware of everything, and I never expected any mercy from poetry.

Fatality plays its villainous tricks on me. In 1984 for the first anniversary of our wedding I bought a grown Japanese bonsai tree in a consignment store on the Arbat. Some call it a "money tree," others a "bread tree," but the late Seryozha Savchenko for some reason called it a "cutlet tree." A thick, scaly trunk, greenish shoots, and glossy oval leaves that seemed to be made of wax. It lived the life of Riley with us, it grew, and we transplanted it about six years later into a fairly hideous plastic wastebasket; it was hard to get clay pots then. Two weeks before I had to go into the hospital, this little family tree started to croak. Already in the hospital, I asked Lena as if by the way, "How's the cutlet tree?"

And my courageous and truthful wife answered, "It died." There were a few other little omens, both rhymed and unrhymed. At the Fortieth Day service for Sasha Soprovsky four years before, I was sitting next to Akhmed Shazzo, and showing off about my decent prophetic skills, I called his attention to the fact that in the line "Velichansky, Soprovsky, Gandlevsky, Shazzo," I had apparently correctly guessed the order in which the characters would depart.[76]

"You're next!" Akhmed laughed.

My operation was scheduled for the 13th; and this too was a gratuitous, feeble, obnoxious joke by fatality.

Now. If I had written those ill-starred lines with hindsight, and in front of me had stood a bookrest holding the CAT scan results, it would be simpler to give the slip to this rhymed rubbish. You could say, the impressionable simpleton writes the way a Kalmyk bard sings: I see a fence,

I sing about a fence. But the point is that the poem was written long before the diagnosis, truly by chance. Because of a certain broad-jump race
run by me and Sanchuk.

Two years ago in the Mayakovsky Museum an evening was planned in
memory of Soprovsky, and as his oldest friend I was supposed to be the
emcee and say a few words. That last week of March school vacation my
family and I were living at the dacha. Toward one in the afternoon my
wife and I were finishing up cooking on the tile stove and washing the
dishes. The children, who had been forcibly thrown out of the house,
were sledding on a forest hill. Charlie was on the slope bothering the
children, tugging at them by their fur coats and felt boots, or yelping at
the occasional skier. Having finished our domestic efforts, Lena and I
were sitting down to have a smoke in the clean, heated, sunny room, but
right at that time, the children came piling in as usual, banging the doors.
They let the cold into the house, tracked in snow, complained about each
other and about the dog, dropped their wet coats, caps, and scarves on
the floor, and brought the results of my household zeal to naught. We
hastily finished our smoke, dressed the little shits in dry clothes, and
hung their wet pants and tights on the oven door, the open panels of the
stovetop, and on chairs pushed up close to the stove. The room immediately became unsightly, and I turned gloomy but Lena didn't. She herself
throws her things wherever she's standing when she stops having need
of them, and it will soon be eleven years that I've been making her life
miserable over it. Then I raised the cry that it was about to get dark out,
and we hadn't yet gotten onto our skis, and my life and talent had been
ruined thanks to the three of them. Shadowed by an invisible curtain
adorned with a "birrud," I mentioned Dostoevsky and Schopenhauer.[77]
Impressed by what they had heard, the children pulled the skis out of
the cold room next door, dropping the poles and racks, and threw all the
equipment out in front of the porch onto the snow bearing the traces of
thrown-out tea leaves and Charlie's urine. I spent about ten minutes on
my haunches fastening the skis on my wife, children, and myself, and
kept repeating to myself, "It's all wrong! It's all wrong!"

Semyon Faibisovich has a diptych, or as one of his relatives calls it, a
twotych: a room with a bath and a room with a toilet in cross section. In
the bathroom his first wife, not Varya, is fervently primping in expectation of the arrival of guests. And in the toilet, with his pants down, as is

the custom, Semyon himself is sitting on the john and hiding his face in his hands. It's all wrong![78]

But what is "right" for me? To drink without stopping? Or, not able to withstand that homeopathic regime—two or three poems a year—to make rhymes beyond my strength, in order to later crumple them up and wipe myself with them when the urge takes me? Lord, what is "right"? Where is it? That's what I was grumbling as I made a big deal out of the ski fastenings.

It's all—right! The lousy wet clothes junking up a room I just cleaned—are right! The goddamned fastenings—are right! Two poems a year—are right! What have you done to merit more than that? And the brain tumor, perhaps, is the main thing in my whole rotten, weak, bad life that's right! And the two tumors and the aneurysm in the brain of five-year-old Alina from the corner ward—are they also right? Why the hell are *you* shitting your pants!

Finally we came out in single file onto the ski track and skied for about an hour and a half, and we ate heartily when we got home. It got dark. The most painful time of our dacha day set in: What should we do until bedtime, if there's only one warm wood-beam room? The children won't let us read or study English. You can occupy them with drawing or reading for an hour maximum, then they start going wild, jumping from bed to bed, riding horseback on the dog. Trying to lure them outside, into the dark and cold, is a lost cause. That's when I wrote my sketch about Sasha, in fits and starts while snapping at my family, and it seems it came out well.

On the morning of March 24, 1992, I left my family in Tuchkovo and set off for Moscow in order to have time to type my remarks and not be late for Sasha's evening. Even in the most favorable circumstances this journey takes three and a half hours. First you have to walk through the whole settlement along the single street. The usual barracks-like poverty of the six-*sotka* garden co-ops doesn't hurt the eyes so much here: the topography helps. Hills overgrown with spruce forests approach from right and left almost right up to the dachas and don't allow the settlement to sprawl out in an ugly way. It's forced to repeat the twists of a long, narrow ravine, at the bottom of which loops the Romanikha, cold even in July, which a kilometer lower flows into the Moscow River. The Moscow River in these parts does not look like itself, the dirty industrial river full of cranes, barges, buoys, and river trams. Here in the upper reaches, it is narrow, shallow, transparent, cold. Toward August, as is appropriate for country rivers, it sprouts vegetation, and the bather has to make his way from the wooden platform into the rapids, squeamishly moving the seaweed away with his hands. But you won't be able to sit long in the river: it's cold. It's useless to try to swim. The current catches you up and carries you with the speed of a bicycle. On the other hand, it's pleasant to kayak in it, and often in the summer the children and I gaze at these fragile boats from the suspension bridge.

Andrei Tarkovsky lived here in his childhood. It was here that he came to shoot *The Mirror.* In the film, Solonitsyn and Terekhova mention the towns of Ignatievo and Tomshino. And those towns are the end point of my unceremonious walks with Charlie. In a word, there's plenty of Tarkovskiana all around. The hazel grove bends with growing sound under the wind, opening onto the green, aquarium-like, half darkness of the fir forest. You expect that any minute now Pergolesi will burst from the skies and someone will read Pushkin's letter to Chaadaev about the fate of Russia.[79] In my youth I was crazy about these filmic beauties and saw *The Mirror* about eight times. But last year they showed it on television, and it made me feel uncomfortable and somewhat bored.

Having come out of the iron gates of the settlement, we turn left and go up a long ice-covered hill. This road was built during my time here, but it was done in a half-assed fashion. They poured some gravel, asphalted only a third of it, and the very first year the rains washed ruts in it and collapsed the shoulders. But it's pretty. Farther on begins the village of Porechie, and we usually take a shortcut through a barely discernible passage between vegetable gardens and tiny homemade storeroom-kennels and come out right next to a glass-walled café, and passing by it on our right, after about 150 meters we end up at the bus stop. Here you have to trust in luck and approximate calculations: the local juvenile delinquents have knocked the schedule out of its iron frame on the telegraph pole.

Smoking, looking now at my watch, now at the curve in the road in expectation of the bus, I rejoiced in my successful sketch about Soprovsky, recalled its best phrases, and made a guess that the evening would not end without a binge. How could it? The friends of the deceased would gather, moneybags Kenzheev was in Moscow, and our apartment was empty, so we could binge right up to morning. And the main thing was that I could now do this without having to fear any family scenes. The happy idea of giving a written oath had come to me only a few days before. Why didn't I do it ten years ago? There wouldn't have been these comings and goings, pouring of alcohol into the toilet, sly promises. It seems simple as pie: "I, Gandlevsky Sergey Markovich, swear that in the case of my very first binge of 3 (three) days, I will go to V. A. Khevronsky and get 'sewn up.' 15 March 1992. Signature."[80] I trust Viktor Abramovich, he knows what he's dealing with. Over the course of thirty years Khevronsky would drink a liter of vodka every day and had no problem until his family caught him on the balcony, combining the backsight and foresight of a hunting gun with a local policeman who was strolling around the courtyard. From that time Viktor Abramovich has run a practice out of his house, sewing capsules of Antabuse under the skin of alcoholics. Now Lena can be calm, and I can drink for two and a half days with my head held high. Toward the end of the third day I'll safely wrap up the business. That means, today I drink, tomorrow I get a good long sleep, recover, clean up the apartment for my family's arrival and for Grisha's birthday, and in the evening I get the 7:25 p.m. train for the dacha—and everyone's happy.

I managed to catch the train before the midday break, in an hour and a half I was at the Belorussky Railway Station, and after seven minutes on the subway I was at the Novokuznetskaya subway stop. At home I took a shower, drank coffee and ate some stale bread, got the essay typed up in two hours—I still liked it—and set off for the Mayakovsky Museum in the best possible mood.

There were a few blunders at the start of the evening. Thanks to the general lack of supervision, some down-at-the-heels local administrator managed to be the first to break through to the microphone under the pretext that he "unfortunately was not acquainted with Soprovsky," and to read something in verse that was shitty, but long and daring by the standards of ten years ago, and which would have made the late honoree throw up immediately. Luckily, by that time I had already chugged some of Kenzheev's firewater in the lobby and had gotten bold enough to take the reins of government into my hands. Then the non-accidental people appeared on stage: Vedeniapin, Sanchuk, Kenzheev, Vankhanen, Sergienko, Nerler. It's true that the loudly tipsy Aleksey Fyodorovich introduced a certain chaos in the course of the evening, but that was in the spirit of the late honoree, and perhaps by then I was pleased by every-thing; after all, Kenzheev and I were sitting next to each other and had surreptitiously put away by turns 0.7 liters of something very strong. Af-ter the program, no less than a half an hour was spent in the lobby on the inevitable stamping around, greetings, and careful negotiations: who's going where, and who knows how to get there. Finally we figured it all out. Proud Sanchuk with his Vilnius friends went off separately, with a stopover to get booze. Kenzheev set off with a second party, with the same stopover plan. And the women got a ride in Mila's and Petya's cars, taking me along to show them the way. On the way we made a detour to an all-night store, and Petya and I got out of the car and bought a few 0.33-liter bottles of vodka.

Lord, what bliss it is without that stinking Soviet regime! As long as you are solvent and prepared to defend yourself, it's possible to live! I remember my father's death, how I scurried to the supermarket in Yase-nevo with the obscene document from the State Registry Office and went to the Order Department that assisted with weddings and funer-als in the Brezhnev district. They gave you a ridiculously small amount of vodka, you had to drip it from a medicine dropper. How I whined and debased myself before the managers there. I was so afraid of losing face, I so wanted for everything to be the way it was when my father was alive—the way other people do it, not like paupers—at those funeral repasts full of guests. I was in despair, because the supermarket people had already stamped the certificate from the Registry Office saying that the client had been issued his goods, and now you could happily roll it into a tube and stick it you know where! But at the last minute—my star is fortunate!—my beneficent father-in-law called and said rumor had it that they would be giving out vodka the next day near them in Strogino, but you had to bring your own bottles to put it in, and you had to register in the morning. I collected at home and from friends twenty excellent vodka bottles, not screwtops just to be on the safe side. I care-fully stacked them in a backpack with newspaper inserted between the rows, and first thing in the morning, making an indecent racket, I blew from my place to the Shchukinskaya stop on the first subway train, then on a bus to the end of the line. I found the right supermarket, and they wrote my number on my wrist with indelible pencil: 372. Most of all I was afraid that they would start checking your district according to your passport—people were making that decisive presumption in the crowd. But the danger passed. For many hours in the nasty December weather the wet line of many hundreds of people stamped their feet, grumbled, concocted pitiful suppositions, worried about a raid by hooligans, worried that they'd be pushed away from the window and there wouldn't be enough for everybody, tried to ingratiate themselves with the ugly sales clerk, who lorded it over us and rudely ordered us around. With what thievish, lascivious, purely Soviet happiness at my own rascally success did I drag that backpack home!

It's possible to live, when you think that the stinking Soviet regime has kicked the bucket!

We went to my place, the others came to join us. We put a leaf into the table, set our trophies out, rustled up some glasses, and it turned out that plates were not needed at all. This was Kenzheev's style of partying: to have a fit of generosity and spend twenty or thirty thousand on alcohol in a kiosk, and be too cheap to buy a couple of loaves of bread. With amazement I discovered the administrator-imposter at the table. What nerve! Everyone started drinking, making noise, and flirting in a disorderly fashion.

I hadn't seen many of them for several years. This group was kept together by Sasha, but now I avoided it, and a different circle had accepted me. My new group didn't drink any less, but there wasn't that atmosphere of the SMOG group's arrogance, of incoherent noise, spontaneous singing and reading of poems.[81] My new friends are drier, they remember their age; their partying is more decorous and orderly. At any rate, they can maintain a conversation in balance without any shouting of insults for an hour and sometimes more. For some time, that sort of gathering had been more to my taste.

But for now I look around with a moved gaze at my old (in both the literal and figurative senses) comrades, I see myself in the mirror with my peripheral vision . . . . And how worn-out, haggard, balding, graying, balding-graying, toothless we all are! I want to get up, listing and spilling my "boglet" (as Pakhomov used to pronounce it when he was a child), and say, smearing the tears all over my kind face: "My dear friends! There is no gerontologist for us!" But I'm kept from performing my toast by the enigmatic signs that Arkady is making at me with his eyes across the table. I follow the direction of his gaze and see that the administrator has taken advantage of the general noisy tenderness and, imperturbably as a Soviet spy (once—okay, no problem; twice—hey, what's going on here?) was putting the 0.33-liter bottles Petia and I had bought into his prudently opened briefcase on the sly. We had to do something about that! Arkady and I sent our uninvited guest packing with extreme prejudice. Not even because he was a graphomaniac and a thief, but because he was so repulsive. And when we returned from the hallway into the room, we saw that during the five or ten minutes we weren't taking part, the company had reached the desired state. Some were singing, some were shouting poetry, some had put music on and were announcing "ladies' choice," and Volodya Sergienko had driven the unfortunate Bakhyt into a distant corner and was speaking the God's truth to Kenzheev about his unfortunate novels. I drink out of the first glass that comes to hand so that I can catch up with the others, but I immediately overtake them since I wasn't starting from scratch, and I go into the children's room, hitting my head in the darkness on the gymnastics rings and trapezes, and lie down fully dressed on my daughter's lower bunk, and I ask Natasha Mazo to sit with me so I won't be lonesome, and I wake up in horror at the realization that I've missed everything and they've all gone home. But with relief I hear voices in the kitchen on the other side of the wall. I come out and see: Masha Chemerisskaya and Vitya Sanchuk are arguing about Kropotkin, and Aleksey Fyodorovich is pestering the debaters, fighting off sleep, and listing on his stool. But there's nothing left to drink. I rush to my wife's money stash in her desk, in Savchenko's iron Havana cigar box. Hurray! Harried Lena forgot to hide her money. Brave Vitya goes out into the hungover darkness with his huge overcoat flung open.

While he's out there in the March night looking for vodka in empty Zamoskvorechie, we can pass the time and gossip a little bit at Vitya's expense, especially since I'm alone, smoking and rattling around the kitchen, and Masha and Aleksey Fyodorovich have gone off to sleep in the children's room.

Vitya and I met in about 1982 at Shteinberg's studio, where one snowy evening Soprovsky and I descended onto the scene and made a certain impression. It turned out, of course, that we had to drink to the general state of inspiration, and everyone chipped in, and Soprovsky and I volunteered to go get the booze, not trusting such a delicate business to the younger generation. When we returned with an abundant catch and stunned the translators and poets with our "Mozartean element," a young man, shaggy-haired, bony, with a martyr's cheerful smile, grinned in approbation: "Now *that* is downright poetic!"[82] That young man was Vitya Sanchuk.

At that time I was renting from old man Beider two rooms and a kitchen shared with Borya Dubovenko in the settlement of Choboty near the Peredelkino station. Although Borya almost never showed up there. I guess that he was simply using this means of lightening my payment out of sincere kindness and a merchant's generosity. Lena would come when I called her from the drugstore or from the station. Instructed by me, she would leave me vodka in secret vials for morning, would sweep up, cook cauliflower sautéed with eggs, and said that she was pregnant. And when on a bright winter morning as the sun was rejoicing on the white tiles of the Dutch stove, lying in bed, I would light up a cigarette after my second drink, and the horror would be receding, and the nausea would be easing, the heart palpitations would be subsiding—and all I could hear was the broom rustling or the skillet hissing in the little kitchen, I would think: "You yourself can see what's become of your wonderful life. But here a good, lonely young woman loves you and is carrying your child. Your sick, doomed mother has been seeing a granddaughter in her dreams year in and year out. Thirty years. Enough. Don't cling to yourself, Seryozha, don't nitpick: you'll be ashamed." Mama. In Peredelkino there's a crossroads. At sunset on a July day, not long before our eternal parting, you were seeing me off to Moscow. You saw me off and looked at me as I walked away. I also turned around more than once. But when I turned toward the restaurant, luckily you had disappeared. Come on already, you train! And I'll go away—come hell or high water—to San Francisco, Marseilles, Yokohama, so that pity doesn't drive me insane. It's the usual sad song.

So now I somehow open my eyes, fight off the kisses of the Saint Bernard and poodle, and Lena says, "In the morning a stranger named Vitya came by, you were asleep, he drank some beer in the kitchen and hurried off for the train."

What bad luck: I'm sorry about the beer, and sorry about Vitya! But several days later Lena's stranger appeared again, and he turned out to be precisely the same Vitya as at the studio. We got some kind of rotgut at the station and we talked, and everything was amazingly to the point, and baring his teeth out of shyness and tormenting the corner of the oilcloth on the table, he recited some very talented poems. He ended the reading with the words "It's shit, in my opinion." And this was not a friendship but a passion. It also shared the fate of passion—a complete calming down over time.

I understood how dear he was to me when he called after having fallen in love yet again, asked whether I believed in God, and asked me to pray for him. Or when he was walking from the Michurinets station against a slanting snow, and I stood by the window of our building in Fedosino and watched him approach.

Lena knows how to be jealous even of my relations with inanimate objects, and here was Vitya's degenerate beauty—a "page's beauty," as Prigov remarked. Soprovsky joined in the adoration, and we even lowered ourselves to the point of slightly bad-mouthing each other to the object of our shared infatuation in each other's absence. And this whole triple masculine pure giddiness dissipated with the appearance of a fourth—Mikhail Sergeevich Gorbachev, General Secretary of the Central Committee of the Communist Party.

Vitya, it seems to me, could not forgive me my innocent official successes, or Sasha his innocent less official ones. I'm not talking about unicellular envy. Vitya became disenchanted with me the way Beethoven did with Napoleon: so even *he* is an ordinary person! We started getting together less and less often and more and more nastily. With my touchiness, to drive me with hints into feeling guilty is as easy as ABC. I would gloomily fidget in front of all reflective surfaces: Maybe I really am part of the literary scum? It all ended ridiculously: with a duel.

Yes, Lyova, yes, my dear, there's no need to wince. We exchange the crosses we wear on our chests, we fight duels, like buffoons, and also— we can barf in a stranger's corridor and in the morning have the effrontery to orate and pontificate, in short, there's more than enough tastelessness to go around. It's good, of course, when our cloak is really too black and our pallor extreme, if we have the nerve to fart out loud. But the surplus of intelligence in that case is made to order, intellectual reflection is prescribed in sparing doses. Your business, though, is also not without a flaw. We may be ridiculous, but we have the courage to be ridiculous, while for you it's like a knife to the heart. Every time you open your mouth you have to run ahead of yourself in order to laugh at yourself before others start laughing. Isn't that tiring, isn't that a kind of dependence? It's amusing: today's innovators in art are good little boys in everyday life, while the people who don't give a damn about the traffic rules when they cross the Stromynka or Bolshaya Cheryomushkinskaya, respect the literary stoplight![83] Vitya himself told me how you were walking with him at night in Mozzhinka and halfway along you crumpled up your newspaper in perplexity and muttered, "Where can I get rid of it? Where's a trash can?" "Just throw it wherever, you're an avant-gardist!" Vitya couldn't resist saying. Or another of Vitya's stories. After a brawl at a meeting of the "Poetry" club, a righteous brawl, but a nonsensical one, in which Soprovsky, acting like some Danton, had put the brand of shame on Prigov, Prigov and Sanchuk were pissing side by side behind a garage. And Prigov, shaking either from wounded pride or from the long-awaited voiding of his bladder, complained, "Aleksandr Aleksandrovich called me a liar twice. They used to exchange shots over that in the old days."

"So you should have exchanged shots," Vitya said to him, fastening his trousers.

Thus I announce out loud in public, slowly and deliberately, which in writing is expressed by boldface type: **You heard right—Sanchuk and I fought a duel.**

We—Grisha Dashevsky, Vitya, Lena, and I—had a good friend, Seryozha Savchenko, a kind and intelligent man. He worked at the Lebedev Institute of Physics, made slide films, went to concerts at the Conservatory, went to film screenings and literary evenings. He wrote poems in imitation of early Pasternak, but only showed them to people occasionally, because he was more enthusiastic about other people's poems than his own. He would go to the mountains either alone or with his parents, was either a Buddhist or a Hindu, didn't eat meat, could cook vegetarian dishes beautifully, was involved in some kind of anti-regime activity but kept quiet about it, had a large beard and shoulder-length hair, and wore shirtsleeves and tennis shoes with no socks all year round, and when he was indoors he took off all footwear. He considered Venedikt Erofeev to be a genius, he was a good listener, and when asked about his own problems he would answer with quotations from Erofeev's *Moscow to Petushki* or obscene catchphrases spoken with a German accent.[84]

You'd come home and Seryozha would already be there playing with the children. Or you'd need to go somewhere right away, but he'd stay.

He was neither my friend nor Lena's, but as they say, a "friend of the family." He was an easy guest, never a burden, and didn't even feel like a guest. He'd go home late, just in time for the last subway train, and I would usually accompany him downstairs to take out the garbage. We would say good-bye, and I would have a cigarette and watch him run—in tennis shoes and a short jacket no matter what the weather, with a small imported knapsack, which was a new thing at the time, on his back. He would shake his long hair and jog along First Novokuznetsky Lane toward Pyatnitskaya Street.

In the Conservatory he met a foreign music-lover, and he turned out to be the Dutch ambassador. The ambassador and his wife took such a liking to Seryozha that they sold him a Canon camera for some trivial sum. Seryozha's usual restraint failed him. He could not hide his ecstasy, and I remember that he dismantled the camera several times to demonstrate its perfections to my indifferent gaze. On October 23, 1989, with his new acquisition at his side and, as always, after midnight, he was returning from showing his slide film at the Glinka Museum and was hit by a passenger car across from his building. His death was instantaneous.

Savchenko's mother called us on the evening of the next day. I wasn't home, and Lena answered the phone.

"Seryozha has died, this is his mama," came through the receiver.

For the first second Lena thought I had died, and that my mother was calling her, but she immediately got hold of herself and realized that my mother had passed away five years ago.

I came home to find Lena crying, I heard the terrible news before I took my coat off, and I set off on foot for Leninsky Prospect to tell Vitya, with whom our mutual hostility was at its most intense. On the way I cried and blew my nose in the Tatar fashion, because I had left my handkerchief at home.

From that time, every October 23, you can drop in from 6:00 to 7:00 in the evening to see Savchenko's parents, Inna Aleksandrovna and Marat Mefodievich, near the Kuntsevskaya subway station, without calling ahead, and find tables set with food and about twenty guests: people of Seryozha's age and people of the older generation who knew him as a boy. It's easy to remember: Myuda died on September 23, October 21 is Soprovsky's birthday, Savchenko died on October 23, my mother was born on November 21, I was born on December 21, and Soprovsky died on the 23rd of the same month.

Behind the glass doors of the bookshelves are many photographs of Seryozha: Seryozha as an adolescent with his father in the mountains; Seryozha—already the way he was when I knew him—is cooking up some grub during an expedition to the Pamirs, making a face; the last enlarged portrait of Seryozha—in it he is unexpectedly serious, even gloomy. There will be groaning boards. After the first glass drunk without clinking, the usual racket will start up around the table. Marat Mefodievich conscientiously accompanies the guests in groups to the subway station as they depart.

In our home we have a cigar box that Seryozha once brought me, full, as a present from Germany; now we keep money in it. I also have a habit I borrowed from him of getting up in the morning and taking a cold shower, and putting my head under it without fail, otherwise some sort of *prana* is lost.

Inna Aleksandrovna and Marat Mefodievich are holding on, they are getting tired and sick. Inna Aleksandrovna continues to work, but Marat Mefodievich has retired, he has trouble with his heart. Last summer the Savchenkos spent Inna Aleksandrovna's vacation in the mountains of Kabardino-Balkaria at the Academy of Sciences tourist camp. They are true to the predilections of their youth: Georgian and Polish film, Slutsky and Korzhavin. They visit the cultural center at the Polish embassy and the Museum of Film. They follow the latest books and periodicals. Musical evenings.

At the mob scenes in memory of Savchenko I never once got truly drunk, thank God. But in 1990, my wife wasn't with me and I apparently overdid it, because after the gathering I didn't go home, but went with Vitya Sanchuk, Anya Ryazanskaya, and Masha Ushinskaya to Masha's place to have some more. We took a taxi and dropped off Grisha Dashevsky on Garibaldi Street on the way. At the entrance to Masha's building Vitya dropped in passing that I probably shouldn't have come. This was too much: in the first place, Masha had invited me, and in the second, I had just paid the cabdriver with my last money and it was too late to get the subway. I became tense.

We made ourselves comfortable in the kitchen. The stages of intoxication of those present did not coincide, or rather, the women were completely sober, and neither the conversation nor the merriment came off. In the midst of the confusion in the kitchen, Vitya said something else nasty to me, and I had to do something about it. With drunken instinct I asked Sanchuk to go into the next room with me, and there I slapped him on the cheek. By my reasoning, I had at once outweighed all his previous insults with this, and let him now try to deal with it. With relief I returned to the kitchen and joined the women. After a while Vitya, who had turned pale, came up to me and said that he considered my little trick to be a challenge to a duel.

"Get a weapon, I don't have any."

"I do," Vitya replied.

The women participated in the choice of weapons and the other details with the liveliest interest and displayed a knowledge of the subject. At about 2:00 in the morning the five of us set off to Vitya's place not far away to get the instruments of killing. In the courtyard the women and I chatted about what had happened while Vitya went up to his apartment and returned with his pocket hanging away from his body. It turned out to be a huge operatic revolver. The ephemeral undertaking had acquired flesh, and the women tried to calm us down. But Sanchuk had developed a taste for it and proposed that we draw lots, and that the one selected should shoot himself, so as to take no chances. I refused. I have a good nose for lousy decadence. After we brawled for an hour in the autumn courtyard mist, they pulled us apart, and I reached home virtually unconscious.

I'm proud of my autopilot, my ability to be in a blackout and produce the impression of being sober. Once I found myself in the airport of Naberezhnye Chelny, where I was in fact supposed to be on that day and at that time, and Inna Limonova, who was meeting me, said, "I think you need to eat something."

As I tucked into her homemade *pelmeni* at her place, I kept trying to remember how I turned out to be so responsible—and couldn't.[85] The last thing I could call to memory was sitting on the floor in the completely empty apartment on First Novokuznetsky Lane, swigging from a bottle of "One Man Show" cologne that my father-in-law had given me as a gift, and Denis Novikov had bent over me and was trying tenderly, as if with a child, to talk me into going with him somewhere, and I just shook my head no. So like a lunatic, I had managed to get up on my hind legs in time, get dressed, take my passport, not forget my tickets, make it to Paveletsky Station, get on the correct train, pass through passport control in Domodedovo Airport . . . .

No, no matter what you say, I do have some good qualities; cleanliness, for example. All in all I spend about a third of the day in the shower. It's true that Yura Kublanovsky considered that I do this as compensation for my inner filth, and if it were in his power, he would introduce restrictions on water use. I don't know. He's in a better position to judge. Kublanovsky is a convenient object for gossip. One of the times he came back from Germany, he treated Soprovsky to some kind of imported booze in a *pelmeni* café on Tverskaya Street where you had to stand to eat, and asked him, while pouring him a drink, why Sasha didn't publish.

"I don't feel like kissing ass," my late comrade answered.

"But these are completely different people," Yura said.

So somehow I must have walked home, like the Golem, from Leninsky Prospect to Zamoskvorechie and am sleeping away. Lena wakes me up in the morning and says, "Soprovsky's on the phone, he demanded that I wake you up."

"Hello," I say, "good morning, damn it to hell, Sanechka."

Sasha dryly and with a solemnity befitting the situation tells me that Vitya had just called him and asked him to be our second and do I have any objections, he is inquiring. And if not, he asks me to be at Neskuchny Park at 1:00 p.m. My God! I dimly remember yesterday's events. What do you mean "duel," when I'm shaking like a leaf! To an unbiased observer I probably looked something like Gogol's Chertokutsky on that unfortunate morning. But I reminded myself of the words of Athos: "Dishonor is more terrible than death," said I'd be there, and got into a cold shower with revulsion.[86] I refused breakfast, got dressed as well and as severely as possible, feeling the glaringly operetta-like nature of everything that was about to happen. I left the house in good time; on the way to the duel I had to stop in to a certain academic institute of natural sciences nearby.

My old acquaintance Tamara Ivanova worked there, and if I asked her very nicely, she would have pity on me and pour out a little pure alcohol from a vial holding some kind of prehistoric insect, otherwise what kind of Voroshilov marksman am I?[87] All you can do with hands like mine is sprinkle salt and pepper, as Volodya Golovkin used to say. Tamara was kind and quick on the uptake that day, and a half hour later I was standing by the

entrance to Neskuchny Park with the triumphant Soprovsky. Vitya was
late, like Onegin to the mill, and I was worrying about my leather coat:
my plans certainly did not include bequeathing my dear new acquisition
with holes and bloodstains.[88] Finally, with apologies for his delay, my foe
appeared. Soprovsky, who adored any kind of ritual of nobility, led Sanchuk aside, then led him up to me and asked whether we would agree to
a reconciliation. But each of the swashbucklers was too far gone in his
binge, and the next stage set in inescapably. We walked into the depths
of the park, and the jubilant Soprovsky started voluptuously pacing out
the distance at which we were to fight. Then he gave instructions to the
adversaries. We drew lots. I was to shoot first.

The weather was conducive to this kind of thing. It was a bright autumn day, the sky was intensely blue, the withered leaves were rustling
underfoot, mamas were pushing baby carriages, jackdaws were calling to
each other. I took off my coat, laid it on a dry hummock, walked up to
the branch that marked the barrier, and shot into the air. The mamas and
jackdaws startled. It was Vitya's turn. But Sanchuk the pedant recalled
that since I was the instigator, I had no right to fire into the air. We re-
loaded. With the muzzle pointing down I carried the ridiculously heavy
piece of crap up to my barrier. The revolver was hanging on my index
finger and fired from its own weight. The dead leaves flew up next to my
shoe. It was a miracle that I didn't shoot myself in the foot. Vitya reso-
lutely took the weapon away from me, stuck it in his pocket, and walked
off in his huge overcoat.

"He didn't say good-bye to his second," Soprovsky said.

Then? What then . . . I again found myself in a seemingly hopeless
situation with my living space when Lena rashly told our policeman
neighbor that he was an animal. But with time everything was resolved
by itself, and for more than two years now we have had our own two-
room apartment in a neighboring lane.

Soprovsky died under the wheels of a car on December 23, 1990, opposite the Shcherbakovskaya subway station, after we had been drinking grain alcohol at Petya Obraztsov's place, talking about death, and
toward midnight had jokingly started courting Petya's stepbrother
Seryozha's girlfriend. We even got down on our knees before her and
vied with each other in exclaiming, "If only I were a little younger and
a little freer!"

Vitya Sanchuk carried corpses out of the rubble after the earthquake in Leninakan. He dropped in drunk to see us with Slon when we were still on First Novokuznetsky Lane and said that Pushkin can't compete with Camoens. He successfully swapped his grandfather's huge apartment for a two-room and a three-room apartment in the same building. He took part in the January events in Vilnius.[89] At one of the anniversaries of Savchenko's death he looked at my Lena for about ten minutes without blinking, then pronounced threateningly that she looked like one of the Fayum mummy portraits. He called my poems shit, then added, "Excuse me, of course." He told us what happened to him in the Vologda-Moscow train, but asked us not to spread it around. We see each other from time to time and seem to be on good terms.

He seems to have returned to the kitchen.

"What do you have to comfort us, Vitya?"

Vitya gets a bottle of vodka out of his immense overcoat, now hanging sideways, and taking it by the neck, he places it slowly and carefully on the soiled kitchen table among the overflowing ashtrays and unwashed cups. Masha and Aleksey Fyodorovich are sleeping. Toward dawn for some reason we are discussing the bombing of Tripoli and the accidental killing of a child and we decide that we, raised on Dostoevsky, require greater precision of aim.[90] Vitya remembers that he has heaps of money back home on Leninsky Prospect, and we leave stealthily, so as not to awaken the guests.

We meet up with Kseniya, we eat something spicy with champagne in the restaurant at Gorky Park, we go somewhere, then somewhere else. From lack of sleep and all that we've drunk we keep nodding off in turn, now at somebody's apartment, now in public transportation, but at midday we both simultaneously jump at the idea that we absolutely have to go see Edik Vidovzorov.

Edik Vidovzorov was our comrade, a defector to Guatemala. I worked with Edik during an expedition on Kamchatka, and the whole three months he studied English from my Bonk textbook. His father was a big shot but an honest man, and at the same time a chronic drunkard. At some point he gave Kosygin two million dollars, which his Western partners had given him to show their gratitude for an illegal deal—to the advantage of the Soviet Union, to the detriment of a certain foreign power. For this he received the Order of the Red Banner of Labor. He'd be brought down

from his binges in the Kremlin hospital. But when he got old and was no
longer involved in business, he had to die in an ordinary ward with fifteen
patients in it. From youth, from the first class in school, Edik was somehow oppressed by his Soviet citizenship. That's what he needed Bonk
for. At one point I worked for him: at the dacha, wearing a gas mask, I
machined keychains out of epoxy resin—skulls, and hands giving the
derisive "fig" gesture of a fist with the thumb placed between the index
and middle fingers. Edik paid me 35 kopecks (old currency) apiece for
them. This was enough money to furnish two adjoining rooms in a communal apartment, the first living space Lena and I had of our own. Five
years ago I caught sight of a familiar "fig" on the stand of a street peddler
on Ben Yehuda Street in Jerusalem, and my heart stopped beating for a
moment: life is short, art is long.

If I had had Edik's looks and manner, I wouldn't have tortured myself
cramming foreign languages, but would just have rolled up to the rusty
iron gates of Hollywood one fine day, exhaled the smoke from my unfil-
tered Gauloise into the piggy little eyes of the unshaven prison screw, and
muttered through my teeth: "Watch your mouth, commander. Where's
the boss here? Take me to him, I'm counting to ten. I'm already at eleven."

But Edik prefers to seek happiness on well-beaten paths: hunting alli-
gators, smuggling counterfeit dollars across the border. But they say that
in comparison with the heroin trade in the capitals of Europe, this is all
just chicken feed.

And now this precious Edik is sitting in the kitchen before Vitya and
me, in the flesh, and has filled the whole table with bottles of German
beer. But he doesn't want to get drunk: the Guatemalan is hurrying
about his urgent affairs, and as he leaves, he puts a rather large sum of
rubles on the same table, considering our status as penniless writers. We
take a little nap, lying wherever we happen to be when it hits us, and
when we wake up, we drink a little more, for strength of character. And
when this too ends and it starts to get dark both inside and out, it dawns
on me that Sasha Borisov fell off the wagon a few months back because
of a toothache and Olya's trip to Borisoglebsk. And that he came to see
me then at night, in a taxi, without a hat, and for two days dammed up
the measured flow of our family life, so that means not everything is so
hopeless. I call him, remind him of the regrettable incident, and say that
one good turn deserves another, isn't that right?

"That's right," Sasha answers apathetically.

Borisov is a story in himself, but I don't have time for sentimentality right now, and Vitya and I meet Sasha at the Akademicheskaya subway station.

"One bottle or two?" he asks at the vodka-seller's stall.

At Sasha's place Olya the friendly hottie is feeding two senseless monsters, and teetotaling Sasha turns on the *St. John Passion* and sits in a wicker rocking chair. He is a Buddhist by nature, he knows how to control himself. After picking apart the delicacies on our plates, we grab the bottles and start to dart off, but imperturbable Sasha gives us a ride in his car. Along the way we forget whose car we're in and who's driving, and in a loud whisper we discuss in the backseat who's going to pay the gypsy cabdriver.

Consciousness returns to us in my kitchen. We are again alone together; the already opened bottle of vodka gives us hope. We renew the conversation that has been interrupted by circumstances out of our control, and Lena comes into the kitchen with the children.

"Why so early?" I ask.

"What do you mean 'early'?" Lena says, and pours herself some vodka. "You've been gone for four days, Sasha has to go to school tomorrow."

The binge is in its fifth day. Everything is ticking: the self-invited grandfather clocks, the alarm clocks, the floor clocks, the watches—they're innumerable as insects. Leaning against the wall I make my way to the john, standing over the toilet I stick two fingers in my mouth, but in vain, the poison has taken hold. "It's a kind of hell," I mutter, assuming a horizontal position on the ottoman next to my wife. I'm dressed, but getting undressed would not be possible right now. The high water of primordial terror is clambering up to the bed. My soul does not yield to persuasion, although this isn't its first time, and in the past I had always gotten away with it. There's no elevator in the building, but I can clearly hear it stop on our floor and someone right by our door wheezing and knocking the snow off his leather-soled felt boots. So that is death itself. You've really blown it, bonehead. Now the game is up: your shaky reason has stumbled upon a line of verse by mistake, and will importunately drill into your skull, squealing always in the same form in your brain like a milling cutter until your hangover torments end. My wife gets up to take the children to their schools. I wait for my family members to leave and again choke vainly over the toilet bowl.

I had to drink for five days and spend a year and a half giving birth, so that the result would resemble the second tercet of the sonnet in *The Gift*![91]

Anna Akhmatova's "If only you knew out of what trash . . ." is one of the most famous and false little lines in Russian poetry. The pronoun messes things up. It assumes that the inert but intrigued crowd is pressing the poet: So is it true that God guides your hand? What is she like, your Muse, captivating but capricious? And with a sad, fatherly smile the poet sets their not too clever heads straight: "They grow out of trash, out of trash. Knowing no shame." Well, nobody cares about that. Well, almost nobody. And it's only the poet who can't believe that out of a tram ticket, out of a slip of the tongue in a line for bread, out of a scrap of newspaper in a rural outhouse this diabolical hallucination could begin.

She was a strange poetess. Anatoly Naiman recollects how enraptured Akhmatova was that in the Gospel of John the disciples didn't suspect anything when they found Jesus conversing with an unknown woman at the well.[92] I have to admit, Akhmatova's train of thought flabbergasted me. Even rotten old me. Although I too stand stock-still, with dry mouth, like an adolescent, in front of the porno stalls, and one of my first worries after my operation was the hormone shots.

I caught Doctor Zolotukhin in the corridor and said that I'd been getting hormone injections for ten days already, and asked him to stop the prescription. "I'm afraid for my temperament," I explained and went off to smoke, and the whole time I was racking my brain: Where did I get that turn of speech? I remembered—and this was the first sign that my memory was returning. Aksakov the elder answered Gogol, when the latter was advising him, an old man, to read Thomas à Kempis: "I'm afraid for your talent."[93] I owe my knowledge about hormone treatment to Solzhenitsyn. When I was in ninth grade I read a typescript of *Cancer Ward* to our blind grandmother, Vera Ivanovna, and she would listen, smoking a "Kazbek" and flicking her ashes now in the ashtray, now in the butter dish. To be precise, she was not our blood relation, but was the friend of our actual late grandmother, Maria Aleksandrovna Orlova.

Before the war there were three or four of them, comrades in misfortune: their husbands had been imprisoned. The friends would get together from time to time. Of course they smoked, *papirosy*, of course. One of them was Vera Ivanovna Uskova, the daughter of a Buzuluk bank employee who had had nobility conferred upon him. She outlived her friends, and thirty years later, completely alone and having gone blind from glaucoma, she came to help my mother around the house a time or two and then settled down to live with us until her death. When my mother and I went over to Vera Ivanovna's room in a communal apartment on the Arbat to gather her clothes for her funeral, out of the folds of her old lady's suit slipped an envelope with an inscription in letters of different sizes: "For Irochka Divnogorskaya for expenses." Two hundred rubles.

Mama was born in Moscow in 1928 and was the granddaughter of two priests—Aleksandr Orlov and Ivan Divnogorsky; one a Muscovite and the other a provincial. Her father, Iosif Ivanovich Divnogorsky, was much older than his wife and died when his daughter had just turned four. Prerevolutionary photographs had been preserved: a storybook-handsome mustachioed military man in a light carriage. From a young age I liked to say that my grandfather had been an officer in the Tsarist army. It's all true, but he served as a veterinarian.

We find the terrible proverb "misfortunes never come singly" in the old Dahl dictionary, and it's true: simultaneously with her father's death, her grandfather, Aleksandr Orlov, the last and only man in the family, was exiled to Solovki. Three women—Aleksandra Vasilievna, the aged wife of the priest; Maria Aleksandrovna, the priest's widowed daughter; and four-year-old Irina—remained alone in the soulless Soviet world. There began a twenty-year stretch of humiliations, keeping quiet about things, lying on questionnaires, timorous vegetating, and ominous hints from the neighbors in the communal apartments. The blinding beauty of Maria Aleksandrovna, which my mother inherited, brought more burdens than advantages, since it deprived her of inconspicuousness, got in the way of her camouflage. When the priest—husband, father, and grandfather—was being transferred from Solovki to exile in Kazakhstan, where he died, there was word that they would be able to meet him briefly in passing at the Kazan train station in Moscow. But the exiled man's wife and daughter were so intimidated that they did not go to this abbreviated rendezvous.

Aleksandr Orlov now looks out from a photograph on the bookshelf—a large man, with thick streaks of gray in the hair over his receding hairline and in his beard, with bushy eyebrows, small rimless glasses on his prominent nose, in vestments, with a large cross on his chest.

Just in case, the return addresses on the greeting cards from the provincial relatives, also disfranchised persons, were carefully crossed out. My mother's Young Pioneer hand, covered with red spots, ink stains, and hangnails, scraped the greetings "Christ is risen!" and "Merry Christmas" off the same old-regime sequined cards with a razor. The whole family was carried by my grandmother alone. She worked sometimes as an accounts clerk, sometimes as a linen-keeper in institutions.

About that time feminine happiness smiled on Maria Aleksandrovna; she got married again to a russified Austro-Hungarian who had been a prisoner of war in World War I. He was called Jan Janovich Bokmiuller. He had a son, Rufa, from his first marriage. Jan Janovich occupied a rather prominent position in a confectionary factory, and shameful destitution receded from Mama's family, but not for long: her stepfather also was put in shackles. They let him out after a year. The results of his captivity were chronic fright, an improvement in his Russian, and a broadening of his horizons—the beneficial influence of his fellow prisoners could be discerned. His twelve-year-old stepdaughter would be offended when, bearded and corpulent, he would return from work, flop into a chair, and say, "Oof, Marusya, I'm tired."

And Mama's mother would get down on her knees before him and take off his shoes.

Right before the war Jan Janovich left her for another woman. But with Austro-Hungarian ingenuousness he would go to Maria Aleksandrovna for advice every time he had problems with bookkeeping.

The stepbrother Rufa was killed in the first week of the war, and my mama was sent into evacuation. There she was undernourished, became covered with scabs, and quit going to school because she was ashamed of her hideousness. When her skin cleared up two years later, Mama continued her studies, but not for long: the well-grown, beautiful young woman had to share her school bench with twelve-year-old adolescents; they teased her, and Mama again quit, worked in a factory until the end of the war, and after returning to Moscow entered a technical college, where history was taught by Fanya Moiseevna Naiman, her future mother-in-law.

Not long ago a packet of my mother's letters from evacuation fell into my hands. Her strange manner of expressing herself, which I perceived as incorrect and even holy-fool–like, immediately reminded me of Leskov. But when I was old enough to be aware, I never heard these turns of speech from my mother. Apparently, this remarkable language died out, became simplified and straightened out under the influence of the neutral speech of my father, a Soviet intellectual.

In the timorous existence of these three women I seem to see such despondency, doom, and wrongful accusation! The misfortunes and burdens of my Jewish relatives were partly justified and expiated by their rash historical optimism, but this priest's family survived only because in the chaos of what was being accomplished the authorities just forgot by mistake to finish them off. When I reveal my unequal sympathies, my interlocutors sometimes suspect me of the anti-Semitism of a half-breed. No. Several years ago, it's true, I got shamefully and hopelessly lost in the problematics of nationalism, but that passed—forever.

Fanya Moiseevna Naiman was an exceptional woman. There is a family legend: in her childhood she was pasturing the Naimans' only goat in an open plot in the *shtetl* of Malin, and a man wearing a boater hat and carrying a cane, a city dweller by his looks, walked by. He sat down in the sun next to the little girl, they got to talking. The stranger asked whether she knew how to read and write.

"No," said Fanya.

He opened a book, read a page, and asked her to retell it.

And she repeated what she had heard word for word. The city man said that he would teach her to read, and he did; he was Sholem Aleichem.

The family had eleven children. The untalented father had a leather shop, but the family was in effect destitute. Only a few of my grandmother's numerous brothers and sisters were lucky enough to grow up; some drowned or perished under the wheels of a cart because of the elders' lack of supervision; others were killed in pogroms. With fatal inevitability the boys who grew up became revolutionaries, and their trace has been lost. To this day there are Yakuts named Naiman in continental Siberia, the descendants of exiled Social Revolutionaries.

Thanks to her talents and sociability, Fanya Moiseevna spoke Russian as well as you and I. I don't remember any specifically Jewish accent. She came to Moscow on a military train, and just as she was, barefoot and wearing a soldier's blouse, she sat sideways on a windowsill in the People's Commissariat of Education (Narkompros) across from Krupskaya's office. And the invisible barrel-organ played an encore—all right, already—of the unpretentious music of luck; the playlet out of a peasant woodcut was repeated, only the composition of the performers changed: now the role of the benefactor was given not to Sholem Aleichem but to Nadezhda Konstantinovna Krupskaya, Lenin's wife. And the next thing she knew, my grandmother was a student in the Academy of Communist Education.

I suspect that before she met my grandfather, Moisei Davydovich Gandlevsky, the level of her ideas and the circle of her interests could be covered by Mandelstam's definition: an insolent "Komsomol cell," an insolent "song of the VUZ."[94] When I knew her I found an incomprehensible proximity of love for and knowledge of Pushkin with a predilection for the anti-clerical song "Sergey the priest, Sergey the priest, Sergey the deacon and sacristan." By the way, such things happen right and left. On a folklore expedition sponsored by the Philology Department, I was perplexed by the way the village women could with the same emotion sing an ancient *magnificat* and without any transition the convicts' song: "In the Mitrofanievsky cemetery a father slit his daughter's throat."

My kind grandmother preserved her Komsomol enthusiasm and a not always appropriate simpleheartedness to her last day, despite all the misfortunes of her life. This old-ladyish liveliness and resoluteness grated on my father the snob and gave him grounds for insulting remarks directed at the thin-skinned and hot-tempered Fanya Moiseevna. She was not pretty, and it seems to me that my grandfather—who came from a prim intellectual milieu—fell in love with my grandmother because she seemed to him to be the incarnation of freedom and spontaneity.

My grandfather Moisei and his younger brother Grigory (called Gorya in the family) were the sons of a conscientious and prosperous district doctor from a long line of the same, David Grigorievich. When he returned from the Russo-Japanese War and bent over the little bed of his firstborn, the child didn't recognize his father and shouted, "A policeman, a policeman, get the cop out of here!"

My great-grandfather sent his wife Sofia Moiseevna, pregnant with Gorya, to Switzerland, believing in the beneficial influence of beautiful landscapes on the course of pregnancy and on the appearance of the newborn. Despite the views of the Alps and the beauties of Lake Geneva, Gorya grew up to be undersized, with protruding ears and a horselike face, and was a kind of wicked caricature of Pasternak. It's true that his health was excellent. He died under anesthesia three weeks before my mother's death, when at the age of seventy-five he was having a cancerous tumor of the kidney removed, the occupational disease of chemists in his specialty. Before then, he had gone to a doctor only once in his whole life.

In 1939 he was making the rounds of the shop floor that had been assigned to him in some kind of chemical factory, and he heard an indistinct noise in one of the gigantic gas boilers. In the twinkling of an eye my courageous relative had shot up onto the enormous vat, bent over the hatchway, and seen that a woman whose job included washing the boilers with a long-handled mop had fallen down and lost consciousness after she gulped the heavy gas on the bottom of the vessel. Gorya jumped into the boiler and managed to lift the inert body of the female worker and push it out through the hatchway, but succumbed to the bad air himself and occupied her place on the bottom of the boiler. People came running at the noise and pulled Gorya out. But for a day and a night after the incident he lingered between life and death and in his unconscious state cried out, "Mamochka!"

My grandfather was born at home, but unlike Gorya he was, according to general opinion, a picture of beauty. The brothers' childhood was completely prerevolutionary and happy, like something out of Lev Kassil's *Black Book and Schwambrania*, about the bourgeois Jewish family of a respected doctor. The preparatory school, languages, father's cello. My grandfather was the first to enter the transitional age and developed a hatred for the "haves." Once, having picked up some freethinking on the side, my grandfather came out to a decorous family dinner in his undershorts. The abundant Judaic vegetation on his legs had been shaved to form rings. In this revolutionary mood Moisei left his parental shelter in about 1920.

While Mozya was shocking his parents, his younger brother had discovered the meaning of life. The truth appeared to the Gandlevsky youth in a dream and was blinding. The coarse light of morning scared off the otherworldly radiance. Gorya rumpled his hair, with his legs hanging off the bed, but the vision was not resurrected. The nocturnal illumination was repeated again, twice, three times, but just like the first time, it left no memory of itself. But Gorya had a strong character. Through fanatical practice he mastered the art of punctuated sleep, learned how to jump up with open eyes at any time of the night; pen and ink were placed at the head of the high-school student's prophetic bunk. "Aha, I've caught you!"—and the sleeping youth would dip the pen into the ink by touch, would blindly trace on the wallpaper the archaic words of the secret knowledge, and would plunge with relief into a sweet, no longer prophetic, sleep with saliva on his pillow. "Titatikapu," he would read while wiping his mouth early in the morning.

His failure in the visionary calling brought in its train a boyish rebellion, and without giving it much thought, Gorya hung upside down with his legs hooked over the mouth of a factory chimney, and hung that way precisely as long as it took for everyone in the neighborhood to crane their necks.

The brothers met up in Moscow. One fine day they up and "consolidated" the living space of their bourgeois Moscow relatives, and it is precisely this that explains the enigmatic absence of relatives on the Gandlevsky side, while there are plenty of Naimans, my grandmother's kinsmen. Most likely, they simply stopped associating with the younger Gandlevskys. Taking into account that the young Land of the Soviets needed specialists, and not petty-bourgeois blabbermouths, the elder Gandlevsky became an engineer and the younger a chemist. Utkin and Selvinsky crowded out Pushkin and Goethe in the original. Soon the brothers had a falling-out that lasted forty years, laying the foundation for a persistent tradition two generations into the future.

Old age reconciled them. At our infrequent family reunions I would condescendingly listen to the two jovial old men's oft-repeated cock-and-bull stories, about this and that, about how the peasants tried to show their gratitude to my great-grandfather the doctor with suckling pigs and geese, and the proud vegetarian Tolstoyan would indignantly chase the visitors out of his office. It's true that the doctor's wife would make eloquent signs to the discouraged patients behind the door, and they would bring the poultry in through the rear. It smacks of my hunt for the Academician Konovalov.

After my operation my grateful and enraptured soul was flying about the Burdenko House of Sorrows like a lawless cabbage butterfly over the first thawed patch of earth, and my body, swollen from lying around, from my wolfish appetite and the hormone shots, undulating its little potbelly and love handles, could hardly keep up with its jerky flight.[95] I would stamp on my weak legs to the smoking room, to the back stairway, along the main stairs into the lobby, and, without bothering to introduce myself, with inadequate pantomime I would tell every Tom, Dick, and Harry the happy story of my deliverance. But this immaterial gratitude needed material proof, and burned-out Lena, with my list in her hands, rushed around the stores in search of symbolic equivalents—in calories and alcohol proof—for my resurrected life. This—for Zolotukhin, this—for Glazman, this—for Olga Arsenievna, this—for the nurses of the first, second, third shift, this, finally—for Konovalov. But what did he look like, this savior-academician? He appeared when I was on a twelve-hour anesthetic leave, and when I returned, there wasn't a trace of him.

The gifts were given after the fact and out of the best feelings. The quality of treatment and care did not depend on our stinginess or generosity.[96] The Burdenko Institute is an amazing oasis of disinterestedness, conscientiousness, and goodwill. And I know what to compare it to. It seems to me that when this enchanted hospital inherited the building of an institute for educating noble maidens, it also inherited both the maidenly purity of manners and the noble skill of not turning poverty into laceration and slovenliness. The old nurse with varicose veins in her legs bends over you: "Sweetie, if you see me in the night standing like this and looking at you, don't be scared: I'm just checking how you are."

The young nurses are not vulgar and rude. And the patient mumbles in his thoughts, "Pinch me, this kind of thing doesn't happen."

The day of discharge came near, and there was no unanimity of opinion about what to give Konovalov as a gift. Lora Grigorievna from the auditing department at work assured me that an academician "doesn't look at your hands" (to see if you have a gift for him); Inna Aleksandrovna and Marat Mefodievich made inquiries and found out that only flowers would be acceptable; my impoverished imagination kept spinning its wheels on the idea of expensive brandy. Wise Misha Aizenberg gave me the best advice. I could combine the idea of flowers with the idea of an expensive bottle: in the New Arbat grocery they were having a sale of collectible Crimean wines. That's it. This would remove the tinge of boorishness from the bottle, since the collectibility, the herbarium flavor of the gift, presumed a certain ephemerality, a flowerlike femininity. So we settled on that. Plus a bouquet of roses, Lena and I decided.

A day before my discharge, at a dark morning hour, when they collect the thermometers and the blood samples, the first patients are shuffling along the corridor, and the smokers are hacking in the bathroom, I went downstairs, like a thief, from the third floor to the first. I was carrying a box with the collectible "Massandra," from 1943, the same year as the infantry that fell "senselessly and in vain"—yet another triumph of my memory![97] I cracked open the first door and went in timidly. Two doctors in starched caps who seemed to be of high rank turned toward me. A middle-aged petitioner with obvious intentions was standing before them: head all bandaged like the Invisible Man. Terry-cloth robe. Light-blue trousers. Bedroom slippers. The ritual gift box clutched to my chest. They forestalled my question:

"If you want to find Aleksandr Nikolaevich, go out into the corridor. There's a door right there."

I went into the corridor and stood before a completely inexpressive door—it could have been a door to a closet. I pushed it and found myself face to face with a man of medium height. He was just taking off his overcoat and hadn't yet managed to pull his left arm out of the sleeve.

"You've gone in the wrong door," he said sternly but with a sense of doom.

I told him my name and extended the box toward him.

"You shouldn't have done that," he said.

I asked him to put himself in my place.

"It's fifty years old," I beseeched, as if I were begging indulgence for the age of the wine. I apologized for the fuss I'd made.

"It's okay," Konovalov said.

I uttered the courtly phrase I had prepared: "Forgive me for making Mozart play 'Twinkle, twinkle, little star.'"

"How do you feel?" he answered.

I said that for some reason my wife was late bringing the flowers.

"Thank God," the academician said wearily, and shook my hand.

In the corridor I thought that the little scene was familiar: the Scarecrow thanks the Wizard for his new brain.

But fate brought me together with the academician one more time. After my discharge I was told to come to Burdenko every three or four days to have my dressings changed. I enjoyed these visits. I would make my way to the institute independently, finding everything along the way moving. I show my transport ticket to the guard—I'm moved, the train comes—I'm moved, I get on the escalator—I'm moved all over again. At the institute gate instead of a pass I would show my bandaged noggin and pass through the fence with dignity. The female coatroom attendant and I would discuss what a difficult thing life is. I would put museum booties on over my winter boots and go up the broad marble staircase, Mr. Sweetness-and-Light, endowing acquaintances and strangers with consoling words. Once they found a brain tumor in Pope John Paul II. What to do? The cardinals brought him a list of the best neurosurgeons in the world. Without giving it a moment's thought, Paul pointed his finger at the name "Konovalov." They sent the Pope's personal plane for Aleksandr Nikolaevich. The operation lasted twelve hours. And a day later the deputy of the Apostle Peter, in his bandages, gave a sermon for the whole Vatican. There you go. Fit as a fiddle.

On my native third floor I would greet the nurses and my acquaintances from the smoking room and in a proprietary way roll the gurney up to the doors of the dressing station. I would knock. Nurse Masha would bring the gurney into the room, I would disrobe and lie down on my back on this wheeled examination couch. The surgical nurse would take the bandages off my shaved head, rub something strong-smelling and cool on my bald pate, and go to get the doctor. Sergey Pavlovich would knead the top of my head, make a puncture, and draw blood and serum out from under my scalp with a syringe. Could I have imagined thirty years ago, swallowing down the fables in Soviet children's books, that it was already preordained that I would become acquainted with the bloody customs of the Iroquois and Delaware on my own hide!

Placidly enjoying myself, I would ask idiotic questions:

"Sergey Pavlovich, you know, I like to have guests, to party (it turns out, that's what it's called now!), what do you think, can I?" (As if I would abstain if he said no.)

"From a glass under a blanket," the gloomy Sergey Pavlovich would answer.

"And birch trees," I'd persist, "I cut down birch trees at the dacha. What should I do now, hire somebody?"

"Cut them down to your heart's content, just don't stick your head under the birch tree. It's all according to how you feel, I tell you, how you feel!"

Once after one of these dialogues the nurse didn't start putting on a new dressing, and Zolotukhin said brusquely:

"You don't have to come back anymore."

"At least give me some cheesecloth to cover the top of my head, my cap will stick to it," I beseeched.

"What would it stick to, you've got a centimeter's worth of stubble there! That's it!" answered the hard-hearted doctor.

The shaven recruit of a second life, I wandered around the floor, mistrustfully stroking my noggin. How can this be? But on the stairway I livened up. One flight below me a doctor of medium height was hurrying with his famous boyish lightness. His hand on the banister, he turned onto the next flight, and I recognized him and started running after my savior, but after passing a few steps I stumbled up against the senselessness of the chase. That's it. I won't go to have my dressings changed anymore, I won't hunt Konovalov anymore, and from now on the guard won't let me through the checkpoint. That's it! I can put this episode on the shelf of happiness in the sunlit dust, right after 28 Studencheskaya and 20 Hampstead Hill Gardens. Will even this hospital at 5 Fadeev Street be lost in oblivion, will the joy lose its edge, and again: the toilet seat, the trousers fallen to the floor, the face in the hands, and the sorrow—"It's all wrong, all wrong!"

In the days of yore, if one is to believe Olesha, successful people got ready in the morning with a song.[98] In fact they say my grandfather used to sing along with the morning roar of the drain in his high-spirited major key. Cheerfulness of spirit would be instilled in himself and in his family by force. In himself and in his family doubts of the rightness of the powers that be would be burned out with a red-hot iron. My grandfather, who was quite intelligent and who had an idea of how the decency of everyday life had been abolished from above, was convulsed by the spasms of his many years of self-simplification, and he tried to cure himself by working round the clock or by disastrous illicit love affairs that were completely devoid of frenchified lightness.

My grandmother, abandoned in her old age and having lost her head, made even me her confidant. At twelve years old, I was burdened by the old woman's garrulous and contradictory sorrow and by her tears, lamentations, and curses, supported by Talmudic references maybe to Clara Zetkin, or maybe to Rosa Luxemburg.

Here's how they lived. Malaya Dmitrovka Street, a room of seven square meters in a communal apartment. The widowed mother-in-law

Sofya Moiseevna with her prerevolutionary haughtiness. Fanya with her Komsomol arrogance. The elder son, Mark, who had hung a portrait of Lenin over his bed to spite his father the Stalinist. The younger son, five-year-old Yura, doesn't eat much and they have to invite—and they didn't have to spend a long time inviting them—the children of the Tatar janitor: maybe Yurochka would swallow a spoonful or two to keep them company. The women's self-sacrificing throwing of the best bits from their plates into those of the children is usually nipped in the bud by the head of the family, the plenipotentiary representative of the Commissariat of Armament, M. D. Gandlevsky, with the disgusted remark "Jewish basketball," but today he has no time for that—he is snarling behind a screen. The doctor is with him. The father of the family is being turned inside out. He took poison in order to attain civic and private integrity. But this is an exceptional case. Normally the Sunday dinners, with the rare attendance of the father, pass rather peacefully, if you don't notice the electricity crackling between the mother-in-law and the daughter-in-law, and if the elder son doesn't stick out his tongue apropos of the domestic and foreign policy of the All-Union Communist Party (of the Bolsheviks). Then an untouched baguette goes flying into his borscht, covering the smart aleck's face and chest with the contents of the bowl.

After the war, catching my father with a wireless radio that was vomiting up sedition, my grandfather crossed the room in two steps and threw the apparatus out the window.

It's no wonder that Mark took advantage of any opportunity to leave for Tverskaya Street. That's where Gorya's branch of the family had established itself.

Gorya got together with Tamara Gambarova, the daughter of a Bolshevik, the Director of the Institute of Oriental Studies, in 1937, precisely at the time when the instinct of self-preservation would dictate that one keep as far away as possible from that family: Tamara's father, Aleksandr Gambarov, had just been arrested and summarily shot. But self-preservation had always been Gorya's weak point. For example, he decided to make himself a test case of how free the Soviet elections were, and he crossed Stalin's name off the ballot. Or he would take a parachute jump.

"Was it frightening?" I asked, as an adolescent at some gathering we had on Studencheskaya Street, when Papa and Myuda were sparring for the second time about the latest article by Lakshin.

"You see, Seryozha," my vain great-uncle answered intentionally loudly, "it's very frightening. But your fear of your own cowardice is even more frightening. And you jump." And the tubby old man with freckled hands would take a stealthy sidelong look at the guests, appraising the impression he had made. But the young partiers didn't hear it and weren't listening, but were making noise: everyone wanted to be friends with Ivan Denisovich.[99]

In one night the arrest of the senior Gambarov turned an important and well-to-do Soviet family into four lost survivors of a catastrophe. Gorya, the boaster and seditious one who had married the eldest daughter, supported both his widowed mother-in-law and the younger school-age children, Nina and Zhora. He also turned a cell of Soviet society into a hornets' nest of freethinking. This is where my young father turned to get away from the forced unanimity of thought in his father's home. There was a special air, merry and risqué, at the Gambarovs' place. For instance, they're visiting Gorya in the hospital after the incident with the chemical boiler. My rebellious great-uncle hangs out of the window of the ward and howls to the whole hospital courtyard, ignoring his wife's warning gesticulations: "I told you that they would get into cahoots!"

He was talking about the Molotov-Ribbentrop Pact. Or Gorya would catch one of Hitler's speeches on the radio and translate it for the young pups, quoting passages from Stalin's speeches in parallel.

The war began. My grandfather Moisei Gandlevsky was inspecting defense plants and had learned from exhaustion on the job how to sleep at odd moments—while walking and with eyes open. Grigory Gandlevsky went to the front as a volunteer, but was soon recalled and assigned responsibility for blowing up the Dorogomilovsky chemical plant if the Germans were to take Moscow.

After the war my grandmother, Fanya Moiseevna, taught history in a technical school. Not without an ulterior motive, she invited her beautiful student, Irina Divnogorskaya, to dinner for the First of May 1950. My twenty-four-year-old father, a snob and a skeptic, swallowed his straightforward mother's bait like a good little boy. After two years of courting and palpitations, my parents got married. Mark, who had endured enough of his father's despotism, preferred not to bring his young wife under his parental roof, but himself moved into the communal apartment in the Mozhaika neighborhood where the old priest's wife and the aging priest's daughter were already living. Nine months later I was born.

By God, it's strange! I never knew Moisei the Terrible. I remember a soft, judicious old gentleman who was a fancier of elegant buffet suppers and composed rather decent verse epistles for the birthdays of his sons, daughters-in-law, and grandsons. He even died as a dandy. He took his suit to the cleaners' before a business trip, was flirting with his acquaintance, the girl behind the counter, and when she looked up from the receipt, Moisei Davydovich was gone. The intrigued clerk bent over the counter—her foppish client was lying dead on the tile floor. Two days before the misfortune, my grandfather's perpetual watch stopped for the first time, indicating to its owner in farewell the precise time of his death.

But my grandfather returned one more time. There were four of us in the kitchen: my father was repairing the iron, cursing to high heaven the Soviet government and its products; my brother was looking at the television schedule; Mama was standing at the stove, in a strange cassock and in the scarf with which she covered her head, bald from chemotherapy; and I was sitting on the windowsill smoking. Grandfather appeared at the door of the kitchen. He was dressed in his distinctive way: a boater hat, a cane, a gaily checked suit, a vest. The dark circles under his eyes harmonized poorly with the versifier's outfit and betrayed the otherworldly citizenship of the visitant. But the guest was cheerful and smiling, as in life. My father kept sweating over the iron as if nothing had happened, my brother didn't lift his face from the newspaper, my mother continued cooking. Praying to be awakened, I pressed my rear into the windowsill.

"Don't be afraid, it's me he's come for," my mother reassured me.

A few days later she died.

It was a holiday morning, May 9, 1984.[100] I was in the kitchen stirring a little porridge for my nine-month-old daughter Sashka, Lena was diapering her in our room, my brother was in his room, my father was in their room, next to my mother. He came running into the kitchen with the words, "Come, Mama has died." I approached. My mother was yawning widely and horribly. My brother the medic tore the scarf off her head and tied up the dead woman's jaw. Lena was standing in the door of my parents' room with Sasha in her arms. My father said in a hoarse voice: "Mama was a deeply religious person," and after a couple of tries managed to light a red spiral candle in a decorative candleholder.

I smelled burned milk and went out to the kitchen.

The transport van came.

"Wait," I said and kissed my mother. It turns out that a person grows cold quickly, like a warm teapot.

Two guys put the naked body into a plastic case, slammed the lid shut, locked it, and carried it out.

"Should Sasha and I drink a shot of brandy?" my father said, meaning that I shouldn't drink.

"Please do," I reassured him, "I'm going to church."

The death agony had started the day before. Mother was unconscious, called out for members of the family by name, asked for her bag.

"Your makeup bag?" I asked, not understanding.

Mother didn't answer me and continued to order: "Give me my bag!"

Ten days before her death it seemed to Mother that she wouldn't live to nighttime.

"Don't go anywhere today, please," Mama asked me.

She told my father to summon those close to her—Myuda, Yura, Katya, Gorya, Yanya, Nina. They didn't tell Mother that Gorya had died a few days before. The loved ones came, Mother was sleeping after getting morphine. Myuda, ill with the cancer from which she would die six years later, was sitting next to the bed of her sleeping friend and was already getting ready to leave when the ill woman opened her eyes and said, "Now we've said good-bye."

"It's getting postponed," Mother said with a guilty smile after the others had left.

The next morning we were watching the May Day demonstrations on television.

"I wonder," I said, "do the old men standing on the Mausoleum know that people go to the parade just to get a day off?"

"Maybe the old men themselves are standing there to get a day off," Mother said.

That year spring was very early, and the courtyard of the Novodevichy Convent was bursting with lilacs. I bought a candle and placed it in front of some icon or other. An old lady church attendant came up and deftly rearranged the candles, and I was upset that I couldn't distinguish mine from the others. But when I came out onto the church porch and lit up a cigarette, I felt the accidental rightness of the church granny. If this is *so-*

bornost', the spiritual community of Orthodoxy, then I'm not against it.

I have had occasion in life to do stupid things, disgusting things, loath-some things. But it's not them—it's one blunder, one oversight that burns my heart. I had come to see my mother in her next-to-last hos-pital, the Second Oncological Hospital on Bauman Street, in order to tell her that I had called Lena and asked her to forgive me and return to Yugozapadnaya.

"Of course, don't treat her badly," my mother said, overjoyed.

Depressed by how she looked, which left no doubts, I hastily kissed Mother and left, almost running away. And only at the subway station did it hit me: she had surely stood by the window of the second-floor ward and waved at my back. Given that she was able to walk, she had stood there and waved, as she had done hundreds of times, letting me out to play in the courtyard, seeing me off for examinations and trips . . . . Wave to me forever! Weak, egotistical, fainting from tenderness, I conjure you: do not lower your hand for an instant, no matter what circle of the universe you are now in and no matter what it costs you. Until under your gaze I turn around, convulsed with sobbing at the unrealizable meeting.

After Mother's death our family fell apart. It immediately became clear who had been the real head, and who had just rattled the attributes of power out of impotence. All their lives Mother, like a guide, had led my father, who suffered from a defect of the heart in both the literal and figurative sense. I hope it's already clear which dough I was made of. A person of principle because of her youth, Lena didn't have any feelings for my father and brother, and you can't get far on principles. The mutual irritation of fifteen years' standing between me and my father flared up. My brother's Soviet passion for swapping apartments, his elemental ego-ism, added fuel to the fire. The hostility in the apartment on Yugozapad-naya made the atmosphere stifling, made you want to tug at your collar.

My father was an intelligent and decent person. He adored his wife and was proud of her beauty. But a happy marriage was the sole gift of fate: maybe fortune was too stingy to offer a continuation, or maybe it overstrained itself, having overrated its own possibilities. A person with inclinations toward the humanities, an erudite Soviet Voltairean, he spent thirty-five years as an engineer, a constant presence on the display board of outstanding workers. Despite his secret shyness with people, he

spent thirty years as a boss at work. A domestic despot, he clashed with
the drunken disobedience of his children. Despite my arrogant attempts
at cultural enlightenment, he mispronounced "to telephone" and "Pasternak" and, forgetting his son's unpardonable didacticism, was able to
shout in the heat of an argument with Myuda, "Even Lunacharsky, who
was a smart guy!"[101]

My best memories of my father, of course, are from childhood. If he
was bringing us good news, his gait would immediately give him away:
he would walk swiftly, with a rocking motion, swinging his arms. This
meant that I had to look very, very hard, and I would find a new bicycle,
covered with a blanket for greater mysteriousness, or that Father had finally found a motorboat that would give all five of us, including the collie, a lift from Uglich upstream to the village of Baskachi. The last fifteen
years of his life he walked in a different way, with his arms lowered like
Pechorin; that was thanks to me.[102]

After Mother's death my father let me know in rather crude terms who
had destroyed her, and his life into the bargain. During our silent, furious
teamwork on the dacha plot we had just received, my father said that he
had a general idea of the underlying mercenary cause of my zeal. I threw
him the keys to the dacha, and the four of us (Grisha had already come
into the world) moved over to live at my mother-in-law's. Besides Tatiana Arkadievna, Lena's brother and his wife and their nine-month-old son
were already living there. What was left for us was a pass-through room.
The three children cried and got sick in chorus, infecting each other. The
television squawked round the clock. Lena's brother would cut through
our room in his long johns during our rare and timorous copulations.
And every time I made a sweeping movement, my mother-in-law's innumerable tsatskes would fall and smash to pieces.

My father died in 1990 from his fourth heart attack. Now for a number
of years my brother and stepmother and I have been receiving belated
payments of my father's foreign currency from the Central Bank. Dollars from Iraq. So a non-Party-member Jew who sympathized with Israel,
who had worked himself to exhaustion for the stinking Soviet government and its wannabe-criminal group of punk pals—Castro, Gaddafi,
Hussein—with similarly Jewish diligence had perfected the rockets that
in their due time would fly to attack Tel Aviv.

Here he is standing in the kitchen at night in his black knee-length boxer shorts. A vial and a cup are trembling in his hands. "Sixteen, seventeen, eighteen," gurgles the heart medicine Valocordin. My father is rather short, bald, his face swollen from his heart ailment. His eyes seem small because of his thick glasses. Fat stomach, an old man's flabby breasts, back covered with gray hair. I come into the kitchen. My father looks back over his shoulder as if cowed, ready for repulsion and attack.

At my mother's wake I went up to the window where Myuda was standing and complained about my father.

"Yes," said Myuda, "the day Arisha died we came, and he was setting out plates and glasses and singing Soviet songs in a strained and challenging way. 'Stop, Mark,' I begged, but he kept singing."

"It's a sort of cursed family," I said in a drunkenly dramatic way.

"All families are cursed," Myuda corrected me.

That family no longer exists, that circle of friends is also gone. I have the habit once a year, on my birthday, December 21, of getting on the No. 39 tram in the morning and going to the crematorium.

When I was born, my father's coworkers congratulated him on his little Iosif, but my father disappointed them. I can imagine how young, beautiful, and happy my mother was, recovering from childbirth, going up to the window of the Grauerman maternity hospital and looking at the already doomed snow-covered roofs of the Arbat.[103] But today, Tuesday, December 21, 1993, I have trouble getting into a filial mood, because my entire soul has been given up to my diagnosis. My empty eyes skim over the Danilov Monastery, the market, the churches on Khavskaya Street.

Peoples' Friendship University. That's my stop. I go through the crematorium gates, walk along the snow-covered path. "The road in a straightforward way set out for the gray crematorium."[104] That's what you have to know how to do: to hammer into memorial lines a banal pun plus internal rhyme. I leave the crematorium building on my right and, skirting a pile of cemetery trash, turn onto the path I want. My head is of course hurting. In my ears there is a dry march without music, only the skeleton of a rhythm. A strange couple is walking toward me. A man of my age, dressed in expensive clothes, is walking arm in arm with an old woman in a fox-fur coat and a crimson Gypsy shawl. Her very bright makeup seems not to fit the outlines of the natural features of a once beautiful face.

"The morning is gloomy and cold," the old woman wheezes from be-low up to her companion, and the chance amphibrach that I catch with my peripheral hearing seems to repeat like an echo the quotation I just remembered.

The farthest niche on the third tier from the ground. Hello. Two por-celain ovals and a little metal shelf for flowers, ordered by my father at work. It's not a solid wall, but a concrete parallelepiped, almost a cube. Its official appearance would be relieved by lilacs, but today everything is bare—it's December. I place my flowers flat on the snow-covered shelf, partly breaking the stems in advance.

(At exactly 10:00 a.m. on a chirping Moscow morning, Gorya's Moskvich gave a dashing beep under the two windows on the first floor of No. 28 Stu-dencheskaya Street. The group came out of the entryway with baskets and bags full of edible provisions: Mother in full possession of her mature charms, Father with a young man's receding hairline and with perpetual irony on his firm lips. My brother was carrying the badminton rackets, and I, a pimply ninth-grader, was carrying a volume of Pasternak with Sinyavsky's introduction.[105] The book had been lent to me for the three days of holiday by my literature teacher Vera Romanovna, who had or-dered me to protect it like the apple of my eye. We had a pass for a recrea-tion camp near Moscow. The whole way there my father, deadpan, made sarcastic comments about a fat lady walking by with a string bag in her left hand and a ficus plant in a tub in her right hand, mockingly mangled the appeals on red banners along the way, and gave Gorya deadly advice on driving, which caused hiccups of laughter in my brother and me.

The resort turned out to be a dozen sweet, freshly painted little plank houses on the bank of a winding stream. I was assigned a tiny single room with a window onto the twilight, the greenery, the trilling of the nightin-gales. Father unlocked the door for me, kissed me goodnight, and with a nod at the dark-blue Pasternak volume, he advised that I not sprain my head on some particularly tricky metaphor. I read for a long time, under-stood almost nothing, but I liked the clear poems of his old age.

> "And the rushing lines of the fiery trunks
> Are so frenzied against the dark blue,
> And we take so long to remove our arms
> From under our bent-back heads . . ."

I shivered from the dampness of the government-issue linen, the pre-dawn cold, and the terrible happiness of life that was coming right up against me. I smiled and fell asleep. And now I've just barely opened my eyes.

> "It's growing dark, and bit by bit
> The moon buries all the traces
> Under the white magic of the foam
> And the black magic of the water."[106]

Is that all? Was that curious dream the long-awaited "life"? A buffoon-ish procession of little people on the wallpaper? A terrifying theater of shadows? A sack race? And I can no longer protest, fix it, exchange my pass? And I can't resurrect a single dead person? And I can't even take my own words back?)

Lighting up a cigarette, I walk around the columbarium, as is my habit. There are names and faces I've known for ten years. The Mitlins. The Derzhavins. And here is Ilya Tsypkin (1953–1975). In about sixth grade he brazenly swiped my series of canceled Río Muni stamps during the long midday break.[107] I was collecting flora and fauna then. Tsypa, it appears we will soon have the opportunity to air our ancient property dispute. There were four of them, four unforgettable colonial stamps: a rhinoceros, a giraffe, a hippopotamus, an elephant. 'Satiable curtiosity.

This past summer the crowd in Tuchkovo stormed the Gagarin–Moscow train. By a miracle I pushed my way through the wheeled luggage, the baskets, and the backpacks into the center of the car, threw my bag onto the luggage rack, and looked around. Resisting the crush with my back, I was hanging right over Tsypa's mother. It's strange—in the course of thirty years she hadn't changed at all: portly, strong, beautiful—a real officer's wife. Through the prisoners' tapping going on between my migraine and the train I could make out that the seated passengers were talking, as is usual in dacha trains, about pickled vegetables. "How weird," I thought in amazement, "here is the mother of a suicide riding along, discussing with her fellow travelers the techniques for conserving tomatoes. So what did you want, for them to share their experience of how to kill oneself most cleverly?" Tsypa's telephone number was G9–16–49. And to think I was almost deprived of such a wicked memory!

I'm overcome by a kind of gloomy housekeeping urge. I see that there's enough room in our niche for a third urn. It would be good to drop this idea into Lena's consciousness under the pretext of black humor. Otherwise they'll send me off to some godforsaken Biriulevo-Tovarnaya, and no one will come to see me, and rightly so.

I finish my cigarette, wrap the butt in a used tram ticket, and shove all these household effects into my pocket. I cast a final glance at the two porcelain ovals and walk to the tram stop. On the way home I again stare unseeing through the window and organize my wake. Lenka will undoubtedly go limp and forget to invite anybody. Thank God, in my life I've made friends by the dozen. I wonder whether that amphibrach will ever leave me in peace today? There's a way to handle it: Natasha Molchanskaya will have to ask permission from Slovesnyi to have the wake in their conference hall, and then the inner circle can go to our place to finish drinking.

Getting out at Vishnyakovsky Lane, I turn onto Ostrovsky Street and buy a freshly baked "Prague" cake in a delicatessen. It's too early to go to work, but there's also no sense in going home, so I go to work. I greet the woman guard, take our key with its green plastic number plate, go up to the second floor, unlock the room, put the cake I bought onto the tea table, sit at my desk still in my overcoat, and propping my face on my fists, bellow from the pain in my head, my terror of death, and the hijinks I'd gotten up to on Friday.

On Friday the 17th, coming out of the Burdenko Institute, I had thought, how appropriate that today Syoma Faibisovich has an opening, and I will see the people dear to me to say farewell, and I'll get nice and drunk, since that's how it is. And I won't say anything to Lena until Monday, why aggravate her nerves for nothing? I was pleased with myself. At home I took a shower, first hot, then cold. But the whole time I was thinking about my disfigured brains: now they're getting warm, now they're cooling down. Grisha Dashevsky called to ask about my health.

"Shall I spoil your mood?" I asked.

"Just tell me everything."

Then I called my friend and boss Natasha Molchanskaya. With her characteristic directness she declared: "Most likely you won't die, but you might be left an imbecile."

Gee, thanks. I started getting dressed, I know what I'm doing in that

area. Red with gray, black with any color. Lena came home from taking
the children to her mother's. I said that the results would be at the clinic
on Monday, and I asked her not to be lazy—to get all dolled up, after all,
it's an opening.

"Just don't be a pain in the ass," she said, "or I'll go wearing galoshes
on my bare feet."

Our armoires won't close because of all the shmattes we bought in
Montreal at a church sale or got for a song at a warehouse in Jerusalem,
but my wife wears any old thing. The style of a tomboy, pants and a man's
shirt. Before introducing us at his birthday party, Soprovsky warned me,
"My friend from the expedition will be there, go easy on her: if there's some
little thing she doesn't like, she'll hit you in the kisser. In Sevastopol—I saw
it myself—they wouldn't let her into the restroom, they said, 'Little boy,
this is the ladies' room.'"

And a little half-pint with big eyes came in, and yet again I thought that
Soprovsky doesn't understand anything about women. That night I fell
asleep in the toilet out of drunken infatuation. That was the beginning
of our acquaintance. My poor little boy! All she wants to do is model
antediluvian idols out of clay or draw something primordial and incomprehensible on bleached cutting boards.

"There are different types of jazz," I say in distress, looking at Lena's
latest piece, "there's some jazz you don't even want to listen to."

I like her realistic style, pen-and-ink drawings: dacha fences, telegraph
poles, old gates in the Zamoskvorechie neighborhood. But I'm afraid
that, sullen out of shyness and pride, she's not the type to sell anything
in Izmailovsky Park or at the Central House of Artists on Krymsky Val.

"How's your head?" Lena asked, her attention diverted from putting
on her makeup.

"E-e-eh, like usual."

My head, my head. Better not think about it.

"Put your fur coat on."

"But it's slushy out."

"Come on, please."

As always, we were a little bit late, but not catastrophically. We almost swore at each other at the Turgenev subway station about which
exit to take. Lena turned out to be right. We moved along the left side
of Myasnitskaya Street in the direction of the Garden Ring. On the

right I could hardly see anything, on the left I was seeing double.

It got dark. A wet snow was falling. It's just hilarious: a cross-eyed half-blind man is dragging himself to an opening. Again we got lost, but suddenly right across the street we saw a huge shining light-blue show window and against its background Misha Zaitsev, Timur, and Lyova smoking and, judging by their howls and gesticulations, already tipsy. That meant we were late for the champagne. Lifting the hems of our coats, I on my heels and Lena on her tiptoes, we made our way across Myasnitskaya Street, dammed up with wet squelching snow, and went into the gallery. Here Lena and I lost each other from sight and wandered each on our own, smiling, saying hello, and dropping friendly phrases.

I always feel out of place at openings and presentations, but now I was additionally constrained by the extra effort of not giving away my impaired state.

Once in Sukhumi I saw a little pack of stray dogs that was crossing the street. One of them was run over by a speeding driver who didn't even bother to hit the brakes, and its sacrum and back legs were crushed. I watched for a minute as the wretched dog, with an artificially cheerful yapping, using just its front extremities and dragging a bloody slush behind it, hurried after its comrades, as if trying to deceive them with its pace and barking, as if to say, everything's fine, I'm still with you, it's just a little hitch.

I seemed to myself to be just such a wretched Sukhumi mutt, when I was yapping out the phrases *du jour* and wandering among Syoma's canvases, squinting my right eye as if for better visibility, when in essence it was there just for show. I like some of Faibisovich's pictures, and besides that, I'm grateful to him for not being a charlatan and not trying to intimidate the spectator.

Once at an opening I was wandering dejectedly past a nonsensical and insensible heap of objects: Composition No. 1, Composition No. 2, etc., and I took up a decorous position in front of the nth composition. A standard-issue magazine table with little plastic cups. One was knocked over. A little puddle of wine or juice had flowed out of it and accumulated on the polished tabletop. Lena and Varya came up to me and they were less pretentious; giggling, they disabused me of my error—this was an extra-aesthetic little table and extra-aesthetic cups, merely the results of the artists' libations.

Squinting my eyes and blinking at the huge pictures, I caught myself thinking that I was looking at the monotonous canvases with great pleasure, and with an intimate joy I suspected the painter of color blindness, the Gandlevsky family defect.

"So tell me, Seryozha, what do you see in this picture?" a woman I was well acquainted with asked me.

Trying to construct the phrase in such a way as not to stumble over her name, which I had completely forgotten, I said, "My head is spinning from those slanting waves."

It was true. And it was hurting. And there was so much noise in it that I couldn't distinguish the inner rumble from the rumble of the crowded hall and the chirring of the video cameras.

Tipsy, with his wife and—Nina-Tanya-Vera-Olya—you're getting warmer! with Olya Trofimova-Tikhonova-Timofeeva, that's it! with Timofeeva, repeat it: Olya Timofeeva, remember that—Genis appeared. Sasha?—that's right, his name is Sasha. Go up and say hello, but don't talk fast, or you'll get tangled up in your words.

"I was at *Foreign Literature* today," Genis answered my greeting. "Your colleagues said that you were having some kind of tests. Everything's okay, isn't it?" And he got distracted by someone attacking him with embraces from the rear.

I was particularly wary of having a lengthy conversation with Genis and was glad I had gotten off easy. Two years ago he and Petya Vail, through the mediation of the all-powerful Lena Yakovich, did an interview with me and Timur for the *Literary Gazette.* It was a little this and that for a freebie of Absolut. Later Krava told me that the two critics had showered me with praise for my conversational reactions. I like for people to like me and I didn't want Genis to see that over the intervening two years I had changed from a rhetorical master into an impaired degenerate. But the danger passed. I started strenuously turning my head and assiduously straining my eyes. Having lost the gift of speech, half-blind, with an aquarium full to the brim with migraine in my trembling hands, I searched for my wife and the vodka that was earmarked for me. Why were there only tipsy people around me, and I, who needed it the most, was sober as a judge? Misha Zaitsev, standing by the window, was stealthily twisting counterclockwise a yellow bottletop that was peeping out of a package he was holding, and excusing myself, I started moving through the buzzing crowd toward the inviting gleam of yellow metal.

I swigged down my couple of shots, and I felt as if a weight had been lifted from me. Here were gathered: the Kalmyk beauty Valya, Koval's wife; the Jewish beauty Alyona, Aizenberg's wife; and the Russian beauty Anya, Zaitsev's wife. To make a harmonious poster all you needed was a beautiful black woman. I settled down in this flowerbed; enough of rushing about the hall like I don't know what.

The twittering of women has a pacifying effect, as if you are lying in a meadow in Tuchkovo and a little birdie is flickering above you in the hot sky and prattling, prattling. And sensitive Charlie is sitting next to you, puffing out his African nostrils, and the embryo of a yelp is moving in his throat.

They were discussing Lena Borisova's fur coat, which Timur had bought for her with the money he got for his Pushkin Prize. Kibirov's wife was charmingly bragging about her new acquisition, and then she shouted at me, "Gandlevsky, give me the coat!"

I bent to the floor, and my head pulsed heavily, as if I were not lifting a light fur but hoisting a heavy weight after rubbing talcum on my palms.

They brought champagne around for a second time. I took two glasses— for myself and for Lena—and put them behind me on the windowsill, as a reserve. My Lena, Timur, and lively Rubinshtein came up. We went out onto the damp street to smoke, we sipped our drinks using our sleeves as canapés, we joked around. Varya Faibisovich whispered in passing, "This will soon be over, and we'll all go to our place."

The opening was folding up, and those who had been invited, in groups of three or four, started moving toward the Garden Ring, in the direction of the Faibisoviches' place.

I ended up walking with Zaitsev and Kibirov. Along the way we discussed a feckless publisher who had paid us in full but hadn't published any books. Timur did most of the talking.

"It's okay for Lyova to claim that he doesn't give a damn whether people read him or not. I want people to read me, I want to publish, and I don't hide it and don't see anything shameful about it."

And Zaitsev echoed him, saying that the contracts were binding only for a set time limit, and that somewhere he had the diskette with the finished layouts of our books, so the work was five-sixths done, if not six-sixths, so all we had to do was find an enterprising publisher.

So what do you think, I asked myself, are these worries repulsive to you with your new interests? No, I answered myself honestly, they aren't. And would you want your comrades to taste such a misfortune, so you wouldn't be so lonely? No, I answered myself honestly, I wouldn't. But don't you even have contempt for this vainglorious blather from the heights of your horror? No, and that's enough about that. And once again I liked myself.

As we talked we managed to jump over the puddles and reach the sought-for building and entryway, we waited for the women and Koval, who, like Prince Vyazemsky, had managed to captivate their souls.[108] We went in and sat down at the table.

I pity those who have never had the occasion to have a drink and a snack at Syoma and Varya's, to learn the meaning of hospitality of a high standard, which is based on cordiality and prosperity. The vaults of their merrymaking are confidently supported on a colonnade of Swedish and Finnish vodkas ("Bad physics, but what poetry!")[109] The eatables are exceptional! On broad platters ham, cold boiled pork, pastrami were like a broad wave frozen in midair; pâtés and garlic-flavored farmer's cheese stood molded into hillocks in crystal bowls. Georgian stewed beans and fresh greens up the wazoo, it goes without saying. Wild garlic. Salads, salads, salads. Crab salad. Prune, raisin, and dried-apricot salad. Olivier salad (potatoes, vegetables, eggs, ham, mayonnaise). *Satsivi* (Georgian chicken in walnut sauce). This kind of pickles, that kind of pickles. Tomatoes. Meat in aspic, by God, with red horseradish and white horseradish. Anya's potato, onion, and mushroom *pirozhki*. Pickled saffron milk-cap and agaric mushrooms. Korean cabbage and cabbage fermented with caraway. For the entrée Varya, shouting for people to clear a space on the table, brings in a platter of unbelievable dimensions holding a mountain of ruddy chicken legs. Fruit drinks in jugs, large bottles of Pepsi and cola—I give up! A more lively feast I have seen only at the fortieth-birthday party of Alik Batchan, where they all but served swans baked whole.

The diligent host hasn't gotten sozzled, like some of us, from excitement and intemperance, but rises to his full height and breadth with dignity at the corner of the long table. Until it's Syoma's turn to burst out in song:

> "We'll go all through the fields
> On a horse made of steel,
> We will reap and we'll sow and we'll plow them."

After three shots I start staring at Varya as if hypnotized, and only fear of Lena forces me to turn my bloodshot peepers in another direction.

We had perched ourselves on the eastern extremity of the long table. To my left, Vitya Koval was meditating, and judging by the pace he was setting, he was getting ready to offer the *tableau vivant* "The sperm whale in labor." In any case, his performance of a song in Chinese was becoming more and more urgent and practicable. On my right, my wife wasn't refusing herself anything, and as a lover of sweets she was lost in conjecture: What would they offer with tea, if they were serving such a luxurious meal with the vodka? My vis-à-vis turned out to be Evgeny Barabanov, a huge philosopher with a ponytail. It suddenly became quiet at our end of the table. I've been sentenced to a life term of lacking constraint when at the convivial table, so I blurted out about fifteen years late that I had read him in the *samizdat* collection *From under the Rubble*.

"What an erudite young man," the philosopher said, putting me in my place.

I snapped that in the first place, I was not erudite, and in the second place, I was not young, and turned to Koval. But he was intently making noises in his throat, getting ready to do the cry of the eagle owl at the full moon; Vitya was no interlocutor for me. Taking advantage of Lena's demonstrative meekness, I silently set about doing a tasting of Absolut, one tall wine glass after another, and soon passed into automated operation mode.

The merriment lost its harmoniousness; it started moving from a dead stop like a rockslide in the mountains, and began sliding, carrying everything along with it.

Lena's forgiving tales on Sunday and my own ragged memories have reconstructed for me my feats on the night of December 17 to 18. My hour struck at a quarter to one Moscow time, when Lena hinted that I had absolutely been saluting the Absolut for long enough: the subway was about to close. I turned my furious bulging eyes to her and muttered through my teeth: "How dare you try to drag me away today? Me! With a brain tumor!"

"You're talking nonsense!" Lena said.

"A meningioma," I retorted.

Lena grasped that this term was a new one for me, no matter how extensive my lexicon was, and she drooped and got submissive. The ice had been broken, the rusty locks had been knocked off, the sluices had been opened—the underground came up to the surface.

With drunken vengefulness and insidiousness I started by degrees turning the ship of the festivities in the direction I wanted, furtively substituting the axe of my misfortune for the compass, like the villain Kokoro in Jules Verne's *Dick Sand, A Captain at Fifteen*. Misha Aizenberg fell as the first and easiest victim. Trustingly and voluptuously—as if to him alone—I disclosed to Misha what had happened and swore him to secrecy. My dear friend covered his face with his sleeve in despair and to the end of the blowout he didn't utter a word but just drank, drank, and drank, so that toward morning he fell asleep on his knees, with his intelligent, balding, and graying head on a kitchen stool. With Timur I couldn't achieve mutual comprehension. I said something to him in passing about the tumor, but he just started laughing, and got even more cheerful than before, and started howling:

> "The yo-o-o-oung cavalryman
> Has a bullet through his he-e-e-ead."

Having bombed the territory the first time, I wasn't satisfied, so I refueled and went for a second run. I sat next to Faibisovich and expressed regret that we had never become friends.

"But it's never too late for that," he said, slapping me on the knee.

In answer I lowered my head listlessly.

Glory to you, vodka, deafening beverage! He who is made drunk by you speaks only of his own affairs, and your effect is more reliable than earplugs! Otherwise I would have notified each and every one of them, like a buffoon!

At dawn Lena shoved me, a creature that did not manifest "the divine bashfulness of suffering," onto the back seat of Batchan's Volvo, and Alik stepped on the gas and took us to Old Tolmachovsky Lane, where neighbor lady–death beats the radiator with the handle of a knife and the trained German alarm clock I bought in Jerusalem for forty shekels comes to life precisely at 7:30 a.m.: fate knocks arrogantly at the door.[110]

I used to consider my morning pangs of conscience a reassuring sign. But I read in Martin Buber that a person who relishes his own filth will never make his way out of it, and—I ceased to respect this melancholy pastime.

Grisha Chkhartishvili comes into the department of criticism and journalism, where I'm miserably smoking without taking off my coat. He greets me and curtly gets down to business.

"Natasha told me," he says. "So what steps have you taken?"

I answer that yesterday we went to the polyclinic and that they had promised to report to us in a few days.

In fact, the day before, December 20, we had gotten up as usual when the alarm went off at 7:30. Lena took the children to school and took Charlie out, and I washed the dishes from the day before and made coffee. We had a quick breakfast, we each had a cigarette, and we set off for Burdenko.

I can't say there weren't a lot of people there. Judging from the fact that some of the patients had such poor eyesight that they couldn't find the right door on the first try, I had come to the right place. At first they called me in to see the oculist. The doctor turned in front of me a half-hoop on a post and hinge that looked like the steering wheel of an airplane. This took no more than three minutes. I couldn't manage the well-known table of letters, not even the first row.

They called me into a second office, and Lena came in too. A wee little gray-haired lady doctor glanced at the medical image, turned over a piece of paper or two, asked a couple of questions.

"Okay, Sergey Markovich," the little doctor summed up, "there's no reason to get fancy, we have to operate. It's no fun, but we have to."

We set off for home. In the middle of the courtyard, around which half-blind people were wandering with guides and without, gaped an open sewer manhole. But that was and remained probably the only thing I could vent my malevolence on.

"That's no good," Grisha Chkhartishvili says decisively. "First of all, you'll wait for a place until the Second Coming, and then you'll lie there just as long, and no one will pay any attention to you. Did you drop from the moon or something? Nobody in this country will lift a finger just like that. You have to make waves. Last year when Kuzminsky landed in the Sklifosovsky Emergency Institute, we made the telephone on the director's desk ring night and day. You have to give them the idea that you are a genius of the first water, that the sun of Russian poetry is setting, and so on. Do you know any 'generals'?"

I answer that I don't know anyone personally. They say that Bitov has read my poems and spoke pretty well of them. Iskander supposedly did the same. But those are just rumors, and I can't call and ask for something on that basis.

"You won't be the one calling," Grisha said, "we'll do the calling, but we have to know who to call."

Meanwhile Natasha Molchanskaya and Olya Basinskaya came in and joined into the conversation to the best of their ability. I dialed Vitkovsky and asked, "Zhenya, tell me, please, is Yevtushenko in the city?"

"Yes, yes, he's in the city," he answered me in his unique voice. "In New York."

Hopeless.

"The biggest celebrity I know," I confessed, "is Kibirov. Bitov awarded him a prize. Maybe we could approach from that side?"

"Natasha, call Kibirov," Chkhartishvili ordered Molchanskaya.

I go out into the hallway. I loiter around, going like a pendulum from one end of the carpeted path to the other and greeting the same colleagues several times. When I reach our door, I hear Natasha's cheerful voice shouting over the noise of Kibirov's staticky phone, "A pretty big goober (*gulya*) is sticking out of his brain."

Gulya Korolyova. The office gets animated: our commercial director, Anya Gedemin (her office nickname is Thumbelina), calls everyone in the directory of the Union of Writers and has already reached the letter F; Izabella Fabianovna is working through the wife of Yury Chernichenko, and now for the first time the name "Konovalov" resounds; Aleksey Nikolaevich Slovesnyi is grieving over the fact that he doesn't have Chingiz Torekulovich's connections; Olya Basinskaya is heating up some tea. And I, steeling myself not to start leaking fluids due to a wave of gratitude and mortal weariness, ask my boss Natasha to cut the "Prague" cake—after all, it is my birthday. In these efforts our irregular workday passes. Before leaving I dropped in to see Aleksey Nikolaevich to say good-bye, and it would have been better if I hadn't: my editorial colleague was convulsed with compassion for the well-known "almost a minute and a half."[111] The courtly condemned man dropped in to say his last farewell to the chief editor, the director of the department of literature, the executive secretary, the acting director of the department of criticism and journalism, and the deputy chief editor.

And now began my great period of lying at home with a book held upside down and Charlie at my feet. This was accompanied by constant telephone calls. Lena would answer, because I was losing the habit of speech not by the day but by the hour. The calls could be divided into two categories: (a) essentially sympathy calls; (b) compassion that took an active form. The female calls of the first sort sometimes ended with suppressed sobs that reached my couch. Then Lena would cold-bloodedly console the ahead-of-schedule hired wailer. The calls of the second sort were drier, and Konovalov was constantly mentioned.

Timur said, based on what the all-powerful Lena Yakovich said, that the Minister of Culture, E. Sidorov, wouldn't write anything himself, but would sign any piece of paper; Lyubov Dmitrievna, my father-in-law's wife, turned out to have a female friend who was a doctor at Burdenko; the critic Pavel Basinsky, Olya's husband, was aiming precisely at the same Sidorov department; Alyona Solntseva found out that a friend of her mother's was a classmate of the academician.

Two days later the chief doctor, L. Iu. Glazman, called. He had apparently been bruised by the "waves," judging by his voice, and he said in bewilderment that I could enter the hospital tomorrow if I wanted to, but what was the use, given that there was a whole train of holidays ahead, and I would be operated on by Konovalov, Konovalov, Konovalov. There was clear evidence of an excess of goodwill, and Lena started asking our friends and some people we didn't know at all to put on the brakes, to ease up on the engine.

Whether I was brushing my teeth, walking the dog, forcing myself to chatter with the children—I did it all correcting for the possibility of death. Occasionally a gloomy playfulness would possess me. Then I would clatter around the dinner table astride a broom, calling myself the "headless horseman." Or I would ask Lena, in case I came back from the hospital an imbecile, to smother me with a pillow, following the example of the giant Indian in the film *One Flew over the Cuckoo's Nest*.[112] That's how we passed the time until New Year's.

New Year's, as everyone knows, is a domestic holiday. For about twenty years I made it a rule to sit up with my parents until 1:00 a.m., and only then go out somewhere else. All the more so now. I thought the four of us would sit for a while, eat some salads and chicken, drink a swallow of champagne each, stare at television for about a half hour, and then go beddy-bye. But the Borisovs took us in hand.

Rubin, a friend of the Borisovs, got it into his head to grill *shashlyk* on a bonfire in the snow. He had done this at one point, and it had stuck in his memory and he wanted to do it again. The Borisovs were tempted into it. They needed a dacha. I said it's easy for you to say "dacha." With the children, with cots, with the dog, eight people in the one heated room— that would be a flophouse, sheer torture, not a holiday. But Borisov was implacable: New Year's is New Year's, he says, if you get the slightest bit indisposed I'll take you back to Moscow, even in the middle of the night. I struggled a bit but gave in: they are such terribly nice people.

We drove out at about 3:00 p.m. in two cars. These hotshots had equipped the expedition with an Opel and a cherry-red Toyota sports car. The children and the dog and I went in the Borisovs' Opel, the women— Lena, Olya, Natasha—in Rubin's flat sports car. While in the city we drove decorously, but on the Minsk highway we drag-raced. The children squealed and rooted for Borisov.

No, it turned out pretty well, I was wrong to balk at it. Borisov and Rubin don't drink, they had gotten themselves sewn up. I drank half a cup of champagne and, exercising my rights as a sick man, I went to bed, moving my son to the wall. The other men also didn't sit up long. Only the women kept drinking little by little in the light of the table lamp, talking in low voices about their female topics, and I couldn't help but eavesdrop with half an ear: Grisha would stretch out, or some goblin would crawl into my head, but toward morning, come hell or high water, I quieted down.

We had adventures on our return trip. We went by a roundabout way, afraid we wouldn't be able to make it up the icy hill. But after we went about five or six kilometers the cars got stuck in the snow on a flat forest road. They all piled out to push the forward car, the Toyota. Sasha Borisov got out of the car cursing, and so that I wouldn't be bored he turned on the tape player, the *St. John Passion*. I watched through the front windshield and through the transparent dome of the otherworldly music as they pushed, argued, pushed again, now together, now discordantly, and I thought something simple, like: they are all there, and they have their own worries, let's say a road incident, and I'm already here, completely alone. Or the other way around: they are all still here, and I'm already almost there. The excessive literariness of the *mise-en-scène* as a whole, with Bach thrown in, didn't bother me at the time, but excited and moved me. Finally the Toyota let out a roar and, wobbling, pulled itself out onto a flat track. It was now the turn of the Opel, where I was sitting. The women had the idea of throwing some pine branches onto the road under the wheels. I shuddered.

With this my essay on the topic "How I Spent the New Year's Holidays" is ended.

At home I took up my usual occupations: I slept, read something light, squinted at the television, walked the dog, but the air around my head ticked and clicked as if a somewhat idiotic joker, a gay blade and a rascal, were bashing out a tune on painted wooden spoons. Imperceptibly I found myself on the homestretch—they were putting me in the hospital on January 4.

To play the staring game with death, as others have already noted, doesn't work, you'll blink after a second. Many of us have had occasion to settle into a comfy seat in an empty subway car toward nightfall, anticipating with pleasure fifteen to twenty minutes of scrutinizing one's fellow travelers, especially young women, with impunity. But today an unpleasant surprise awaits the gawker: he's not going to get to do the scrutinizing, but he's going to be scrutinized, and point-blank, to boot. An insane man with a tense back and jumpy wrists has perched on the seat directly opposite and is all mad interestedness. We note, averting our eyes: pupils dilated with sick enthusiasm, saliva on the garrulous lips of the dervish, the bare neck and hairy Adam's apple, the second-hand overcoat buttoned crookedly on the left side, the worn and untied shoes gaping open on his sockless feet. We can catch with our peripheral hearing the scratched record of his mutterings. It's a simple motif—from sobbing laments to piercing threats; we can't make out the words. We avoid looking with all our might. We're not looking at you, see, we're not looking. We stare with pronounced diligence at your neighbor to the right. And now we've shifted our gaze with a leap over to your neighbor on the left, we're interested in his muskrat-fur hat. Just please, be a good boy, turn your bulging eyes away at least for a moment, at least blink. But he doesn't turn his eyes away, he doesn't blink. In such cases a fellow traveler, a neighbor and interlocutor, is irreplaceable. An unconstrained travel conversation, after all, helps you express sincere indifference to the half-mad person opposite. But it was precisely with my fellow traveler that I had no luck.

"Shpakov, Erast Eduardovich," was written by hand on a slip of paper taped over the head of his bed. A similar little square had been stuck over the head of my bed as well. I had been given a corner bed in a ten-bed ward, and the garrulous Erast Eduardovich got me into his clutches and trapped me from the first moments of our acquaintance.

The dim black-and-white television had the imprudence to mention Yegor Gaidar, and my politicized neighbor perked up and let me know, as an obviously like-minded person, that Gaidar would soon be so fat he wouldn't be able to fit in a chair. He wasn't at all bothered by the fact that in the department of obesity of waist and thighs he was still a few points up on the hated reformer. This jumped right out at me, but I kept silent.

My neighbor had two symmetrical tumors in the temporal lobes. He was admitted at the same time I was, and we were nearing the time of our operations neck and neck. Our operations were held up for a week because of a lack of blood. There was a blood-donor center right there on the first floor, but my neighbor stood on principle and said that for that kind of money (his employer was paying for his treatment) he had the right to a half liter of standard-issue blood. They refused Lena at the blood-donor center because of her period. Aizenberg, Molchanskaya, Tanya Poletaeva volunteered to donate, but I thanked them and said that a day or two wouldn't make any difference. That's how it turned out: they took the blood from me before the operation, and they used that blood on me.

I spent the week before the operation, for the most part, playing hide-and-seek with my sociable neighbor. Or rather, it felt like playing cat-and-mouse. And he was always the leader, and with unfailing pleasure. He would effortlessly catch me coming out of the stall in the latrine, find me smoking in the stairwell, or ambush me making a phone call from the staff lounge. At night I was at his full disposal simply by virtue of the way the beds were arranged. He was drawn to me as an equal to an equal. He disdained hobnobbing with the other riffraff in our ward. Erast Shpakov took my stubborn silence as the like-mindedness of one white person (me) with another white person (him). He had enjoyed being a white person in India, where he was a gofer in a trade delegation for several years. He showed me again and again with a juicy snap of his fat fingers how he would send one of the natives to get him a smoke. Meeting me in

the evenings coming from the shower, he would nod sagely and say that
it was high time for him too to have a little wash. As far as I can remember
he never got around to it.

It was hard to sleep in the stuffy ward. And on top of it there was the
nightly monologue to my right:

"Blood will be spilled. Of course, I'm not in favor of it, but it will be
spilled. Judge for yourself, Sergey. Two market stalls. They're both selling lemons. The Russian guy is selling them for 3,000, and the Azeri guy
right next to him is selling them for 3,500. They've really gotten uppity!
Or television. I don't have anything against the people of your nationality, and I've had contact with them at work. But do you think it's right for
them to be 60% of the people on Russian television, if not more?"

"How did you find out that I'm Jewish? My last name is Polish, my first
name is a common one, maybe only my patronymic (Markovich) has a
Jewish ring to it. My mother was Russian."

"I can tell hybrids right away," he snickered in the darkness with the
self-satisfaction of a disciple of Michurin.

With trembling hands I rummaged for my cigarettes and lighter on
the night table, threw on a robe, and went out to the toilet. But my tena-
cious neighbor wouldn't let me remain above the fray even there. He had
probably decided to console me, and, scratching his red-haired armpits,
he said, for the sake of objectivity, that wherever there is one Khachig
(Armenian), two Abrahams (Jews) won't be able to do anything.

Fuck! I'm going to die, maybe he's going to die, everybody here is
beating about the same bush! Do I really have to waste the week before
my most serious trial on mediocre—I don't know what to call them—
Khachigs and Abrahams!

He also snored, violently. Was I afraid of death on those hospital nights
to the accompaniment of resounding snoring to my right? You bet I was.
But I noted with approval the absence of any animal horror, or an insect's
clinging to life, in myself. Or maybe I just hadn't thought it through to
the end. Did I pray on those nights? No one ever taught me any prayers,
and I never learned by myself. I drop into a church only occasionally,
although I'm baptized and wear a little cross on a silver chain. At services
I'm mostly bored, unless they sing.

"So here You see all of me," I would say to Him. "You can cut short the
total mess of my life, and I won't be offended: I've had forty years, all

the same. And I have nothing to reproach people, or circumstances, or Heaven for. I'm to blame for everything myself. But I'd like to live a little bit more, if possible. I have a family, and I love them; I have a wife and children. I'd like to live. Please."

On January 12 they told my neighbor and me that it would be the next day. We both signed a Xeroxed consent to the operation, and his wife came to see him and shave him with a cunning little foreign machine. I went down to the first floor, knocked at the barbershop door, which was locked, contrary to the posted hours, and started waiting for Lena.

My brother came, then Lena. We wandered for about three hours from the ward to the smoking room and back, warmed some water in a jar with an immersion heater, drank instant coffee. My brother, the kind heart, kept putting off leaving and tried to instill courage in me assiduously, as if reading from a copybook. Finally he left. Lena and I caught a moment when the bathroom was free and went in. There was a draft from the window.

First Lena used scissors to cut my beard over a newspaper. My wife thinks I have an unmanly chin, and I referred to this misfortune in order to get the doctor to agree that I didn't have to shave my face cleanly. Then I got undressed and squatted in the rusty-bottomed bathtub and soaped my chest and underarms. I raised each arm in turn, bent at the elbow, and Lena shaved my underarms, I couldn't do it well myself. Then my chest.

It was about 10:00 in the evening, and we all waited for the barber, sitting on my bed and agreeing for the hundredth time about all kinds of trivial things. The door opened.

"Boys! Who am I going to shave for tomorrow?"

Lena and I came out to the summons. It was a big, sprightly gal with gold teeth and dyed hair with gray roots. Similar to the buffet attendant Chumak and I fenced the coffee to at half-price.

You couldn't turn around in the barbershop on the first floor, but Lena found a place for herself in the corner and didn't leave. The whole she-bang cost a hundred rubles, but my wife gave her five hundred rubles and didn't ask for change, and I sat in the crooked, shaky chair. It smelled unbearably of burnt cooking.

"Did she forget the kasha on the stove or something?" laughed the sociable old gal and made the first cutting in the mop covering my hydrocephalic skull.

That's it. And my everyday life with my wife was finished. We couldn't reduce the fraction any further. The sense of utter peace was not a theft, as it feels to adults—there just wasn't a decent replacement for it, nothing else we were supposed to be doing. I had finally coincided with the primordial masculine mission—to be subjected to danger. My children, my son Grigory and my daughter Aleksandra, were sleeping in my home. Like the original woman, my wife Elena was standing behind me, and there was no need to turn around to be assured of this. The Big Mama, the favorite progeny of the supreme Shakespeare, scraped and joked, and didn't try to sweeten the pill: her shaving brush was an old-timer, almost bald; the dull razor in her jaunty hands scraped painfully in rhythm; and the torn sheet thrown over me from the front was stiff from the blood that had been shed in close shaving—there had been predecessors. Now they'd scalped me, the wise guy, too.

After midnight I went down into the dark lobby with Lena.

"You have a beautiful skull," she said, "you should keep it that way."

I agreed and helped her into her coat. We kissed each other, waved to each other—she, standing in the door, and I from the main staircase—and I went to brush my teeth before bed.

The lights had been turned out long ago. The ward breathed and snuffled in various rhythms. My jovial tormentor was sleeping, but he wasn't snoring now. I stole up to my night table on tiptoe, found my toiletries, and slipped into the corridor in which every other lamp was turned out. The toilet was also empty. On my right—three sinks with a mirror over the middle one. On my left, right by the door—a leatherette-covered couch with a tin can for cigarette butts; this is where people would lie down for their pre-op enemas. Farther to the left in a large alcove were three stalls. You couldn't use the second one—it was clogged. The windows were whitewashed over. I washed with soap, and brushed my teeth for a long time, now lengthwise, now crosswise. Then I looked up at myself: what a clean-freak, with a week's reddish-and-gray stubble, student glasses, and gauze stuck to a cut on my naked head.

But my cursed neighbor wasn't sleeping. Forestalling ideological conflict, I turned the conversation to sports, Tuchkovo, skiing in March. He didn't interrupt me, was silent for a minute when I stopped talking, and finally said in a low voice, "Let's dream that we are young and healthy and we're skiing together."

The anesthesia definitively wore off and I realized that my fussy collecting of large and small bags and knapsacks had been premature. It was easy and peaceful, only I was bothered in my nether regions. I tried to relieve myself while lying down, with the help of the urinal, but my muscles wouldn't obey me. I began complaining out loud that I couldn't go Number One. I had been reduced to smallness, and I couldn't get my tongue to express itself more manfully: to void myself, to urinate, let alone to take a leak. Two nurses in white bent over my dick with a long rubber tube.

"I seem to have put it in the wrong place," the first one said.

"Try again," the second one answered.

The first one tried again and got it in the right place. She started pressing her warm palm on my stomach above my privates, and I felt relief. I closed my eyes, and two tears crawled down my temples, because the same thing had happened to me once before.

Long, long ago in a certain sovereign state there lived a certain decent boy named Seryozha. He lived as safe as in God's pocket with Mama, Papa, his younger brother, and a dog. And then he disappeared somewhere. He would get sick at times, as often happens, and if his temperature went higher than 102 degrees, nausea would set in. Seryozha would whimper and fuss, and Mama would put a basin next to his chair-bed. The little lad would hang off the pillow, and he would retch again and again, tormentingly and sweetly. His head on its thin neck would waggle from side to side, and his forehead, wet from weakness, would butt into his mother's palm, feeling her wedding ring . . . .

Lord, without admitting it to myself, how I was afraid, was frightened, was apprehensive, was cowardly, was timid, was wary, shivered, trembled, froze with fear, shook, showed the white feather, broke out in a cold sweat, didn't dare to breathe, to make a peep, to open my mouth, got weak in the knees, feared like the plague, feared the way the devil fears incense—I will take the liberty of supplementing the list of synonyms with the little expression "shit my pants"! How else can you explain the fact that the high water of foolish ecstasy just doesn't recede. My appetite after I was discharged? I ate like a starving man, seven times a day—and I never got full. I would get up at night and gobble, gobble, gobble, squatting in front of the open refrigerator, and my ears would move under the bandages.

You jubilant, brainless D-student! They didn't kick you out, but let you repeat the year, and you're peacefully enjoying yourself and recklessly talking nonsense about how you're going to make up what you missed over the vacation and end up an A-student! Don't you know that your little mind is skimpy and your will is weak, and your laziness and mischievousness are boundless, and in a week you'll already start slacking like crazy, leaving shreds of your trousers on the fence and a piece of carbide bubbling in a puddle covered with a tin can to cause an explosion.

You slacker, they haven't canceled the exam, but postponed it: the silver cord will be loosed and the pitcher will be broken at the fountain . . . You were picking your nose during the lesson and didn't hear, but it is precisely you, the bunny rabbit in the school reading program, squinting and gray, raised up over the ruinous abyss by the merciful hand of Nekrasov's grandfather![113] Your ears are pulled back and are pulsing in his fist, your eyes are bugged out, your incisors are bared from anguish and torment, your front paws are tucked in, a dark-blue vein is pulsing on your belly, and your genitalia, your main pride and enjoyment, have contracted into a pitiful lump, your back extremities are stretched out and buck from time to time. . . .

But that implacable woman with the face of an assistant principal and an agricultural implement in her hand will still unlock my door with a duplicate set of keys, will pull up a chair in an unceremonious way to my desk, where under the scratched plexiglass are scattered—not so much like mementoes as with the secret design of covering the stains on the cloth—photographs of my children, wife, Lili Pan, Savchenko, Soprovsky, Golovkin, the Israeli philosopher Yoel Bin-Nun and his wife Esther; and in the center of the table—my favorite faded, fringed, prerevolutionary pink napkin, which I inherited from my mother, with inconceivable flowers embroidered in pale-blue thread by a diligent maiden, and next to them a little verse embroidered in the same thread:

> "You wish to strike a chord
> Full of living sounds
> But unexpectedly—a dissonance resounds . . ."

and she will begin studying my papers with mockingly heightened interest, sticking out her lower lip and opening her eyes wide, those papers full of complaints, requests, whims, claims, and pretensions. She will squeamishly leaf through them, and reluctantly, with the grimace of a literary consultant, will fold them, neatly tapping the edge of the sheaf on the table and at the same time making the sides even with her palms, will sigh and tear it in two, then into fourths, then once again, and with a theatrical gesture will scatter it over her shoulder, so that the scraps settle smoothly onto the floor covered with a green palace rug, onto the sideboard, the couch, the round dinner table covered with an unbleached linen tablecloth . . . .

Here's what I want. I want to learn English; I want to get rich off my writing and buy a three- or even a four-room apartment right here in Zamoskvorechie; I want my literary gift not to abandon me. . . . And if it turns out that I can't have that, and I have to merge with all the other people on the trains, streets, and the subway and earn my living in some ordinary way—it's no catastrophe, so be it. Then I want to work until retirement at *Foreign Literature* and I want all the more to learn English and become a good editor; I want to live to see grandchildren, to have a cheerful old age and die suddenly, because I am very afraid of pain; if, God forbid, my wife dies before me, I want not to quarrel with my children over assets and real estate; I want Grisha, my son, not to get lost, not to get dirty, and not to spread dirt for as long as I have, and about my daughter for some reason I have no worries; I want the Sanitary & Epidemiological Service to allow them to bury me at the dacha, but that's probably asking too much; and also, I very much want, when I die, for God to raise me to that height where there is powerful joy and it becomes clear why tumors appear in the brains of children too young to understand, and that He find it possible after all to have mercy on you and on me.

1994

PEOPLE MENTIONED

Aizenberg: Mikhail Natanovich (Misha) (b. 1948), poet and essayist.

Aleichem: *See* Sholem Aleichem.

Aleinikov: Vladimir Dmitrievich (b. 1946), poet and translator, one of the organizers of the 1965 poetry group called SMOG, which originally stood for the Russian words for "Boldness, Thought, Image, Depth," but as a freestanding word means "I was able to." It has later been interpreted as standing for the Russian words that mean "The Youngest Society of Geniuses."

Alyosha: *See* Tsvetkov.

Arkady: *See* Pakhomov.

Bagritsky: Eduard Georgievich (1895–1934), Soviet poet and dramatist, member of the Odessa and Constructivist schools of writers; died of asthma.

Bakhyt: *See* Kenzheev.

Batchan: Alik (1953–2000), journalist for Voice of America and Radio Liberty.

Bazhanov: Leonid Aleksandrovich (b. 1945), art historian, specialist in contemporary art.

Bitov: Andrei Georgievich (b. 1937), major prose writer of the second half of the twentieth century; author of *Pushkin House* (1978).

Bonner: Elena Georgievna (1923–2011), human rights activist and wife of Andrei Sakharov.

Bukovsky: Vladimir Konstantinovich (b. 1942), dissident who spent twelve years in Soviet prisons and psychiatric hospitals.

Chemerisskaya: Mariia Ilin'ichna (Masha) (b. 1948), poet, part of "Moscow Time" group, once married to Tsvetkov.

Chkhartishvili: Grigorii Shalvovich (b. 1956), literary critic, translator from Japanese and English, and since 1998, under the pen name Boris Akunin, the author of wildly popular novels featuring the Tsarist police investigator Erast Fandorin.

Chukhontsev: Oleg Grigor'evich (b. 1938), poet, editor at journals *Iunost'* (*Youth*) and *Novyi mir* (*New World*).

Chukovsky: Kornei Ivanovich (1882–1969), important children's book writer and literary critic.

Dashevsky: Grigorii Mikhailovich (1964–2013), poet and translator.

Dubovenko: Boris Borisovich (Borya) (1945–2013), poet associated with SMOG group (*See* Aleinikov), later a Russian Orthodox priest.

Faibisovich: Semyon Natanovich (Syoma) (b. 1949), artist who worked in both official and unofficial spheres in the Soviet period; in 2013 came out publicly in support of LBGT rights.

Gaidar: Egor Timurovich (1956–2009), economist, deputy and acting prime minister and finance minister under Boris Yeltsin, who worked to move the economy from a command to a market system ("shock therapy"), and was bitterly blamed by many Russians for the economic chaos that resulted. Grandson of the children's book writer Arkady Gaidar.

Genis: Aleksandr Aleksandrovich (b. 1953), writer, essayist, and broadcaster who emigrated to the United States in 1977 and has long hosted a show on Radio Liberty; often collaborated with Pyotr Vail.

Iskander: Fazil' Abdulovich (b. 1929), major prose writer known for his stories of life in the Abkhaz village of Chegem.

Kassil: Lev Abramovich Kassil' (1905–1970), Soviet writer; Gandlevsky refers to his novel *The Black Book and Schwambrania* (*Konduit i Shvambraniia*, 1928–1931), about an idyllic childhood in the prerevolutionary bourgeois Jewish family of a respected doctor.

Kazintsev: Aleksandr Ivanovich (b. 1953), journalist, known for his work on the journal *Nash sovremennik* (*Our Contemporary*).

Kenzheev: Bakhyt Shkurullaevich (b. 1950), poet of Kazakh origin, now in Canada, who in the 1970s was one of the participants in the poetry group "Moscow Time," along with Gandlevsky, Soprovskii, and Aleksei Tsvetkov.

Kibirov: Timur Iur'evich (pseudonym of Timur Zapoev, b. 1955), postmodern poet of Ossete origin, author of friendly epistle *To Seryozha Gandlevsky, on Certain Aspects of the Contemporary Sociocultural Situation* (*Seryozhe Gandlevskomu. O nekotorykh aspektakh nyneshnei sotsiokul'turnoi situatsii*, 1991).

Klimontovich: Nikolai Iur'evich (b. 1951), playwright and prose writer; like Kozlovskii, he participated in the underground collection *Katalog*.

Konovalov: Aleksandr Nikolaevich (b. 1933), neurosurgeon of international renown, director of the Academician N. N. Burdenko Scientific-Research Neurosurgery Institute since 1975. There is no evidence that he operated on Pope John Paul II.

Korolyova: Marionella Vladimirovna (Gulya) (1922–1942), film actress since childhood, died heroically at Battle of Stalingrad, where she served in a medical battallion.

Korzhavin: Naum Moiseevich (real last name Mandel') (b. 1925), dissident poet and prose writer, emigrated to United States in 1974.

Kosygin: Aleksei Nikolaevich (1904–1980), premier of the Soviet Union from 1964 to 1980.

Koval: Viktor Stanislavovich (b. 1947), poet and artist.

Kozlovsky: Evgenii Antonovich Kozlovskii (b. 1946), Russian writer, playwright, theater director, and journalist; participated in the 1980 almanac *Katalog*, published in the West by Ardis in 1982. He was arrested in 1982 and spent seven months in prison. In recent years he has written books and journalistic articles about computers.

Krava: Nickname for Valentina Kravchenko, once married to Tsvetkov.

Krupskaya: Nadezhda Konstantinovna (1869–1939), Bolshevik revolutionary married to Lenin, instrumental in founding the Soviet educational and library system and the Komsomol.

Kublanovsky: Iurii Mikhailovich (Yura) (b. 1947), poet, essayist, one of the organizers of the 1965 poetry group called SMOG (*See* Aleinikov).

Kushner: Aleksandr Semyonovich (b. 1936), major poet, associated with the image of St. Petersburg–Leningrad.

Lakshin: Vladimir Iakovlevich (1933–1993), literary critic and memoirist, early champion of Solzhenitsyn's *One Day in the Life of Ivan Denisovich* (1962). From 1990 until his death in 1993, he served as chief editor of *Foreign Literature*.

Leskov: Ivan Semyonovich (1831–1895), Russian novelist and short-story writer known for his complex narrative style, which incorporates dialectisms and other marks of the oral speech of sometimes uneducated narrators.

Luxemburg: Rosa (Rosalia) (1871–1919), Marxist theorist, economist, and revolutionary activist, murdered in Berlin while in police custody, revered by the Soviet state.

Lyova: *See* Rubinshtein.

Mezhirov: Aleksandr Petrovich (1923–2009), poet, in United States from 1992; Gandlevsky quotes his poem *Thanksgiving* (*Blagodaren'e*).

Michurin: Ivan Vladimirovich (1855–1935), horticulturalist who specialized in hybridization; his name was invoked after his death to promote the dubious theories of Trofim Lysenko about the inheritance of acquired characteristics, which had a stranglehold on Russian biological science in the mid-twentieth century.

Molchanskaya: Natal'ia (Natasha), director of the department of criticism of the journal *Foreign Literature*; killed in an accident in the late 1990s.

Myuda: *See* Yablonskaya.

Nerler: Pavel Markovich (real last name Polian) (b. 1952), poet associated with "Moscow Time" group, author of works on the poet Osip Mandelstam, also a geographer and historian.

Novikov: Denis Gennadievich (1967–2004), Russian poet, member of "Almanac" group.

Orlov: Iurii Fedorovich (b. 1924), nuclear physicist, human rights activist, and former Soviet dissident; founded the Moscow Helsinki Group in 1976 to monitor Soviet adherence to the Helsinki human rights accords; arrested and imprisoned in 1977, freed in 1986, and deported to the United States, where he became a professor of physics and government at Cornell University.

Pakhomov: Arkadii Dmitrievich (1944–2011), poet, member of SMOG group (*See* Aleinikov*).

Poletaev: Vladimir Grigor'evich (1951–1970), poet and translator who killed himself by jumping out a window.

Prigov: Dmitrii Aleksandrovich (1940–2007), important poet, artist, and performer, one of the founders of the school of Moscow Conceptualist art. Prigov was still alive when Gandlevsky wrote *Trepanation of the Skull*, so the direct address to him in the work reads somewhat differently now than it did at the time.

Rubinshtein: Lev Semyonovich (Lyova) (b. 1947), important experimental poet, one of the leaders of the Moscow Conceptualists, known for his poems in the form of a "card catalogue" that combine verbal, visual, and performative art. His first publications appeared in the West in the 1970s.

Ryashentsev: Iurii Evgen'evich (b. 1931), poet, lyricist, translator.

Sanchuk, Genrikh: Genrikh Eduardovich (b. 1917), father of Viktor, historian specializing in Slavic-German relations.

Sanchuk, Viktor: Viktor Genrikhovich (Vitya) (b. 1959), poet, member of the group "Moscow Time."

Selvinsky: Il'ia L'vovich Sel'vinskii (1899–1968), poet associated with the Constructivist group.

Sholem Aleichem: Pseudonym of Sholem Naumovich Rabinovich (1859–1916), important Yiddish writer who spent his formative years in the Russian Empire; most famous for his cycle of stories *Tevye the Dairyman* (1894).

Shteinberg: Arkadii Akimovich (1907–1984), poet, translator, artist; conducted workshops on poetic translation at the Central House of Writers that involved both translators and poets engaging in poetic translation.

Slovesnyi: Aleksei Nikolaevich (b. 1929), chief editor of *Foreign Literature* (1993–2005).

Slutsky: Boris Abramovich (1919–1986), greatly talented Soviet poet of the War generation. In the post-Soviet period his poetry containing Jewish and biblical themes and subtexts has led to his reevaluation as an important postwar Jewish Russian poet who had a considerable impact on Joseph Brodsky. See Marat Grinberg, *"I am to be read not from left to right, but in Jewish: from right to left": The Poetics of Boris Slutsky* (Brighton, MA: Academic Studies Press, 2011). I am grateful to Alexandra Smith for this reference. See also Boris Slutsky, *Things That Happened*, ed. and trans. G. S. Smith, Glas New Russian Writing, vol. 19, 1998.

Solonitsyn: Anatolii Alekseevich (1934–1982), stage and film actor, star of films by Andrei Tarkovskii, including *Andrei Rublyov* (1966) and *The Mirror* (1974).

Soprovsky: Aleksandr Soprovskii (1953–1990), poet and essayist who like Gandlevsky worked at various jobs while pursuing his unofficial literary career. In a 2004 interview, Gandlevsky said that Soprovskii was "the main influence on my life, other than my parents, of course."

Tarkovsky, Andrei: Andrei Arsen'evich Tarkovskii (1932–1986), major filmmaker, director of *Andrei Rublyov, Solaris, The Mirror,* and *Stalker,* son of poet Arsenii Tarkovskii.

Tarkovsky, Arseny: Arsenii Aleksandrovich Tarkovskii (1907–1989), poet and translator, father of the film director Andrei Tarkovskii.

Terekhova: Margarita Borisovna (b. 1942), stage and film actress and director, star of Tarkovskii's *The Mirror* (1974).

Timur: *See* Kibirov.

Tsvetkov: Aleksei Petrovich (Alyosha) (b. 1947), major poet, one of the founders of the "Moscow Time" poetry group with Gandlevsky, in the United States since 1975.

Utkin: Iosif Pavlovich (1903–1944), poet of the War generation.

Vail: Pyotr L'vovich (Petya) (1949–2009), journalist, writer, broadcaster, in the United States from 1977 to 1995, when he moved to Prague; broadcaster with Radio Liberty; often collaborated with Aleksandr Genis.

Vankhanen: Natal'ia Iur'evna (b. 1951), poet and translator.

Vedeniapin: Dmitrii Iur'evich (b. 1959), poet and translator, associated with "Moscow Time" group.

Velichanskii: Aleksandr Leonidovich (1940–1990), poet and translator, associated with SMOG group (*See* Aleinikov).

Vitya: *See* Sanchuk.

Volgin: Igor' Leonidovich (b. 1942), poet, historian, Dostoevsky scholar; ran a literary workshop at Moscow State University (called "Luch" ["Ray of Light"]) starting in 1968 that was important for Gandlevsky, Soprovsky, Tsvetkov, and other writers.

Yablonskaya: Myuda Naumovna (1926–1990), art historian, specialist on women artists, friend of Gandlevsky's mother.

Yakovich: Elena (Lena) (b. birth date not made public), journalist and documentary filmmaker.

Zetkin: Clara (1857–1933), German Marxist theorist and advocate of women's rights, close friend of Rosa Luxemburg; died in the Soviet Union after Hitler's rise to power.

PLACES MENTIONED

All-Russia Exhibition Center (VDNKH): Subway station near the exhibition complex in northeast Moscow.

Andijon: Town in Uzbekistan.

Arbat: Historic neighborhood in west central Moscow.

Baskachi: Town in Yaroslavl Oblast, on the Volga River.

Biriulevo-Tovarnaya: Railway station in far southern Moscow.

Borisoglebsk: Town in the Voronezh region.

Brezhnev District: Region in southwest Moscow named for Brezhnev from 1983 to 1988, otherwise known as Cheryomushki.

Buzuluk: Town in Orenburg Oblast, on the Samara River.

Chardzhou: Town in Turkmenistan.

Choboty: Region to the west of Moscow, near the writers' colony of Peredelkino.

Danilov Monastery: On the Moscow River in southern Moscow.

Domodedovo: Airport in far southeast Moscow.

Dunaevsky Street: Southwest central Moscow, near Studencheskaya Street, where Gandlevsky grew up.

Dzerzhinskaya: Subway station in north central Moscow; renamed Lubyanka in 1990.

Elista: Capital of Kalmykia, autonomous republic within the Russian Federation, on the Caspian Sea.

Fadeev Street: Street in northwest central Moscow, location of the Academician N. N. Burdenko Scientific-Research Neurosurgery Institute, where Gandlevsky had his brain surgery.

Fedosino: Region in far western Moscow, part of Peredelkino.

Fili: Western suburb of Moscow, once a village. It was in Fili that General Kutuzov held the council of war after the Battle of Borodino in September 1812 at which it was decided not to defend Moscow from Napoleon in order to save the Russian Army for as long as possible.

First Novokuznetsky Lane: Street in south central Moscow, where the Gandlevskys lived in a communal apartment from 1987 to 1991.

Fomicheva Street: Far northwest Moscow.

Fort Shevchenko: Town in Mangystau (Mangyshlak) Province, on the Caspian Sea.

Gagarin: Town in the Smolensk region, known as Gzhatsk until 1968, when it was renamed in honor of Yurii Gagarin, the first cosmonaut. It is located near Tuchkovo, where the Gandlevskys have a dacha.

Garden Ring: Circular avenue around central Moscow.

Gazli: Town in Uzbekistan.

Glinka Museum: Museum of musical culture named for Mikhail Glinka, one of Russia's greatest composers, on Fadeev Street in northwest central Moscow.

Gorky Park: The Gorky Park for Culture and Leisure in southwest central Moscow.

Gunt River: Tajikistan, in the western Pamirs, a tributary of the Pyandzh.

Izmailovsky Park: Large park in far eastern Moscow.

Kabardino-Balkaria: Region in the northern Caucasus.

Kamchatka: Peninsula in the Russian Far East.

Kashirka: Region in far southeast Moscow.

Kazan train station: Northeast central Moscow.

Khorog: City in Tajikistan.

Kiev-Radial subway station: Southwest central Moscow.

Klimentovsky Lane: South central Moscow, near Tretyakov Gallery.

Kon'kovo: Region in southwest Moscow.

Krymsky val: Southwest section of the Garden Ring; location of the Central House of Artists, the exhibition center of the Union of Artists.

Kutuzovsky Prospect: Major street in west central Moscow.

Leninsky Prospect: Major street in southwest Moscow.

Lyublino: Region in far southeast Moscow.

Malaya Dmitrovka: Street in northwest central Moscow by Pushkin Square; called Chekhov Street from 1944 to 1993.

Malin: Village in Ukraine (98 km WNW of Kiev).

Mangyshlak: Peninsula on the northeast edge of the Caspian Sea, in western Kazakhstan. Its modern name is Mangystau.

Mayakovsky Museum: Central Moscow, near the Lubyanka.

Michurinets station: Train station in the far west of Moscow, in Peredelkino.

Mozhaika: Neighborhood in west central Moscow, near Kutuzovsky Prospect, which was once part of the Mozhaiskoe Highway.

Mozzhinka: One of the dacha settlements established by Stalin after World War II to reward scientists and scholars (members of the Academy of Sciences) who had helped in the war effort; located west of Moscow, near the ancient town of Zvenigorod.

Murghab: Town in Tajikistan, in the Pamirs.

Myasnitskaya Street: Northeast central Moscow; officially called Kirov Street from 1935 to 1990.

Naberezhnye Chelny: City in Tatarstan.

Neskuchny Park: Largest park in the historical center of Moscow, a remnant of estates that belonged to the noble families Trubetskoi, Golitsyn, and Orlov; considered part of the Gorky Park for Culture and Leisure.

Novodevichy Convent: Sixteenth-century convent in southwest central Moscow.

Old Tolmachovsky Lane: Southeast central Moscow, where the Gandlevskys lived from 1991 to 1998.

Osh: Second largest city in Kyrgyzstan.

Ostrovsky Street: South central Moscow; before 1948 and after 1992 called Malaya Ordynka.

Otradnoe: Region in the far north of Moscow.

Pamirs: Central Asian mountain range.

Peredelkino: Dacha settlement west of Moscow; in the Soviet period, it was the province of the Union of Writers and home to Boris Pasternak and other literary figures.

Pevek: Town in the far northeast of Russia, above the Arctic Circle, in the Chukotka Autonomous Okrug.

Porechie: Village on the Moscow River near Tuchkovo, where the Gandlevskys' dacha is located.

Pyandzh River: Tributary of the Amu Darya; forms part of the Afghanistan-Tajikistan border. Modern name Panj.

Sevastopol: City on the Black Sea coast of the Crimean peninsula, now in Ukraine.

Solovki: Prison camp located in a former monastery on the Solovetsky Islands in the White Sea.

Studencheskaya: Street in southwest central Moscow, where Gandlevsky spent the first fifteen years of his life in a communal apartment with his parents and brother.

Sukhumi: Capital of Abkhazia, which during the Soviet period was part of the republic of Georgia.

Svoboda Street: Far northwest Moscow.

Tuchkovo: Town 80 kilometers west of Moscow, where the Gandlevskys' dacha is located.

Tverskaya Street: Major street in central Moscow; officially called Gorky Street from 1935 to 1990, but often called Tverskaya by Muscovites even then.

Uglich: Historic town in the Yaroslavl oblast, on the Volga River.

Urgench: Town in northern Uzbekistan.

Vanch: Small town on the river Vanch in eastern Tajikistan (modern spelling Vanj).

Yugozapadnaya: Subway station in southwest Moscow.

Zamoskvorechie: Historic district in south central Moscow.

Zhdanovskaya: Subway station in the far southeast of Moscow; since 1988 called Vykhino.

Zvenigorod: Ancient town west of Moscow, the site of the Savvino-Storozhevskii Monastery.

MAP 1—Moscow

map designed by Olga Monina

128

MAP 2—Environs of Moscow

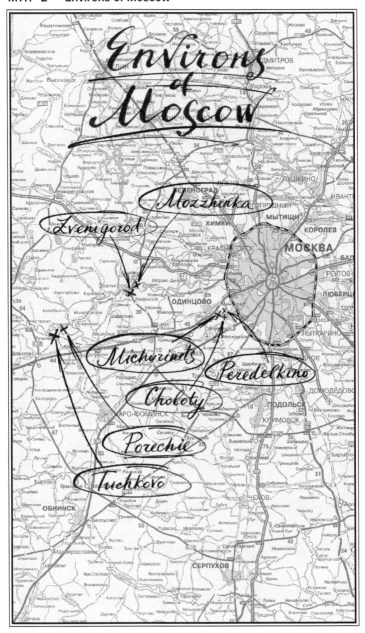

map designed by Olga Monina

MAP 3—USSR

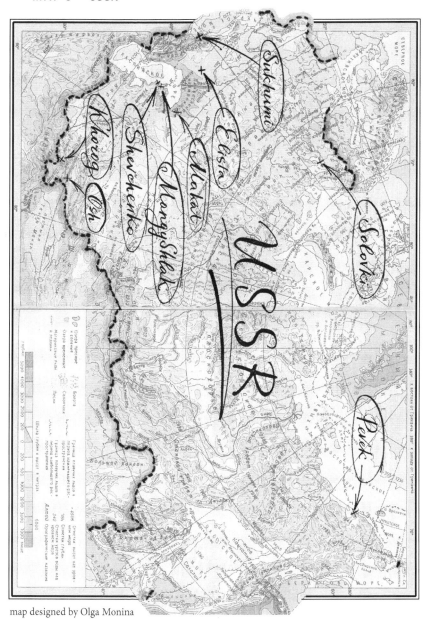

map designed by Olga Monina

NOTES

1. The quotation is from Dostoevsky's 1866 novel *Crime and Punishment* (*Prestuplenie i nakazanie*). The speaker is Razumikhin, a friend of the hero Raskol'nikov. The next line he speaks is "If you talk enough nonsense, you'll get to the truth!"

2. The Young Pioneer Organization of the Soviet Union was a mass youth organization for children aged ten to fifteen (1922–1991). Part of its emblem was the bonfire, which symbolized eternal readiness. Singing songs around a campfire was a typical activity in a Pioneers' camp.

3. "Take off my pants and run away" is one of a series of typical Russian children's nonsense rhyming answers to boring questions, in this case, "What should I do today?" The other joke is inserting the nonsense phrases "in pants" and "without pants" into the popular song "Garland of the Danube," written by O. Fel'tsman and E. Dolmatovskii, most famously performed by Edita P'ekha (or Piecha, b. 1937), a Soviet singer popular in the 1960s and 1970s. The song tells of a garland to be woven of flowers and dropped into the Danube by people in the Soviet bloc (Hungary, Slovakia, Bulgaria, Yugoslavia, Romania), and finally the Soviet Union.

4. The neighbors are employees of the KGB (Committee for State Security [Komitet gosudarstvennoi bezopasnosti]), the Soviet secret police. Employees of the KGB were given military ranks. Efim Alekseevich Cherepanov (1774–1842) and Miron Efimovich Cherepanov (1803–1849), actually father and son, built the first Russian steam locomotive in 1833–1834.

5. Formerly an overseas province of Portugal, the Democratic Republic of São Tomé and Príncipe is an island nation in the Gulf of Guinea, off the western equatorial

coast of Africa. Its strategic location made it a site of interest for both the United States
and the Soviet Union during the Cold War.

6. Iurii Vladimirovich Andropov (1914–1984), Chairman of the KGB 1967–
1982, General Secretary of the Central Committee of the Communist Party 1982–
1984, and Chairman of the Presidium of the Supreme Soviet 1983–1984. The idea that
he would be holding up Americans as a positive example for Soviet spies is a scandal-
ous one. The retired spy's meter at the dacha reads only "eight rubles" because he's been
stealing electricity by hooking up directly to the communal network and bypassing his
own meter.

7. Fili is a western suburb of Moscow, once a village. It was in Fili that General
Kutuzov held the council of war after the Battle of Borodino in September 1812 at
which it was decided not to defend Moscow from Napoleon in order to save the Russian Army for as long as possible.

8. A 1977 film about the mafia starring Gian Maria Volonté, *Io ho paura*, directed by Damiano Damiani (1922–2013), international title *The Bodyguard.*

9. It is of course illegal to drive down the centerline, but KGB agents can disre-
gard such niceties. Gandlevsky grew up near Kutuzovsky Prospect, on Studencheskaya
Street. "Borozdina's house" refers to Irina Borozdina (1954–1997), whom the narrator
refers to later in the text as "my almost first love." "Youth. . . . Childhood and boyhood"
alludes to *Childhood, Boyhood, Youth* (1852–1857), an early work by Lev Tolstoy that
combines autobiography with fiction.

10. "Porfiry" refers to the investigating magistrate Porfiry Petrovich, who pur-
sues the murderer Raskol'nikov in Dostoevsky's *Crime and Punishment* (1866). Vladimir Al'brekht (Albrecht), mathematician and prominent Moscow dissident, imprisoned from 1983–1987, now in the United States, wrote a famous *samizdat* text, "How
to Be a Witness" (sometimes called "How to Conduct Yourself in an Investigation"),
in which he described strategies for dealing with interrogation. The first step in his
system is to request that each question be entered into a written record (protocol). The
interrogator addresses Gandlevsky as "Sergey Markovich," the polite form of address
in Russian that uses the first name and patronymic (a middle name consisting of the
first name of the person's father plus the suffix *-ovich* or *-evich* for men and *-ovna* or
-evna for women). Elsewhere Gandlevsky is called by the familiar nickname Seryozha,
and Chumak uses a more unusual and folksy nickname, "Seryi," which coincidentally
is also the word for "gray."

11. 1980 Soviet novel by Vladimir Orlov (b. 1936), in the genre of "fantastic
realism," about a virtuoso musician whose talent comes from his father, the devil.

12. *Kontinent* was a journal founded in Paris in 1974 as a venue for "free" Russian thought. Smuggled into the Soviet Union, it served as an important source for the
intelligentsia to keep up with unofficial Russian literature.

13. The work ID is a document that certifies every citizen's work record and
length of service. Every Soviet citizen over the age of sixteen also had an internal passport that was to be carried at all times and served as means of identification as well as
certification of place of residence. The "military ticket," translated here as "draft card,"
is a certification either of military rank or of deferment for health or other reasons.

14. Pechorin is the aristocratic officer hero of Mikhail Lermontov's 1840 novel *Hero of Our Time* (*Geroi nashego vremeni*), who fails to respond warmly when he encounters his old comrade, the lower-class captain Maksim Maksimych.

15. "Andropovka" is a nickname for a cheap type of vodka that appeared in 1982, when Iurii Andropov was leader of the Soviet Union. The use of the term here seems to be an anachronism, since the scene is taking place in 1981.

16. Article 2B indicates that the cardholder has been diagnosed with epilepsy, which exempts him from military service but is also supposed to exclude him from participating in expeditions. Gandlevsky, who suffered from seizures as a child perhaps as a result of a difficult birth, was able to circumvent this restriction and travel the whole country on expeditions.

17. Pevek is a town in the far northeast of Russia, above the Arctic Circle, in the Chukotka Autonomous Okrug. The narrator is referring to an earlier expedition.

18. Volodia Teleskopov is a character in Vasily Aksyonov's 1968 novel *Surplussed Barrelware* (*Zatovarennaia bochkotara*). He carries on a running monologue of stories from his picaresque life.

19. A classification yard is a railroad yard found at freight train stations, used to separate railroad cars onto one of several tracks.

20. The narrator and Chumak are using a typical criminals' toast.

21. The "letter to the Turkish sultan" is a reference to Ilya Repin's famous painting, *The Zaporozhian Cossacks Write a Letter to the Turkish Sultan* (1880–1891), based on a legendary incident. Every Russian schoolchild would be familiar with the vivid image of the jovial and daring Cossacks dictating to a scribe their bold reply to the 1676 ultimatum of Ottoman Sultan Mehmed IV. This mental image would help capture the flavor of the scene Gandlevsky describes.

22. Komsomol is an abbreviation for Vsesoiuznyi Leninskii Kommunisticheskii Soiuz Molodezhi (All-Union Leninist Communist Union of Youth), an organization for people aged fourteen to twenty-eight that prepared Soviet youth to be members of the Communist Party. It was difficult to make a good career without being a member in good standing.

23. A *kishlak* is a Central Asian village.

24. Onegin is the hero of Pushkin's novel *Eugene Onegin* (*Evgenii Onegin*, 1825–1833), who begins the novel as a bored but dashing aristocrat.

25. "New Russians" is the somewhat scornful term for people who flourished financially and socially in the aftermath of the collapse of the Soviet Union. It bears something like the stigma of the Western term *nouveau riche* and may have been derived from it.

26. Nikita Sergeevich Khrushchev (1894–1971), the premier of the USSR from 1958 to 1964, was long an advocate of the cultivation of corn in the Soviet Union. His efforts were largely unsuccessful due to poor implementation. Khrushchev's biographer William Taubman writes, "Before long, his crusade turned into an irrational obsession" (*Khrushchev: The Man and His Era* [New York: Norton, 2003], 373).

27. *Marxism and the Problems of Linguistics* (*Marksizm i problemy iazykoznaniia*) is a 1950 work by Stalin in which he denounced the linguistic theories of N. Ia. Marr (after the latter's death) as anti-Marxist.

28. The term *raznochinets* was used in the nineteenth century to refer to people of non-gentry origin who had become educated and entered the ranks of the intelligentsia. They were often of clerical origin and tended toward political radicalism. Perhaps the most famous *raznochinets* was Nikolai Chernyshevsky, author of *What Is to Be Done?*, the handbook of the young radicals in the 1860s and 1870s. The usual land allotment for ordinary Soviet citizens to use for their dachas and kitchen gardens was 0.06 hectares or 600 square meters, called "six *sotka*s" (from *sto*, the Russian word for "hundred"). The "latifundia" (great landed estates) ironically referred to by Gandlevsky are the more generous allotments given to the high-profile scholars and scientists in the dacha settlements established by Stalin as a reward for service to the Soviet state.

29. Oak leaves were featured in some of the highest decorations awarded by the Third Reich.

30. At the Twentieth Congress of the Communist Party of the Soviet Union in February 1956, Khrushchev gave his "secret speech" denouncing the Stalinist cult of personality.

31. In Pushkin's 1830 verse drama *Mozart and Salieri* (*Motsart i Sal'ieri*), based on apocryphal stories about the relationship between the two composers, Salieri is consumed with jealousy over Mozart's divine talent and poisons Mozart.

32. The quotation is from the section of Dostoevsky's *The Brothers Karamazov* (*Brat'ia Karamazovy*, 1880) entitled "The Grand Inquisitor." In Ivan Karamazov's literary fantasy, the Grand Inquisitor has arrested Jesus Christ and is explaining to him how the Church hierarchy has improved on his mission. Quoted here from the translation by Ignat Avsey, *The Karamazov Brothers* (Oxford: Oxford University Press, 1994), 319.

33. The Hutsuls (var. Huzuls) are Ukrainian inhabitants of the Carpathian region. In the Russian imagination, they are wild mountain people with curly hair.

34. Johan Huizinga (1872–1945), Dutch cultural historian, author of *Homo Ludens* (*Man the Player*, 1938), on the element of play in culture.

35. The phrase I have translated as "beachside card games" is "Sochi bullet" in the original text, a variant of the card game "preference" named for the Black Sea resort. The phrase "Sochi bullet" also evokes Gandlevsky's poem "Neither *sika*, *bura*, nor Sochi bullet" ("Ni sika, ni bura, ni sochinskaia pulia," 2007), which combines references to these somewhat plebeian beachside card games with a hidden quotation from Pushkin's noble masterpiece *From Pindemonte* (*Iz Pindemonti*, 1836) (Gandlevsky, personal communication).

36. In 1968, in reaction to reforms instituted by the Czechoslovak government, known as the "Prague spring," the Soviet Union and other Warsaw Pact troops invaded and occupied the country.

37. The World Festival of Youth and Students was held in Moscow in 1957. It was part of the regime's attempt to overcome the legacy of Stalinism and to recognize the importance of youth culture.

38. Cosmonautics Day, celebrated on April 12, was a Soviet holiday in honor of the first manned space flight made on April 12, 1964, by Yuri Gagarin.

39. The April Theses were directives issued to the Bolsheviks by Vladimir

Lenin in 1917, after the February Revolution. They provided much of the ideological groundwork for the October Revolution. The second and last all-Union strike of coal miners was declared in early March 1991 and suspended two months later.

40. In Lev Tolstoy's novella *The Death of Ivan Il'ich* (*Smert' Ivana Il'icha*, 1886).

41. The journal *Foreign Literature* (*Inostrannaia literatura*) was founded in 1955 for the publication of literature in translation. The journal's promulgation of Western culture in a Soviet milieu that was often hostile to such activities gave it an aura of liberalism.

42. A quotation from *The Twelve Chairs* (*Dvenadtsat' stul'ev*, 1928) by Ilf and Petrov. The main characters are in furious search of twelve chairs, one of which supposedly contains a prerevolutionary treasure. The pursuit is difficult, because the chairs have been sold off in various places after being expropriated by the Bolshevik state. When one of the characters, the legendary con man Ostap Bender, locates some of the chairs and tries to buy them from a workman, the following exchange takes place: "'When will you bring the chairs?' 'The chairs come in exchange for money.' 'That's possible,' said Ostap without thinking. [The workman replies] 'Money in advance. Money in the morning, chairs in the evening; or, money in the evening, chairs the next morning.'" Like many passages from the novel, this one became proverbial in the Soviet vernacular.

43. Gandlevsky refers to Chekhov's devastating 1895 story "The Spouse" ("Supruga"), in which a man finds a telegram in his wife's bedroom and uses an English-Russian dictionary to laboriously decipher what turns out to be a message from her lover. The "Piccinni" passage is a quotation from Pushkin's "little tragedy" *Mozart and Salieri* (1830): "No! I have never known envy, / Oh, never! Not even when Piccinni / Was able to captivate the hearing of the savage Parisians, / Not even when I heard for the first time / The opening sounds of *Iphigenia*." Niccolò Piccinni (1728–1800) was an Italian composer, extremely popular in his day. "*Iphigenia*" probably refers to *Iphigénie en Tauride* (1779) by Christoph Willibald von Gluck (1714–1787), Salieri's mentor, although Piccinni also wrote an opera called *Iphigénie* (1781) as part of a kind of competition between the two composers organized by the directors of the Paris Grand Opera. See also note 31 above. "Alyosha" refers to Aleksei Tsvetkov (see People Mentioned).

44. Gandlevsky says (personal communication) that he does not remember the context of the "main Dostoevsky thought," but the most famous quotation that seems apposite is Dostoevsky's statement in a letter to his niece S. A. Ivanova about his 1868 novel *The Idiot* (*Idiot*): "The main thought of this novel is to depict a positively beautiful person. There is nothing more difficult than this, especially now" (letter of January 1, 1868 O.S.). "I am real" is a quotation from Osip Mandelstam's 1911 poem "Why is my soul so melodious" ("Otchego dusha tak pevucha"), from his collection *Stone* (*Kamen'*): "Am I really real, / And will death truly come?"

45. "Stop up the fountain" is a rude way of saying "Be quiet," analogous to "Put a cork in it," but it also derives from one of the humorous aphorisms of Koz'ma Prutkov, a parodic persona created in the 1850s–1860s by the poets A. K. Tolstoi and the Zhemchuzhnikov brothers: "If you have a fountain, stop it up; let the fountain rest

too." Benjy is one of the narrators of Faulkner's 1929 novel *The Sound and the Fury*. His mental defects are the motivation for the incoherence of his narrative voice.

46. The Russian Booker Prize, modeled after the Man Booker Prize, was established in 1992. *Trepanation of the Skull* won the 1996 "Little Booker" Prize for the best debut in prose. This prize is no longer awarded along with the Booker Prize.

47. Russians often use the name of Russia's greatest poet as a humorous scapegoat for all sorts of household misfortunes.

48. "Dahin" ("To there") is the refrain of Mignon's song "Kennst du das Land," in Goethe's novel *Wilhelm Meister's Apprenticeship* (1795–1796). Mignon's romantic longing for "the land where the lemon trees blossom" contrasts grotesquely with Gandlevsky's trek over ice-covered Moscow streets to get alcohol.

49. The term "port wine" is in quotation marks because the Soviet *portvein* bears little resemblance to the fine aged wine drunk by English lords along with Stilton cheese after elegant dinners. It was a cheap, sweet fortified wine drunk by Russian alcoholics at any time of day.

50. In his 1924 poem *Jubilee* (*Iubileinoe*), in which he converses with Pushkin, Mayakovsky labels poetry "the most bastardly thingumajig ("presvolochneishaia shtukovina"). The phrase "cynical and spicy" comes from Aleksandr Blok's *Poets* (*Poety*, dated July 24, 1908). Blok describes the life of poets in terms that are consonant with Gandlevsky's vision: "When they would get drunk they would swear their friendship, / They would babble cynically and spicily. / Toward morning they'd vomit. Then they'd shut themselves up / And work dully and fervently." At the end of the poem Blok assures the reader that despite this ugly picture, the poets' lives are still superior to those of the ordinary philistine: "No, dear reader, my blind critic! / At least the poet has / Braids, and little clouds, and the Golden Age, / All that is inaccessible to you! . . . Let me die in a ditch like a dog, / Let life trample me into the ground— / I believe: it was God who buried me in a snowbank, / It was a blizzard that kissed me!"

51. "The Blue Cup" is a canonical Soviet children's story by Arkady Gaidar (pseudonym of Arkadii Petrovich Golikov, 1904–1941), in which the breaking of a blue cup comes to symbolize guilt and forgiveness in a small Soviet family during the rise of Nazism (the story was first published in 1936). In the Soviet context there is an element of blasphemy in using this title to refer to a drunken brawl. (I am grateful to Alexandra Smith for bringing this reference to my attention.) Gaidar was the grandfather of Egor Timurovich Gaidar, the economist mentioned later in *Trepanation of the Skull* (p. 109).

52. The *fortochka* is a small hinged window above the regular window in Russian houses and apartments, which is sometimes opened for ventilation even in the depth of winter.

53. Gandlevsky's phrase "kolot'sia i kolot', baldet' i otrubat'sia" (lit. "to spill one's guts and to expose, to get high and to black out") is a parody in convicts' slang of "Borot'sia i iskat', naiti i ne sdavat'sia" ("To struggle and to seek, to find and not to give in"), a key phrase in the popular Soviet novel *The Two Captains* (*Dva kapitana*, 1938–1944) by Veniamin Kaverin (1902–1989). Kaverin's phrase itself is a translation of the last line of *Ulysses* by Alfred, Lord Tennyson (written 1833), "To strive, to seek, to find,

and not to yield." The last three lines of Tennyson's poem were inscribed on a cross at Observation Hill, Antarctica, commemorating the explorer Robert Falcon Scott and his party, who died on their return journey from the South Pole in 1912. Kaverin's hero, who dreams of polar explorations, makes the line his motto. I have chosen to parody a line by Tennyson that is more current in the West, from "The Charge of the Light Brigade".

54. Bakhtin first presented his influential theory of carnival in his 1940 dissertation on Rabelais, which was published as *Rabelais and His World* in 1965.

55. Ferdyshchenko is a character in Dostoevsky's 1868 novel *The Idiot*. At an evening gathering, he proposes a game in which each person present tells "something about himself out loud, but the kind of thing that he himself, in his sincere conscience, considers the worst of all his bad actions in the course of his whole life; but it has to be sincere, the main thing is that it's sincere, no lying!" Predictably, emotional chaos ensues.

56. In August 1991, a group of Communist hard-liners attempted to take power from Gorbachev. The coup lasted only a few days, thanks to a vigorous campaign of civil disobedience in which Boris Yeltsin played a prominent role.

57. At the press conference given by the coup leaders on August 19, 1991, the camera focused repeatedly on the shaking hands of Gennadii Ivanovich Ianaev (1937–2010), the "acting president." Most viewers attributed the tremor to drunkenness, the "flapping tremor" of alcoholism.

58. Evgenii Aleksandrovich Evtushenko (known in the West as Yevgeny Yevtushenko, b. 1933), poet who enjoyed broad popularity in the "Thaw" era of the 1960s and who continued to be an influential literary figure through the perestroika period. Poets of Gandlevsky's generation had complicated feelings about Yevtushenko due to his semiofficial status and the compromises that went with it. Yevtushenko's verse is marked by its assonant "root" rhyme.

59. The reference is to Milosz's landmark essay on the struggles of the intellectual in Communist society, *The Captive Mind* (1953).

60. *And Quiet Flows the Don* (*Tikhii Don*, 1928–1940), by Mikhail Aleksandrovich Sholokhov (whose authorship is questioned), depicts the life of the Don Cossacks during the turbulent time at the beginning of the twentieth century. Sholokhov won the Nobel Prize for Literature in 1965.

61. The monument to Feliks Edmundovich Dzerzhinskii (1877–1926), founder of the Soviet secret police (the Cheka), was toppled by a cheering crowd in Lubyanka Square at midnight on August 22, 1991.

62. "Your tongue will take you to Kiev" is a proverb that means "As long as you can ask questions, you can find the way anywhere." The expression "The elderberry-bushes are in the garden, and uncle is in Kiev" is used to describe a narration that jumps from subject to subject without logical connection.

63. Leonid Aleksandrovich Latynin (b. 1938). The reference is to his 2003 trilogy of novels *Russian Truth* (*Russkaia pravda*), in which he traverses the entire history of Russia. Stribog is god of the winds, sky, and air in the Slavic pre-Christian pantheon.

64. Bobchinsky and Dobchinsky are characters in Nikolai Gogol's 1836 play *The Government Inspector* (*Revizor*).

65. "Almanac" was a literary group in the 1970s consisting of Gandlevsky, Kibirov, Koval', Novikov, Prigov, and Rubinshtein.

66. C. S. Lewis, *The Problem of Pain* (New York: Macmillan, 1945), chapter 9: "Now it will be seen that, in so far as the tame animal has a real self or personality, it owes this almost entirely to its master. If a good sheepdog seems 'almost human' that is because a good shepherd has made it so. . . . And in this way it seems to me possible that certain animals may have an immortality, not in themselves, but in the immortality of their masters" (127–28).

67. Andrii is a character in Gogol's 1835 novella *Taras Bulba*, the son of a Cossack chieftain who falls in love with a Polish maiden and is killed by his father for his betrayal. In 1978 Yevtushenko married Jan Butler, who was English. In the Orthodox tradition, the eighth commandment is "Thou shalt not steal."

68. In 1969, dissident Andrei Alekseevich Amal'rik (1938–1980) wrote *Will the Soviet Union Survive until 1984?* The essay, published abroad in 1970, predicted the collapse of the system in the year in which Orwell's 1949 dystopian fantasy *Nineteen Eighty-Four* is set.

69. Aleksandr Arkad'evich Galich (real last name Ginzburg, 1918–1977), poet, screenwriter, and playwright, one of the most important of the Russian "bards" whose performances of their own songs with guitar accompaniment were a significant cultural phenomenon of the 1960s–1970s, was expelled from the Union of Writers in 1971. This expulsion, which he describes as a "flogging" in the Oak Lodge, is portrayed in his song "From my trivial misfortune" ("Ot bedy moei pustiakovoi"). For more on Galich and the tradition of Russian guitar poetry, see Gerald Stanton Smith, *Songs to Seven Strings: Russian Guitar Poetry and Soviet "Mass Song"* (Bloomington: Indiana University Press, 1984).

70. The words "young tribe" are from Pushkin's 1835 poem "Again I have visited" ("Vnov' ia posetil"), and would be perceived as pretentious and patronizing.

71. In *A Writer's Diary* (*Dnevnik pisatelia*), Dostoevsky often discussed his aspirations for Istanbul to be the Orthodox capital, with Russia in control. For example, in the issue for November 1877, chapter 3, Dostoevsky wrote, "Constantinople must be ours, conquered by us, the Russians, from the Turks, and it must remain ours forever" (Fyodor Dostoevsky, *A Writer's Diary*, vol. 2 1877–1881, trans. Kenneth Lantz [Evanston, IL: Northwestern University Press, 1994], 1208).

72. The reference is to Gandlevsky's 1982 poem "The lynch law of unexpected maturity" ("Samosud neozhidannoi zrelosti"), which contains the lines, "Silence / Has long lain in wait for my speech."

73. The poem about prison-camp songs is *To A. Magarik* ("Something about prison and parting"; *A. Magariku* ["Chto-nibud' o tiur'me i razluke"], 1984). The poem that mentions the *Admiral Nakhimov* is *To O. E.* ("There was a downpour in Batumi. The puddles were higher"; *O. E.* ["Liven' lil v Batumi. Luzhi byli vyshe"], 1981). The Soviet passenger ship the SS *Admiral Nakhimov* collided with a freighter near the Black Sea port of Novorossiisk on August 31, 1986, killing 423 of the 1,234 people on board. The ship had been built in Germany in 1925 and converted several times during its period of service.

74. In the collection *A Kindred Orphanhood: Poems by Sergey Gandlevsky*, trans.
Philip Metres (Brookline, MA: Zephyr Press, 2003), this poem is dated "1994," but
Gandlevsky says that he was mistaken in this dating and that the poem was written
before his diagnosis and operation (personal communication). "Before a great parting
/ Custom requires that one sit for a little while": when people are leaving for a journey, the Russian custom is for both host and departing guests to sit quietly for a few
moments before the departure. The custom is probably related to pagan beliefs about
house spirits. "Fathers, teachers—this is what hell is!": a reference to the final dis-
course of the saintly elder Father Zosima in *The Brothers Karamazov*. In his last hours,
he addresses his monastery colleagues as "fathers and teachers," and discourses on the
true meaning of hell and hellfire, which he considers to be not a physical state but the
spiritual condition of having missed one's chance to love actively while on earth.

75. The Italian title of Luchino Visconti's 1969 film *The Damned* is *La caduta
degli dei* [The Fall of the Gods or Götterdämmerung], which is closer to the Russian
title. The film centers around the fate of a rich industrialist family during the rise of the
Nazis. It depicts the "Night of the Long Knives," called the "Röhm-Putsch" in German
after Ernst Röhm, the leader of the *Sturmabteilung* (SA), who was executed along with
many of his henchmen during this purge in July 1934. The film depicts it as a massacre
of SA men who have fallen into a drunken sleep after an orgiastic night.

76. In the Orthodox church, a memorial service is held on the fortieth day after
a person's death. The poem Gandlevsky refers to is "May God grant me the memory to
recall my labors" ("Dai Bog pamiati vspomnit' raboty moi," 1981). In it he lists his various places of work, including the theater, the construction-site watchman's shed, and
expeditions, where he "learned the ancient science of talking nonsense / And forgot
how to ask about the weather without using obscenities."

77. In act 3 of Anton Chekhov's 1897 play *Uncle Vanya* (*Diadia Vania*), Vanya
says, "My life is ruined! I'm talented, intelligent, courageous. . . . If I had had a normal
life, I might have become a Schopenhauer, a Dostoevsky. . . . I've let my tongue run
away with me! I'm going mad!" Chekhov's plays were first performed at the Moscow
Art Theater. In honor of Chekhov's *Seagull* (*Chaika*, 1895), the seagull became the emblem of the theater and is depicted on its curtain, hence the reference to the "birrud."

78. In the typical Soviet apartment, there were two "bathrooms," one with the
bath and sink and the other with the toilet. Gandlevsky's lament here that his whole life
has been "wrong" ("ne to") echoes the thoughts of Tolstoy's Ivan Il'ich on his deathbed
(see the earlier reference to *The Death of Ivan Il'ich*, p. 26).

79. In Tarkovsky's 1975 film *The Mirror* (*Zerkalo*), music by Pergolesi, Bach,
and Purcell is incorporated into the score by Eduard Artem'ev. In one scene the hero's
son reads him an excerpt from Pushkin's famous 1836 letter to Pyotr Iakovlevich Chaadaev about the fate and mission of Russia.

80. In Russia an accepted medical practice is sewing a capsule containing the
drug disulfuram ("Antabuse") under the skin. (In other countries, it is used as an oral
drug, and there is no evidence that it can have long-lasting effect when inserted this way.)
This procedure has given rise to the slang term "to get sewn up" (podshit'sia). It is widely
considered that the procedure is a kind of placebo; it is the fear of adverse reactions that

keeps the patient from drinking, not any actual long-lasting chemical effects.

81. SMOG was a poetry group organized in 1965 by Leonid Gubanov, Iurii Kublanovsky, Vladimir Aleinikov, Arkadii Pakhomov, and others. "SMOG" originally stood for the Russian words for "Boldness, Thought, Image, Depth," but as a free-standing word means "I was able to." It has later been interpreted as standing for the Russian words that mean "The Youngest Society of Geniuses."

82. This is a reference to Pasternak's words about the poet Sergei Esenin in his 1956 autobiographical essay *People and Situations* (*Liudi i polozheniia*): "Esenin was a living, pulsing lump of that artistry that we call, following Pushkin, the higher Mozartean element."

83. Gandlevsky's note (personal communication): "Lev Rubinshtein [Lyova] is a conceptualist, that is, a writer with a deliberately heightened level of literary-critical reflection—that is how I, at any rate, understand this method. It's an intelligent art, even cerebral and calculating, in which it is hard to get carried away and say some tasteless or unintelligent thing in heat. For these advantages one may have to pay with over-rationality and even tedium. And then there is the poetry of the Romantic confessional tradition, which cultivates passion and ardency of expression. This captivates the reader, but there is a risk of saying something tasteless or stupid in heat, to take for example the last two strophes of Blok's poem *Poets*, which I mentioned. In order somehow to balance out the excessive pathos and beauty of the Romantic method, some authors use an ironic lowering. That's what Blok does in effect, when he writes, 'Toward morning they'd vomit.' That's what I have in mind when I write that it's not at all bad to balance out the Romantic attributes—the cloak and paleness—with some kind of lowering detail, for example, farting. . . . All I am doing is jokingly hinting at peculiarities of our different artistic methods and modes of behavior that are well known to Lyova and myself."

84. Venedikt Vasil'evich Erofeev (1938–1990) wrote *Moscow to Petushki* (*Moskva–Petushki*, 1969, not published in the Soviet Union until 1989), a phantasmagorical novel that follows the adventures of a drunk on a train journey from Moscow to the suburb of Petushki. The novel was highly prized in intellectual circles for its lively, untranslatable language.

85. *Pelmeni* are meat-filled dumplings of Siberian origin, usually frozen and then boiled and eaten with sour cream. They can be a gourmet delight when made at home by a skilled cook, but the *pelmeni* that are eaten while standing up in a café (as mentioned later, p. 71) are not as elegant and tasty and are considered fast food.

86. Chertokutsky is a character in Gogol's 1836 short story "The Carriage" ("Koliaska") who gets drunk with a group of cavalry officers and invites them to come the next morning to see his new carriage, which he describes in exaggerated terms. When they show up at his estate, he is still sleeping off his binge, and to avoid embarrassment he hides in the carriage. The story ends with the officers deciding to take a look at the carriage, opening the door, and finding the ridiculous Chertokutsky "sitting there in his bathrobe and bent in an unusual way." Athos is one of the "three musketeers" in the novels by Alexandre Dumas.

87. Starting in 1932, the civil-defense organization Osoaviakhim awarded badges for marksmanship named for Kliment Efremovich Voroshilov (1881–1969), a Soviet military hero and politician.

88. In chapter 6 of Pushkin's novel *Eugene Onegin*, the hero oversleeps and arrives late at the mill, the assigned meeting place for the duel in which he kills his friend Vladimir Lenskii. His insulting insouciance is manifested both by his lateness and by his bringing his valet as a second.

89. A devastating earthquake took place in northern Armenia (then part of the Soviet Union) in December 1988, killing about 25,000 people. In January 1991, in the aftermath of the declaration of independence by Lithuania, Gorbachev sent troops to quell unrest; they killed thirteen civilians in Vilnius.

90. In 1986 the United States bombed Libya in retaliation for a terrorist attack at a Berlin discothèque. Among the casualties was an infant girl claimed to be the adopted daughter of Gaddafi.

91. The second tercet of the sonnet in chapter 4 of Vladimir Nabokov's novel *The Gift* reads, "And with a woman's smile and a child's care / Examines something she is holding there / Concealed by her own shoulder from our eyes" (translated from the Russian by Michael Scammell with the collaboration of the author [New York: Paragon, 1963], 224).

92. Gandlevsky's reference is to Anna Akhmatova's 1940 poem "I have no need of odic armies" ("Mne ni k chemu odicheskie rati"), part of her cycle *Secrets of the Craft* (*Tainy remesla*). In it she writes, "If only you knew out of what trash / Poems grow, knowing no shame, / Like a yellow dandelion by a fence, / Like burdock and goosefoot." The poet Anatolii Genrikhovich Naiman (b. 1936) published his memoirs about Akhmatova in 1989. The story refers to John 4:6–8, 27.

93. In January 1844, Gogol wrote to his friend the writer Sergei Timofeevich Aksakov (1791–1859), father of the famous Slavophile Ivan Sergeevich Aksakov (1823–1886), sending him a copy of the *Imitation of Christ* by Thomas à Kempis and advising him to read it, one chapter a day, and meditate on it. In April Aksakov replied from Moscow, "I am 53 years old, and I read Thomas à Kempis before you were born." The phrase "I am afraid for your talent" does not appear in the letter, but a similar sentiment was often expressed by Aksakov in the 1840s.

94. From Mandelstam's 1933 poem "The apartment is as quiet as paper" ("Kvartira tikha, kak bumaga"). Mandelstam's line is "More insolent than a Komsomol cell / and more insolent than a song of the VUZ." VUZ stands for *Vysshee uchebnoe zavedenie* [Institution of higher education], part of the Soviet educational system.

95. Gandlevsky's phrase "like a lawless cabbage butterfly" refers to Pushkin's 1828 poem *Portrait* (*Portret*): "With her flaming soul, / With her stormy passions, / Oh, women of the North, among you / She appears at times / And rushes to the point of exhaustion / Past all the conventions of society, / **Like a lawless comet** / In the calculated orbit of the heavenly bodies" [emphasis mine].

96. In the Soviet period, it was customary to give gifts (usually alcohol) to doctors to ensure the best care. Gandlevsky is remarking on the fact that in the Burdenko this was not a requirement; he just wanted to do it out of pure gratitude.

97. The reference is to Galich's 1962 song *The Mistake* (*Oshibka*), about the Battle of Narva in World War II.

98. Iurii Olesha's 1927 novel *Envy* (*Zavist'*) begins with the perfect Soviet man Andrei Babichev singing in the bathroom to express his senseless joy in life.

99. Ivan Denisovich is the hero of Alexander Solzhenitsyn's landmark novel *One Day in the Life of Ivan Denisovich* (*Odin den' Ivana Denisovicha*). The novel, published in 1962 in the Soviet journal *Novyi mir* (*New World*), was the first to openly confront the legacy of Stalinist repression and seemed to harbinger a new openness in Soviet life in general. It describes in telling detail the life of a peasant political prisoner in a labor camp from morning to bedtime of a single day (a perhaps more accurate translation of the title than the accepted English one would be "One of Ivan Denisovich's Days"). The phrase "friends with Ivan Denisovich" is a reference to Vladimir Lakshin's article "Ivan Denisovich, His Friends and Enemies [Ivan Denisovich, ego druz'ia i nedrugi]," *Novyi Mir*, 1964, no. 1: 223-45.

100. May 9 is the day on which the German capitulation to the Soviet Union in World War II (the Great Patriotic War) is celebrated.

101. Anatolii Vasil'evich Lunacharskii (1875–1933) was the first Soviet Commissar of Education (lit. Enlightenment) and Culture, and an outspoken literary critic. Gandlevsky notes, "For my generation, enlightened by forbidden literature, Lunacharsky was no longer an authority, but for my father, against the background of ignorant hangmen like Yezhov and the others, he was an authority. There was a boundary here: for our generation, Lenin and the Bolsheviks were in principle criminals, but for the generation of our fathers and our older brothers, the people of the 1960s, the criminals were Stalin and company, and Lenin and his followers were idealists. In short, we had read Khodasevich's *The White Corridor*, but they had never even heard of Khodasevich" (personal communication). Vladislav Felitsianovich Khodasevich (1886–1939) was an influential émigré poet and critic, considered one of the most important Russian poets of the twentieth century. *The White Corridor* (*Belyi koridor*) is a memoir in which Khodasevich depicts Lunacharsky in a highly unflattering light, as "a liberal minister of a very un-liberal government," warning a group of writers in 1918 that they must write only the kind of literature that is acceptable to the "rule of workers and peasants."

102. In *Hero of Our Time*, Lermontov's narrator describes Pechorin: "His gait was careless and indolent, but I noticed that he did not swing his arms—a reliable sign of a certain reserve of character."

103. Gandlevsky was born on December 21, Stalin's birthday, so his father's coworkers expect him to honor the leader by naming his son Iosif. The phrase "the already doomed snow-covered roofs of the Arbat" refers to the demolition of small streets and houses in the Arbat region of Moscow to make way for the building of the major thoroughfare Kalinin Prospect (now the New Arbat). When Gandlevsky's mother looked out the window of the Grauerman maternity hospital, she would have had a view of this charming neighborhood that was to be destroyed. Gandlevsky's note (personal communication): "I remember the sorrow of old-time Muscovites that for this construction they were destroying a very beautiful neighborhood of Arbat lanes. . . . I've been told that this maternity hospital also no longer exists—there is now a drugstore and offices in that building. But it was a famous maternity hospital: to be born in the Grauerman was cool!"

104. The line is from Pasternak's 1931 poem in memory of the pianist and composer F. M. Blumenfel'd (1863–1931), "The reproach has not yet fallen silent" ("Esh-

che ne umolknul uprek").

105. The publication of a collection of Pasternak's verse in the "Library of the Poet" ("Biblioteka poeta") series in 1965 was a cultural landmark (the books in the series had dark-blue covers). The introduction by Andrei Siniavskii was that critic's last legal publication in the Soviet Union. He was arrested the same year the book appeared and emigrated to France in 1973.

106. The two quatrains are from Pasternak's 1941 poem *Pines* (*Sosny*).

107. Río Muni, on the west coast of Africa, was a province of Spain from 1959 to 1968, when it combined with the island of Fernando Po to become Equatorial Guinea. It issued its own stamps, which often depicted local flora and fauna, only from 1960 to 1968.

108. In chapter 7 of *Eugene Onegin*, the provincial heroine Tatiana is taken to Moscow, where Pushkin depicts his real-life friend the poet Pyotr Andreevich Viazemskii (1792–1878) meeting her at a party: "Meeting Tania at the home of her boring aunt, / Viazemskii happened to sit near her / And managed to captivate her soul."

109. The quotation is from Pushkin's own note to the fifth poem in his 1824 cycle *Imitation of the Koran* (*Podrazhanie Koranu*). The poem begins: "The earth is immobile—the vaults of the sky, / Oh Creator, are supported by you, / And they do not fall onto the dry land and the waters / And they do not crush us with their weight." These lines are glossed by Pushkin with the words, "Bad physics, but what daring poetry!"

110. From Fyodor Ivanovich Tiutchev's 1830 poem "There is in the brightness of autumn evenings" ("Est' v svetlosti osennykh vecherov"): "[On an autumn evening] on everything / There is that gentle smile of fading away, / That in a thinking creature we call / The divine bashfulness of suffering."

111. Gogol's play *The Government Inspector* ends with the famous "mute scene": according to Gogol's instructions, the actors are to stand frozen in various poses for "almost a minute and a half."

112. In Miloš Forman's 1975 film based on Ken Kesey's 1962 novel *One Flew over the Cuckoo's Nest*, the Native American character "Chief" Bromden (played by Will Sampson) smothers the hero Randle McMurphy (played by Jack Nicholson) with a pillow when he realizes that he has been given a lobotomy.

113. Ecclesiastes 12:6: "Or ever the silver cord be loosed, or the golden bowl be broken, or the pitcher be broken at the fountain, or the wheel broken at the cistern." In Nikolai Nekrasov's 1870 poem *Grandfather Mazai and the Rabbits* (*Dedushka Mazai i zaitsy*), an old huntsman tells the narrator about how he saved as many rabbits as he could from a spring flood. As he lets them go in a meadow, he warns them not to cross his path in winter; the reprieve is only temporary, and if he sees them then, he'll shoot. The poem ends: "I don't kill them either in spring or in summer, / Their pelt is poor—the hare is shedding then."